DESTINED DARKNESS

NEPHILIM'S DESTINY: BOOK 1

TESSA COLE

Gryphon's Gate Publishing

Destined Darkness

Cover Design by Melody Simmons

Gryphon's Gate Publishing

550 King St. N.

PO Box 42088 Conestoga

Waterloo, ON

N2L 6K5

ebook ISBN978-1-988115-65-8

Print ISBN978-1-988115-66-5

CHAPTER 1

I RECOGNIZED THE FREEZE IN THE AIR THE MOMENT I opened the pharmacy's door. Fear. A fear so cold that, if the chill got any stronger my weird next-to-useless empathic magic would manifest it in full and I'd see my breath—while no one else would see theirs.

I fought a shiver and swore under my breath. I hadn't even gotten to the precinct to start my shift, but it looked like my patrol was starting right now. This kind of fear could only mean the pharmacy was being robbed.

The cashier, Pam, a middle-aged woman who'd been happy to see me from the moment I'd moved into the neighborhood two years ago, flashed me a smile. It lit up her heart-shaped face and crinkled around her eyes like it always did. She was completely oblivious, which meant whatever was happening had to be at the back of the store.

"Essie, the usual?" she asked, reaching for the box of nicotine patches on the shelf behind her.

"Yeah, but I need to get something from Abe first."

Maybe the pharmacist was worried about something else, or maybe he was angry. Sometimes a person's rage manifested to me as cold. But it was stupid to try to convince myself that the cold biting my cheeks was anything but fear. Sometimes I had no idea what the change in temperature meant, but this was perfectly clear.

Except I couldn't just tell Pam to leave the building and call 911. Not without having to explain how I knew about the robbery. And no way in hell was that going to happen. Which meant I had to call it in where Pam couldn't see me, and keep control of the situation to ensure she, Abe, and anyone else in the pharmacy were safe until backup arrived.

"I'm glad you quit," she said, "but maybe you should consider weaning yourself off of these, too?"

"I'll ask Abe about that," I said as I hurried to the farthest aisle, so she wouldn't see me pull out my phone to call for backup.

"Two years is a long time," she called after me.

And it would be if I'd actually been using the patches to quit smoking, but I wasn't. They were the only thing that seemed to partially ease the constant, painful buzz in my body that had manifested two and a half years ago. It was like I was always in contact with a low voltage electric fence or something. Weaning myself off the patches wasn't even close to being an option. I'd go crazy within the week. Hell, probably a few days.

When the buzz had first started, I'd been terrified it meant I was developing another magical ability, something I wouldn't be able to hide. But when nothing had appeared—thank God—and the hum had lasted more than two weeks, making it impossible to concentrate, or sleep, or do my job, or have a normal conversation with anyone, I'd started looking for a cure, anything to make it stop.

I'd tried everything legal and illegal—not going insane was worth jeopardizing my job with the Union City police department—but nicotine was the only thing that helped, and thank God I'd stumbled across it.

I also had no idea why it had started and couldn't just search the internet for answers since I was a nephilim, half angel and half human, and even if I was supposed to exist, there was little to no information on my type of supernatural being. And I didn't want to start poking around and raise suspicion. I didn't know what the agents of the Joined Parliament would do with me if they found me. Probably lock me up or execute me as a war criminal for a war that had happened twenty-three years ago that I hadn't even been involved in. Hell, I'd barely been seven twenty-three years ago. Or worse, they'd lock me in a laboratory and test me like a lab rat because I wasn't like the other nephilim.

Twenty-three years ago, Michael and Rafael had freed Lucifer and led an uprising of angels to cleanse the earth of the human parasite and—unbeknownst to humans—all non-angel supernatural beings as well. They had found a dark magic that ensured the unnatural conception and rapid maturation of thousands of nephilim, and had grown their army within months. Because of the magic creating them, these nephilim were ferocious, mindless soldiers, more beast than human or angel.

The fact that I wasn't a mindless beast had to prove that I wasn't *made* during the war, that I was somehow conceived naturally even if the angelic powers-that-be claimed it was impossible. Except I wasn't sure that little detail would be enough to protect me, and I wasn't planning on revealing myself just to find out.

The nephilim had slaughtered thousands of humans and angels before Gabriel, the leader of the Angelic Defense, decided to make a deal with the supers to join the fight. No more living in the shadows, representation in government, and, as along as they abided by the laws they helped create, they'd be left to live in peace.

So now everyone knew about supernatural beings.

And nephilim were the new monster-in–the-dark to be hated and feared.

Leaving me to live my life as a normal nothing-to-see-here human who only wanted to serve and protect.

Just, jeez, did it have to be before I'd had my first coffee and replaced my nicotine patch?

I pulled my phone from my purse and eased up to the end of the aisle near the back of the store. I wasn't carrying my off-duty sidearm—my neighborhood was pretty safe so I usually didn't—but that didn't mean I couldn't monitor the situation or talk to the robber and buy time for backup to arrive.

In the convex overhead mirror, my aisle and the store's two others stretched toward the front. The pharmacy counter sat forty-five degrees to the aisles, recessed to my left with its narrow shelves, and a door to the stockroom leading to the only other exit in the store. A rake-thin man with pale grayish skin, ripped jeans, and a dark blue hoodie—the hood down revealing greasy brown hair—pointed a revolver at Abe, Pam's middle-aged, balding husband.

My empathic cold billowed, making my teeth chatter, and the buzz in my body grew stronger, now tiny nips under my skin indicating it wouldn't be long before I really needed a new patch.

"Come on, come on," the guy said. He jerked a step closer to the counter, his movements twitchy, his breath fast, and a sheen of sweat on his forehead catching the glare of the fluorescent light. It was either nerves or he was coming down from some kind of high. Probably both.

Great. Served me right for thinking whatever trouble I found myself in while off duty wouldn't require a weapon.

I inched back from the edge of the aisle, hoping a few feet would make a difference and he wouldn't be able to hear me, and called in the armed robbery. Then I shoved my phone into my pocket, set my purse on the floor, and slunk back into position.

"The Divifend, too." The guy raked a hand through his messy locks and glanced over his shoulder—thankfully not thinking to look up at the mirror. "I don't see Divifend."

Shit. If his high of choice was zip, a concoction of the magical immune enhancing drug Divifend combined with an amphetamine, the situation just got more dangerous. The mixture of upper and magic gave the user an incredible high heightened with the exhilaration of spurts of magically enhanced strength, speed, and vitality. But the low, if it didn't kill you, came with aggressive mania and sometimes violent hallucinations.

"We didn't receive our order yesterday," Abe said, shoving a plastic bag over the counter toward the robber. It was likely true. Divifend wasn't easy to make and with a slew of recent robberies in town, it likely meant the supplier was working double-time to make up for the lost dosages. And that still meant some cancer patients right now were going without and that pissed me off as much as this idiot pointing a gun at Abe.

"This is all we have," Abe added.

"No, you're lying." The guy waved his gun, his breath coming faster, his movements jerkier.

"I'm not. We didn't get it." Abe's fear deepened, so cold now it felt like my skin was burning.

"Where is it?" The guy slammed a hand on the counter, his voice screeching and desperate. "Where's the Divifend?"

He was going to lose it and no way in hell was I going to let him shoot Abe.

"Hey." I rounded the corner and raised my hands. It was one of the stupidest things I could have done, given that I was unarmed, but all I needed was to buy time. Less than seven minutes.

The guy wrenched to face me, pointing the revolver in my direction, but his hand was shaking too much for him to keep his aim. His eyes were bloodshot and wild, his face sunken and pockmarked. Definitely zip. And definitely coming down.

"He has to have it," the guy said.

"How about you put the gun down and we talk about that."

"Talk about *that*?" The guy's breaths were now short, desperate gasps, and he slapped his head with his free hand. "I'm not going to talk about that." His gaze whipped back to Abe. "He's hiding it."

The guy leaped over the counter, faster than humanly possible, grabbed Abe around the neck, and shoved the gun's muzzle against Abe's temple. "Tell him to tell me where it is."

Frost formed on the backs of my hands, Abe's fear so strong the emotion was manifesting on my body. I forced myself to stay put. I didn't have a gun and jumping in to tackle the guy risked Abe getting shot. Seven minutes was all I needed. Hell, probably six minutes now.

"How about you let the pharmacist go," I said. "I can get you help."

"I don't want help. I want Divifend." The guy's grip around Abe's neck tightened.

The pharmacist gasped, fighting to breathe, his wide eyes locked on me, begging me to save him.

"I want the drug now or I swear—"

"I'll get it for you," I said, telling him what he wanted to hear and praying it would calm him down.

"You better," he snarled.

"But you have to put the gun down."

"Do you think I'm stupid?"

A girl could hope—even if it was ridiculous to think that without a weapon I could convince him to put his down. But I still needed to get the gun off of Abe, so I did another stupid thing in the "don't be an idiot cop" book. I took a step forward and said, "Point your gun at me, then. You can only keep it pointed at one of us and I know where Abe's shipment is."

Abe's fear grew, frosting over my wrists, and I ground my teeth, fighting to keep my expression even. This guy could mistake any twitch as an attack and lose his shit, and I didn't want a chance of that happening until I had him in the alley behind the store. Six minutes? Probably more like five and a half. Of course, more cops showing up might set the guy off, so the faster I got him into the alley, the better.

"I saw the delivery guys drop it out back just before I arrived," I said.

The guy dug his gun's muzzle into Abe's temple. "I knew you were a liar. I should shoot—"

"Abe doesn't know about it," I said as fast as I could to stop him from shooting. "He was in here with you when it arrived. I can show you." *Oh, please work. Just get away from Abe.* I took another step toward him. "Point your gun at me and I'll show you."

"You better." He shoved Abe, slamming him against the narrow shelves with a force that made the pharmacist cry out in pain before sagging to the floor gasping. "Show me."

The gun jerked back to me and the buzz in my body crackled stronger, stinging under Abe's frost, now up to my elbows.

"It's out the back." I eased through the half-door at the end of the counter while the guy glared at me, his body trembling. I drew open the door to a small, packed stockroom. "Through here to the back door."

"Come on. Come on." The guy jerked forward, his magical speed snapping him a step then stalling out, making him stagger the final two. "Stop moving so fucking slow."

He shoved me into the stockroom, the force knocking me off my feet and crashing me to the concrete floor.

"I said move faster." He clawed at his scalp and the gun dipped away from me.

I scrambled to my feet. If I jumped now, I might be able to disarm him. There was still at least five minutes before help could arrive and I'd hoped to stall him here in the stockroom, since once we were out in the alley he'd know I'd lied about the delivery.

But another burst of speed hit him before I could lunge at him and he shoved me again. I struggled to keep my balance, slamming into the back door and managing at the last minute to hit the crash bar. I stumbled into the alley, smacking against the concrete wall opposite the door, with the robber close at my heels, and a blast of cold hit me so hard the frost swept over my face and neck, defying the early morning sunlight and late-spring warmth.

I wrenched around and my thoughts stuttered, unable to fully comprehend what I was looking at. Swirling, viscous smoke roughly in the shape of a man churned a few feet away, and a body crushed almost beyond recognition lay on the ground before it. Blood pooled around the corpse and painted the alley walls. A sickening sense of power and darkness swept over me, making my stomach want to instantly reject this morning's cereal, and the buzz in my body ignited into an inferno.

The robber screamed, his eyes wild, and he fired three shots at the—

I had no idea what it was. It didn't look like any supernatural being I'd ever come across. Best guess was that it was a demon, but it didn't have the telltale heat, which meant casting a divine light strike might not work. And from its size and emanating power, if this was a demon, it should have been radiating heat like a furnace.

The guy's shots went wide, his panic making him shake, and the monster lashed out a smoky tentacle. It snapped around his neck, slammed him against the pharmacy's wall, and smashed his skull with a sickening crack. The gun dropped from the guy's hand, clattering to the asphalt at the edge of the blood pool. For a ridiculous split-second, I actually considered going for the weapon. If it had been fully loaded before the guy had fired, then there'd be three rounds remaining. But I didn't even know if normal ammunition would hurt this thing, since I doubted the robber's was enspelled. Hell, I had no idea if an enspelled bullet would hurt it.

I turned to run, but a whip of darkness snapped for me. I twisted out of the way, somehow managing to avoid a pile of rotting boxes and not trip, and forced myself to run faster. Another whip flew toward me. I twisted again, lost my balance, and careened into the alley wall. The creature howled, the sense of nausea deepening, making me gag, and three whips shot toward me.

Oh, shit.

I dodged one, but two more seized my leg. I hit the

asphalt, managing to protect my face with my hands, and was tossed back down the alley toward the monster's two victims. Half of my back and right shoulder slammed into the alley wall and searing pain screamed through my chest and neck. My knees hit the ground and I fought to stand and run. Hell, I fought to just breathe past the agony.

The monster swept toward me, and I scrambled back unable to get up on my feet, and instead falling onto my butt. My hand slapped into something warm and sticky. The blood from the crushed victim. Bile burned my throat, but now I was within grabbing distance of the gun.

Two more tendrils swiped at me. I threw myself to the side and snatched the weapon as the tendrils seized me around the chest. The monster jerked me up and agony screamed through me, threatening my consciousness. I gasped for air. The buzzing in my body joined the screaming pain and I felt like I was going to light on fire.

The monster jerked me closer, its writhing mass licking against my body, curling around my neck, and sliding over my face. I gasped out the spell that summoned a divine light strike. My very human level of power warmed the palm of my free hand and I slapped it against the tentacle around my chest.

White light snapped from my hand.

The monster hissed, the blast not even strong enough to make it cry out, and it slammed me against the alley wall, shooting agony through my chest, then jerked me close again. Its sense of power and darkness grew, and so did the buzz within me.

I fought to breathe, to think past the pain, but I couldn't break free. What little divine power I possessed wasn't strong enough. The only thing I had left was the gun. At least I was at point blank range. *Please, God, let a normal bullet kill it or something, anything.*

I fired.

The darkness screamed and more smoke swept around me, pouring into my mouth, suffocating me. I fired again and again and again, pulling the trigger even though I knew I was out of ammo, but the thing kept pouring into me, choking, engulfing, and making me want to scream and vomit. Except I couldn't get enough breath for either.

Far away, someone yelled.

A gunshot roared.

The monster screamed and jerked.

Three more shots, louder and closer, and the monster howled.

The darkness surged out of me, dropping me to the ground, face-first into the viscous puddle of blood, and flew away.

My stomach churned, the creature's nausea and darkness clinging to me, and the alley around me spun.

Two sets of feet pounded toward me, but I couldn't raise my head high enough to see who'd come to my rescue.

"Shit, Shaw." That sounded like Brant Keels, an officer in my precinct. "I couldn't see you behind it. If I'd known you were there, I wouldn't have fired."

Brant's partner, a rookie whose name I couldn't remember, knelt beside me and called for EMTs on his radio. His pale eyes were wide. He reached to touch me, his hand shaking, but stopped as if he was afraid to. "What was that?"

"I have no idea," I gasped. And I had no idea why it hadn't bashed my brains out like it had with the robber. Which scared the shit out of me.

CHAPTER 2

Ten minutes later an ambulance arrived and so did a horde of officers from my precinct—it being the closest one to the pharmacy. They swarmed the area, my captain sending out teams to search for the monster while Detectives Snyder and McLellan examined the scene.

Shaking and sliding in and out of consciousness, I was lifted onto a gurney. My chest was on fire, my stomach queasy, and my head spinning and spinning and spinning as I was rushed to the hospital.

I flirted with unconsciousness and didn't try to fight it. If I was unconscious, I wasn't feeling pain and I couldn't feel the buzz. It had eased, back to its normal non-nicotine level, but that was still painful.

I wasn't sure how I ended up in a hospital gown, but one minute I was in my blood-soaked clothes, the next I wasn't, and I was fuzzy on if I'd had X-rays taken or not. All I really remembered was feeling gentle hands, hearing a soothing voice, and looking into warm brown eyes in a devastatingly handsome face.

I woke with what felt like the worst hangover of my life—and I really wished it had been because I'd been an idiot and partied too hard last night. The buzz crawled in my skin and pain stabbed me in the chest and neck every time I took a breath. I was in a hospital bed, an intravenous needle in the back of one hand attached to a bag of something clear—saline?—with my other hand captured in a sling immobilizing my arm. My light brown hair hung loose, tickling my cheeks, and I was grateful someone had taken pity on what was probably a tangled half-ponytail and taken out the elastic. Above and beside me, a heart monitor beeped, sure and steady, and beside me sat the most gorgeous man I'd ever seen. Correction, demon. Little horns poked through his stylishly disheveled hair, indicating he was a supernatural being from the Realm of Celestial Darkness.

He slouched in the bedside chair, one leg up—ankle on his thigh—his attention on a folder of papers in his lap, his posture doing nothing to diminish his aura of lithe sexual danger. He reminded me of a cat, sprawled and half asleep but ready to pounce. From what I could see of his face, he looked young, mid-twenties, but being a demon, he could be much older. His black hair hung low, veiling his eyes and curling around his ears and the base of his neck, the color a stark contrast to his pale skin. He wore a black T-shirt stretched tight across a chiseled chest and muscular arms, leaving little to the imagination save for maybe what all that muscle would feel like under my hands or wrapped around me—

His gaze rose as if he could hear my thoughts. Heat flooded my face, and I was captured by his warm brown gaze, so unlike a typical demon. My pulse stuttered and the heat turned sultry, sinking low into my chest.

And then I remembered those eyes had been with me when I had entered the hospital, and I was certain now that he wasn't a doctor. Had he been there for my change of clothes? I shifted, trying to secretly determine if I still wore underwear. Had he seen me naked? I didn't know if I'd been in that blood pool long enough for it to seep through my pants and into my undies. God, that would be mortifying. If he was going to see me naked, I wanted to be conscious for it.

Which, jeez, shouldn't be something I was thinking.

It had to be the buzz, and the pain, and whatever medication I was on.

"You're awake," he said, his voice sliding over me like silk.

My brain stalled.

He closed the folder and leaned forward. "Officer Shaw, I'm Kol, an agent of the Joined Parliament."

...

"I need to ask you a few questions."

...

...

He pursed his lips and my brain jerked back into gear.

"Questions. Right. Yes." It made sense the Joined Parliament would take over the investigation into whatever it was that had attacked me. At least three rounds of department-issued enspelled ammunition hadn't taken it down. The officers in my precinct weren't prepared to deal with anything like it. My division had less than ten percent of supers living within its boundaries, and the most we had to deal with was the odd witch or minor demon causing trouble.

The door eased open, revealing an angel, the soft glow in his eyes giving away his divine nature. His wings were hidden, somehow absorbed into his body—that was part of the magic that made an angel an angel—and he wore a pale blue button-down—matching his eyes—and black slacks. His blond hair was perfect, not too short to look military, but not too long to look sloppy, and his chiseled jaw was clean-shaven. With broad shoulders—broader than the hot-as-hell demon—and narrow waist, he looked like the poster boy for angels: handsome, strong, divine, even if most of the angel population wasn't blond-haired and blue-eyed.

"Finally," he said, his tone brusque and edged with frustration. He strode into the room and turned his attention to Kol. "Has she said anything?"

"I was just about to," I said, pissed that he didn't bother to ask me. Typical angel. I knew they'd risked everything to save humankind, but they still acted like dicks around us. I was still an officer of the law, even if I didn't make everyone follow the rules as strictly as an angel did. Sometimes there really were shades of gray on the spectrum of right and wrong. Good thing most of the angels had returned to the Realm of Celestial Light after they had ensured the war was over and the humans and supers were playing together nicely. "And gee, sorry I got the shit beaten out of me and couldn't answer your questions right away."

Kol smirked, a hint of red hellfire flickering in his eyes.

The angel glared at me. "Ms. Shaw—"

"Officer," I corrected, unable to stop myself even though it was smarter not to draw unnecessary attention to myself.

"Been a beat cop for five years," Kol said. "She's not a rookie."

The angel shot him a dirty look. "Could have fooled me. What made you think you, a human, could take that perp on your own?"

"I hadn't been given much of a choice." I bit the inside of my cheek, yanked my gaze away from him, and glared out the window. Clearly the angel was a part of Kol's team, probably the boss, and I wasn't an idiot. I didn't just jump into danger thinking I was invincible. I'd already learned that lesson the hard way. That was why I'd taken the advanced combat training for dealing with supers and discovered I could summon a bit of divine light with one of the combat spells—and yes, I realized there was a risk of someone discovering my true nature by my being able to summon any kind of magic. But after a disaster that had nearly gotten me and my partner killed four and a half years ago, I wanted every tool in the toolbox so that never happened again.

The training had only taught me that I hadn't wanted to go up against that thing. And while my nephilim nature let me heal a little faster than the average human, it wasn't *that* fast.

I was also smart enough to remember to not piss off JP agents, even if the buzz and the pain and nausea were making it hard to concentrate. Especially if that agent was an angel.

Outside, it was bright, but there was almost no sunlight streaming through the glass onto the floor. Which meant the sun was high and it was around noon. Almost six hours since I'd walked into the pharmacy and thought I could stall a junkie long enough for backup to arrive.

I drew in a breath, trying to calm myself, but pain sliced into me, forcing me to take shallow, quick gasps. "I was in the alley before I knew the perp was there," I said through gritted teeth. "I'd been working on getting a hopped-up junkie with a gun away from civilians when things went sideways."

"That was the second body in the alley?" the angel asked.

"Yeah." I shuddered, the memory of the monster's essence churning my stomach.

The angel looked like he was trying not to roll his eyes at me, probably thinking I was shuddering over the gore. If I was smart, I'd let him continue believing that, no matter how much it grated on my nerves. Honestly, I was smart.

"You know you're lucky to be alive," Kol said, his voice tender and sensual and drawing my attention back to him. He leaned even closer to me. The warmth in his eyes and the heat gently radiating from his body made my heart flutter.

My thoughts stalled and for a second there was only him, no pain, no angel, and no worry about being discovered, then everything evened out. I could think, and while both the buzz and pain were still there, they'd been relegated to the back of my mind.

"That better?" he asked.

"What did you do?"

"Nothing you need to worry about," the angel said before Kol could answer. "Now I need you to give a detailed description of the perpetrator. The other officers didn't get a great look at him, but you were up close."

"Him? It could have been female for all I knew. I'm not even sure what it was." And God, I'd had it pouring down my throat.

I shuddered again, making myself gasp in pain.

"Stop thinking about the bodies and concentrate on the killer," the angel snapped.

"I'm not thinking about the bodies," I snapped back. "I'm thinking about the smoke tentacle monster who cracked a man's head open with one swing and crushed someone to a pulp. I'm thinking how I have no idea how the hell I'm still here, how it didn't rip me apart or crush me or just beat me to death against the wall when it had me in its grasp or when I managed to shoot it."

The angel's eyes widened. "It held you? For longer than a few seconds at a time?"

"Yeah." Why hadn't it killed me?

Someone knocked on the door, opening it without waiting for an answer, and a massive man entered. He was bigger in every way than the angel, with shoulder-length light brown hair pulled back at the nape of his neck. The intensity in his dark eyes was breathtaking, captivating me as much as the demon beside me but in a different way, and his black calf-length duster made him look just as dangerous but more like a Wild West outlaw than a JP agent.

He moved to stand beside the angel, allowing another man behind him to enter, and my heart skipped a beat with a stuttering bleep on the heart monitor, my breath stolen.

"Marcus."

My thoughts stalled on his name. It had been four and a half years since we'd worked together. And four and a half since the biggest mistake of my life, which had gotten Marcus bitten by a werewolf, and the reason I'd taken the advanced training for supers. There'd been a one in a million chance that he'd be susceptible to lycanthropy, so the odds had been in his favor that he'd gotten through my fuck-up okay, but he'd still demanded a transfer and left. He hadn't even cleaned out his locker or said anything to me. Not a word after the incident. But then I'd been the rookie who'd nearly gotten him killed. I wouldn't have wanted to talk to me, either.

His beautiful green eyes narrowed, a muscle in his jaw twitched, and the temperature in the room rose.

Yeah, four and a half years wasn't enough for forgiveness, and given that my empathy had instantly connected with it, his anger toward me was still strong. Not that I deserved forgiveness. The next time, if I hadn't outright killed him, he could actually have been infected or enspelled with something that would have taken his humanity and turned him into a super. And while there was a small percentage of the population who wanted that, most didn't, and Marcus hadn't struck me as someone who did.

He eased his lean-muscled body against the doorframe and crossed his arms, not even willing to step all the way into the room. God, he was just as handsome as I remembered, rich skin tone, piercing green eyes, his perpetual five o'clock shadow darkening his cheeks and making him mouth-wateringly sexy. Not to mention the way his gray T-shirt stretched across his muscular chest and his jeans hugged his narrow hips.

There'd been something between us. Hell, there'd been a whole lot of something. An attraction that had sizzled and stolen my breath the moment we'd first met. Every time we'd worked together the temperature had always been a little too warm, a little too sultry, whispering to me that he felt the connection, too. But he'd always kept his emotional and personal distance, and I'd messed everything up before fully establishing a working partnership, let alone the intimacy the attraction promised.

Except that sizzle was still there, instantly flaming a need for him within me that I thought had long been snuffed out, as if four and a half years and the biggest mistake of my life had never happened.

"Are we done here, Gideon?" he asked, his attention turning to the angel.

"No. We need to transfer Ms. Shaw—"

I glared at the angel. "Officer."

"—*Officer* Shaw," Gideon said. "We need to transfer her immediately to Operations. She's survived extended contact with the perp, which means we can examine her memories and get his essence."

My pulse picked up, the heart monitor revealing my fear. Shit. If I went into the Joined Parliament Operations Building and let them read my memories, they could learn the truth about me and I might never come out. "I'm a human. I can't sense magical essence."

"You don't have to," the Wild West guy said, his voice a deep rumble, his gaze jumping from me to the heart monitor and back again. "You're alive, so your memories are, too. The lethe demon will be able to sense details your mind isn't able to register."

"A memory demon?" I made my voice crack—I didn't have to work too hard at it—hoping it would make them think that was what I was afraid of, and then pulled the heart monitor's sensor from my finger.

The monitor squealed.

Marcus winced. But at me or the monitor? "She's clearly refusing consent."

"You saw what this thing can do," Gideon said, and a hint of emotion, fear and need, seeped through his chilly expression. The emotions weren't enough to shift my empathy from Marcus's anger, but it did surprise me. Angels were warriors who knew how to lock their feelings away and do what needed to be done. It made them efficient officers of the law, but not overly compassionate. Which meant whatever this monster was, whatever it had done, was enough to break through his icy emotional shield.

"She said she doesn't want to do it," Marcus said, his voice low.

Why was he trying to protect me? Except the moment I thought that, I was sure he wasn't protecting me, he was probably trying to get the hell away from me. Taking me to the Joined Parliament Operations Building meant spending more time with me and he'd made it perfectly clear after that horrible night that he wanted nothing to do with me. Which, if I was being honest, still hurt.

"Technically she hasn't refused, just had a panic attack about it." Kol turned off the screaming heart monitor, leaned forward again, and captured my hand. Heat pulsed from his grip like a heartbeat, sending a wash of warmth up my arm, adding to the heated emotion in the room that no one else could feel. "The lethe demon isn't that scary. It won't hurt. It's just like—"

"It's not consent if she doesn't have free will," Wild West guy said.

"Jeez," Kol said with a huff. "I'm not even doing *that*. I'm just trying to calm her."

Gideon's gaze dipped to our joined hands and Kol huffed again and released me.

"I've been a part of this team for over a year. When have I ever mixed business with pleasure?"

"There's always a first time," Gideon said.

"And you did insist on being the one to sit here until she woke up." Wild West guy raised an eyebrow, clearly not believing Kol. "You've never been interested in watching over a damsel in distress before."

Marcus snorted. "She's hardly a damsel."

"Dude, you seriously need to have your eyes checked," Kol said. "And yes, I did, because this guy has dropped three supers in five days. We need to get on top of this."

And now that I knew they were after a serial killer, refusing to have my memories examined only made me look suspicious. I was a cop. I was supposed to want to do anything within the law to save people.

And I did. But I couldn't let them know the truth about me.

"It doesn't hurt. You'll even feel better about what... happened." A hint of sadness crept into Kol's gaze, and he slid it over my body, warming my insides and confirming that Kol had been there when they'd stripped me down and assessed my injuries. "And the lethe demon won't look at anything he's not supposed to."

Yeah, right. I didn't believe that for a second. Lethe demons fed on the emotions around memories. Technically they fed on the whole memory, but since they could survive on the emotion alone, the law prevented them from full consumption. Some people actually used them as a form of therapy to purge the emotions around horrific events, but that didn't mean this lethe demon wouldn't take a sip from other memories with strong emotions while in my head. And I had some strong emotions, particularly from my childhood, where I was terrified of someone learning what I was. Hell, I was still scared about that. I was just better able to compartmentalize it so I could hold down a job.

"Will you consent?" Gideon asked.

"I—" I was torn. Saying yes could save lives. It could also end mine.

"Will you?" Gideon's eyes narrowed, as if he was trying to will me into compliance without breaking his precious rules.

"Give her a moment to think about it," Wild West guy said. "She's probably still in shock."

Gideon jerked his attention to him. "We both know we don't have a moment. We've already wasted hours waiting for her to wake on the slim chance she has a lead. Well, she does." More emotion seeped into his voice. This felt like it was more than just an angel determined to find justice. It felt personal.

Gideon's gaze swept back to me, his pale eyes icy with determination. "I *can* get a court order."

The temperature in the room dropped, but I couldn't tell what it meant or who it came from. Useless stupid empathy.

"Whoa." Kol straightened, his expression shocked.

The angel pulled his phone from his pocket, likely to call a judge to get the order.

Marcus jerked a step into the room. "Gideon, really?"

"It's safer for everyone if you consent," Gideon said.

Except it certainly wasn't going to be safer for me. And now it pissed me off that he hadn't even given me a chance to say yes... not that I would have. Jeez, couldn't he wait until my head wasn't throbbing and I could think straight?

"Officer Shaw—" The pain in Gideon's eyes was shocking. This was deeply personal for him. "People are dying."

Which is what it came down to. Whatever had attacked me scared me to death. I didn't doubt that with its strength it could murder any number of powerful supers, maybe even an angel, and if it was on a killing spree and I could help stop it, I had to let the lethe demon see what had happened and get the monster's magical essence. The God damn angel in me couldn't let the murders continue even if it meant putting myself in danger.

Another shiver swept through me, slashing agony through my chest. Maybe I'd get lucky and the lethe demon wouldn't find out I was a nephilim. Without a doubt he was going to know that thing had poured down my throat.

Jeez, I wasn't even going to think about what these JP agents would do when they learned that. Would they consider me lucky or become suspicious because I wasn t dead? What it really came down to was that I couldn't live with myself if more people died.

Fine. God help me.

"I'll do it."

CHAPTER 3

MARCUS GLARED AT ME, THE HEAT IN THE ROOM GROWING, and I met his glare. He was just going to have to put up with me for however long it took for the lethe demon to reveal my secret. Then he could have a party when Gideon arrested me.

My insides churned at the thought. This was a nightmare. There wasn't a way out of this and I could be spending my last free minutes with a man who hated me.

"Let's get this over with," I said through gritted teeth.

"Kol, arrange Officer Shaw's release from the hospital and let Amiah and Yadveer know we're coming. Jacob, a word." Gideon jerked his chin to the door and Wild West man turned to leave. "Marcus, keep an eye on her."

Wonderful. Now I was going to be left alone with him and his rage, which was so strong it burned.

Kol, Gideon, and Jacob left, closing the door on me and Marcus. His presence filled the room, more masculine and powerful than I remembered, almost ferocious.

There'd always been something overwhelming about Marcus. That had to be why I'd screwed up all those years ago. I'd been distracted by him. A part of me had wanted my attraction to him to be purely physical. The guy was hot with the sexy scruff along his jaw and those eyes that could capture my soul. But there'd been something else with him, something deeper. I couldn't put it into words then, and I couldn't now.

The buzz inside me bit into my skin and the heat in the room continued to grow. I fought the urge to push the sheet back to help cool down. I didn't know how little clothing I had on and I didn't want him to think my sudden rise in temperature was because I was attracted to him. Even if part of it was. Nothing was ever going to happen between us. I'd screwed up while working with him. We weren't friends, we didn't really know each other, and from his emotional heat it was clear he didn't want that to change.

His gaze dipped down my body, making the heat of desire billow within me. The sense of ferocious power about him grew. "Five broken ribs, a broken collarbone, and most likely a concussion," he growled.

"No wonder I feel like I want to throw up."

"Kol says you did. Nearly got his boots." A hint of a smile curled Marcus's lips. "Serves him right for trying to enthrall away your pain so he could interview you before the doctors dosed you with painkillers."

So Kol had tried to enthrall me. That meant his demonic nature gave him some kind of mind magic. Probably, given his looks, he was an incubus who fed on sexual energy. No wonder just looking at him turned me on. I shuddered, spiking pain through my chest, and gasped.

The muscles in Marcus's jaw twitched, his smile gone, and the heat turned humid. Sweat pricked on my forehead, under my arms, and between my breasts. Jeez, I was going to turn into a puddle and then evaporate with this heat. And God damn it, I needed a nicotine patch. It was so hard to think past everything. Easing the buzz would at least help. Easing the heat would as well.

Fine. To hell with how much clothing I did or didn't have on. I couldn't handle this on top of the pain and the nausea. I tugged the sheet up just past the knee of my left leg, praying that uncovering even this little bit of skin would help cool me.

Marcus's gaze leaped to the massive bruise on my knee and the temperature in the room jumped to sweltering. God, he was so mad at me.

"What the hell were you thinking in that alley?" he said, his voice low, his body tense.

"What?"

"What were you thinking?" His hands fisted. "Haven't you learned anything since you were a rookie?"

"This wasn't like what happened to us." No. I'd been smart this time and tried to run. The monster just hadn't let me.

"They said you didn't even have your sidearm."

"I hadn't started work yet."

"So you just decided to confront a super who could squash a human without breaking a sweat before you started your day? God, Essie—" He raked a hand through his black locks. "What is wrong with you?" Accusation and frustration filled his voice, making me feel just like I'd had that horrible night four and a half a years ago.

And I deserved his anger. I'd screwed up and he had a right to confront me about it whenever he was ready. I had called and left over a dozen apologies on his voice mail when I'd realized I wasn't going to see him again, but he'd never called back. And even if he had, I could never have made it up to him for almost infecting him with lycanthropy and nearly killing him. The problem was, if he'd returned my calls and demanded answers, I wouldn't have had any for him, just like I didn't have any now.

"Well?" he growled. "You're going to get yourself killed."

"You mean I'm going to get someone else killed."

"That's not what I said."

The door opened and Kol entered, pushing a wheelchair. "A chariot for the lady. Oh, and some pants." The incubus held up a pair of green scrub pants.

Marcus held his glare at me, as if daring me to say something. But I didn't know what to say. There wasn't anything I could say. All I could do was not screw up so badly with any other partner.

"Fine." With a growl, he turned and shoved past Kol. "I'll get the car." He strode from the room, taking his ferocious heat with him and leaving me cold and a little empty.

"Don't mind him. It's just getting close to that time of

the month," Kol said. "Makes him ornery. I'll go get the nurse to help you change." Kol flashed a wicked grin. "Unless you want me to stay?"

As much as a part of me really wanted him to stay... "The nurse, please. But I think you've forgotten something."

"Clothes and a wheelchair. Pretty sure that's everything." The playfulness softened out of his expression and turned to sympathy. "The clothes you arrived in were covered in blood and the docs cut them off you. I didn't think you'd want them back."

"I don't. But I could use a shirt." I didn't want to be walking around in a hospital gown for who knew how long.

"Until Amiah mends your broken collarbone, I'm pretty sure you don't want to be pulling on a shirt. Trust me." He shuddered and a hint of darkness clouded his expression before he flashed a heart-pounding smile. "But that's your first stop at Operations, so you'll be out of the gown soon enough."

He hurried out the door and I contemplated sitting up. The bed was at a bit of an angle, but I wasn't sure if I was forward enough for my battered body to pull me up. If it hurt to breathe, it was going to hurt sitting up, and I only had one good arm to help me.

A nurse entered, her face flushed and her eyes bright, and I couldn't help but wonder if that was what I looked like every time Kol talked to me. She helped me slide on the pants—and yep, I'd lost my underwear. Then she sat me up so my legs hung over the side of the bed and unhooked the IV from my hand. My body screamed in agony, every gasping breath as shallow as I could make it. The room spun and the contents of my queasy stomach sloshed, but I managed to not pass out or throw up. Somehow I fought through the pain of just moving and got into the wheelchair. God, I had no idea how I was going to manage getting into a car, let alone getting out of it or anything else.

The nurse helped me put on my running shoes and turned me to push me out as Jacob opened the door, as if he'd known we were ready to leave. Gideon stood a few feet away, gave a tight nod, and headed to the elevator without waiting for a response. Jacob dismissed the nurse and took over pushing me, while Kol bounded down the hall toward us, leaving a group of nurses at the floor's station desk flushed and excited.

Gideon rolled his eyes. Not the response I expected. But then, if they'd been working together for over a year as Kol had said, the icy angel would have had to accept the incubus's nature or kicked him off the team.

The elevator doors opened. We took it down to the parking garage, where Marcus waited in a running chunky dark gray SUV.

This wasn't going to be fun.

I tried to take in a deep breath to steady myself and was painfully reminded that a deep breath was a terrible idea. The pain sent the parking garage spinning and my stomach churning. *Oh, Lord, was it too late to go back and ask for stronger painkillers or hell, something to just knock me out?*

"Get the door," Gideon said to Kol, then he bent, slid one arm under my legs and the other across my back, and

picked me up. His strong arms held me with ease and
cradled me against his muscular chest. The scent of
springtime enveloped me, the air after a rainstorm, fresh-
cut grass, and sun-warmed skin. His scent was warm and
comforting. There was nothing frozen about it.

He set me in a seat in the middle row as gently as he'd
picked me up, a stark contrast to how he'd talked to me
earlier. Of course he hadn't said anything to me or looked
at me, so he wasn't acting completely out of character. He
took the front passenger seat ahead of me, while Kol slid
into the seat beside me. Jacob folded up the wheelchair,
put it in the back, and took a seat beside it, then Marcus
drove us out of the parking garage, his emotions
simmering around me again.

The hospital wasn't far from the Supers' Quarter, but
it didn't cater to supers. They had their own facility,
which was probably a good thing. I couldn't imagine the
average human doctor or nurse trying to help a vampire
or werewolf or even demon in medical distress. They
might be living out in the open now, but that didn't mean
they were any less powerful or dangerous. And while
some humans were adjusting well to this new norm, most
hadn't. Just under a quarter of a century had passed since
everything humankind knew had been turned upside
down. Being happy that your new next door neighbor
only came out at night and preferred a diet of O negative
was still a long way away.

Of course, the supers weren't thrilled to be living
beside neighbors who started growing wolf's bane or
installing silver door handles, and even adding all the
supernatural species together, they were still a small

percentage of the earth's population and outnumbered by the humans—the very reason they'd been living in secret for so long. So the Joined Parliament had expropriated areas at the edges of a few of the largest cities and created neighborhoods catering to supers. Most had at least one high rise apartment/office building with UV filtering glass and a park covered with a UV filtering glass canopy for vampires, as well as dense forested areas for shifters to release their beasts and help their children deal with the first five or so years of their transition.

Not all members of the supernatural community lived in the Quarter, but most did, and it was enough to maintain a peace between humans and supers. Of course, it hadn't hurt that the supers had come to humanity's defense when half of angelkind had tried to eradicate us.

What the members of the Joined Parliament hadn't expected was for the Supers' Quarters to regularly draw human visitors—the few of us who'd embraced the idea that supers lived among us—and an eclectic mix of businesses had moved into our city's Quarter, catering to all kinds. For those humans who were brave or didn't care about the Supers' dangerous natures, the area was a pretty happening place and had a rocking nightlife. Or so I'd been told.

I'd never crossed through the park surrounding the district, which ensured a clear separation between humans and supers, as agreed upon by the Parliament. I hadn't wanted to run into one of the few angels living in Union City.

So much for that.

Now I was going into the heart of angel central where

every angel in town—thankfully not many, but still every angel—lived and worked. The Joined Parliament Operations Building.

Marcus turned a corner and headed to the park at the end of the street. The delineation from towering residential high rise and park ring was almost shocking, as if the city had just stopped at the edge of a forest. No series of strip malls leading out of town or farmers' fields. Just blam, mature maples and oaks and blue spruce right up to the chain link fences at the edge of the last properties. But that was part of the magic that made the Supers' Quarter. I didn't know what super had made the trees rapidly mature, but my mother said that within six years, the park ring had looked as if it had always been there.

Sunlight filtered through the canopy above, sending bands of light cutting across the road and into the SUV for a few minutes, and then we were through and the metropolis continued. This had been an older part of town, since the city officials hadn't been willing to let the Parliament expropriate newly built properties, so most of the buildings didn't tower as high as the rest of the city. Artistic scrollwork and wide ledges ornamented the façades of the buildings on either side of the street. The bricks were stained with age, but modern signs hung above the doors of the ground floor businesses and the roads and sidewalks were in good condition.

People drove, rode bicycles, and walked up and down the sidewalk, coming or going from stores, window shopping, and just looking everyday normal. Save for the few demons with horns, onyx skin, or tails, and the odd person with features that didn't look quite human, this could have been any street in the downtown core.

Marcus turned at the first intersection and pulled into the short driveway of a converted 19th century two-story warehouse with a five-story high rise added to the back. The big garage door ahead of us rose on silent tracks and we drove inside, parking in the first spot. There were two other SUVs parked a few spots down as well as about two dozen other vehicles, mostly sedans and hatchbacks.

Much to my surprise, Gideon picked me up and eased me back into the wheelchair, his fresh, warm scent wrapping around me again. Not surprising, though, that as soon as I was seated, he marched away, expecting everyone else to follow.

"I'll go check on Yadveer," Marcus said, also storming away.

The temperature in the garage dropped, the air cooling but still holding a hint of dampness. I hadn't realized how hot Marcus had been making me feel until he was gone, and, if I was being honest with myself, the heat was from both his mood and his body.

"And I'll find you that shirt." Kol darted after Gideon and Marcus, and I was left with Jacob, once again my chauffeur, pushing me toward the door.

One of the chair's wheels squeaked. I hadn't noticed it in the hospital, but in the quiet of the garage it was nerve-gratingly clear. That, along with the buzz, the fear of being discovered, and Jacob's silence, and I was squirming by the time we reached the door only a few feet away.

"So... ah... have you been a JP agent for long?"

"Since its inception," he said in his soft rumble. He hit the button to automatically open the door and we waited for it to slowly... draw... open, then he wheeled me into a long institutional hall with white walls, a frosted-glass sliding door about twenty feet down, and pale gray flooring.

Silence again.

The buzz continued to nip at me and my nerves tightened until I wasn't sure if it was the concussion nauseating me or not, and the squeaky wheel cr-creaked, cr-creaked, cr-creaked—

Oh, my God! This was a terrible idea. I needed a distraction and damned if I wasn't going to force Jacob to be one.

"What makes a—" I had no idea what kind of super he was. "—a super become an agent?"

"I fought in the war. It was a natural transition."

"I'm not sure soldier to investigator is a natural transition." Sure, in the case of being an agent of the Joined Parliament, it wasn't as much of a leap as a human soldier becoming a detective, since often criminal supers were more aggressive than humans and military training would likely be used more often. But I was trying to distract myself before I went insane.

Jacob shrugged. "It's as natural as anything else about me."

I wasn't sure if that was self-deprecation or a clue about the kind of super he was. If he wasn't a natural super, that meant he'd been made, and the pool of possibilities shrank to a shifter of some kind, a witch who'd made a demon-deal, and a vampire. There were a few other kinds of supers that could be made instead of born, but those were the top three.

I tried to get a better look at his face, but couldn't turn my head far enough with the agony of my broken collarbone. With his bulky size and tanned complexion, I'd guess shifter. I'd heard that the JP liked to make their teams diverse to help ease tensions among the various communities. Marcus was clearly the human on the team —as rare and dangerous as it was for a powerless human to be on a JP team—Kol the demon, Gideon the angel, which left Jacob.

Yeah. He had to be the shifter.

We reached a T-intersection, and Jacob pushed me around the corner and through the first door on the right into an office. The room was packed with books and papers and plants with just enough room for the wheelchair and Jacob. An angel sat behind a desk covered with paperwork, the papers and folders and notepads piled on top, on the floor against the legs, and on the chair beside it. She could have been Gideon's sister with her long blond hair, sharp blue eyes, and sculpted features, and a part of me wondered if I'd been told a lie all my life and all angels really were blond-haired, blue-eyed beauties. But then that would have made my mother a liar. She'd said my father's hair had been brown with a hint of copper if the sun hit it just the right way and his eyes were brown with flecks of gold. And while I had the brown hair with a hint of copper, my brown eyes were just brown. Boring and thankfully very human.

The angel closed the file she was reading and her expression turned icy. "Officer Esther Shaw."

"I'll wait outside," Jacob said.

"No need." The angel stood and strode around the desk. "I'm Amiah, and Marcus Diaz has told me all about you."

Just great.

CHAPTER 4

Amiah crossed her arms and stood just out of reach, looking down at me. "The humans agreed to protocols regarding supernatural criminals. This is at least the second time you've ignored that, Officer Shaw." She raised an eyebrow, but I didn't get a sense of angel iciness about her, more of an anger under tight control. The temperature in the room didn't change, so under very tight control. "If I looked at your service file, would I find more disregard for protocol?"

"No." And the incident with today's monster hadn't been on purpose—neither really had been the one with Marcus. But I was smart enough not to say that out loud. That would only start a fight, and I didn't want to draw any more attention to myself than necessary. What was it with everyone assuming I was stupid enough to think I could have taken that thing on by myself? Or at all?

Jacob cleared his throat and Amiah's attention jumped to him. "We're in a bit of a hurry. If you would?"

"She doesn't deserve this," Amiah said, but she

stepped forward and clasped my broken shoulder. Lightning shot through me, white hot agony. It turned the buzz into an inferno, screaming in a dissonant resonance to Amiah's magic.

I clenched my teeth against the grating vibrations and every muscle jerked taut. It was like that time we had to go through Taser training and each of us had to experience what over 1,200 volts felt like surging through our body. I couldn't move and couldn't breathe. There was only agony and my whirling thoughts. And at the forefront was the fear that somehow, by using her healing magic on me, Amiah would know I was a nephilim.

Then she jerked her hand back. I sagged in the wheelchair, my muscles twitching, but was unable to tell if the agony of broken bones was gone. The nausea certainly wasn't, and now my buzz was stronger and the room was spinning.

"Healing her like that wasn't necessary," Jacob said, his voice low.

Amiah strode back to her chair behind the desk and sat. "You said you were in a hurry."

"Gideon wouldn't have been impressed if you'd damaged her mind while fixing her bones."

"I didn't." She flipped open the file she'd been reading. "Now get her out of my office."

A hint of a growl rumbled from Jacob, but he pulled me out into the hall and shut Amiah's office door.

"She shouldn't have done that," he said, leaning closer to me. "Are you okay?"

Even with only seeing him from the corner of my eye, the intensity radiating from him made me shiver.

The hall twisted, but the pain in my chest was gone.

"I think I just need a moment."

"You can have a moment when you're done with Yadveer, the lethe demon," Gideon said. He stood in a doorway at the end of the hall.

I opened my mouth to protest then snapped it shut. The sooner I dealt with this, the sooner I could get out of there. Maybe if things moved quickly enough, Gideon and everyone else wouldn't notice the truth about me. This monster was killing supers and if the crack in Gideon's icy angel emotions was an indication of anything, capturing this monster was personal.

And maybe I had nothing to worry about. Maybe I didn't have enough angel in me for anyone to notice. Amiah hadn't, and I was sure she'd have said something if she had. Maybe the lethe demon wouldn't either.

Which only provided a stronger incentive for hurrying through this. In and out and I could go back to being a beat cop in my mostly human neighborhood.

Jacob pulled the wheelchair back, drawing me closer to him and making my long hair brush against his clothes. "She can have a moment."

Gideon stiffened. "Which of us do you think he's hunting next? Prudence and Javan could have been a coincidence, but now Paul is dead. That's a pattern."

"And we won't get anything if her mind shuts down," Jacob growled. "You've more patience than this."

Gideon gave him a withering look, only adding to my impression that this investigation was personal.

Here was hoping that would be enough to distract him and dismiss me.

I drew in a shallow breath to try to steady the whirling room and confirmed that yes, I could breathe without pain.

"Let's just get this done." I considered standing and walking the distance between us but thought better of it. I didn't want to collapse halfway there and draw out my stay at angel central.

I glanced up at Jacob. His expression was pinched, but he gave a tight nod and pushed me into a dimly lit room, past Gideon standing near the door. It was twice the size of Amiah's office, but the walls, floor, and ceiling were painted black, and it didn't have any furniture except for four long benches, one tucked tight against each wall.

Kol and Marcus sat on the one to my right, and the temperature plummeted as my empathy locked onto someone, probably Marcus. He still looked angry, ready to start a brawl, his body tense, his muscles bunched, and his rage had probably swung from heated fury to cold and calculating.

Beside him, Kol leaned against the wall with a folded shirt in his lap, his posture relaxed and sensual, but a sense of tension radiated from him as well.

An elderly man sat in the center on a black pillow, the fabric satiny, reflecting the illumination from the single-bulb light fixture above him. Shadows accentuated his lined and weathered features and a prick of red hellfire glowed in his dark eyes.

"Sit." He pointed to the floor in front of him.

My insides lurched at the idea that I was actually going to go through with this. Not that I had much of a choice, but inevitability didn't necessarily do anything for nerves. And as much as I'd tried to fool myself that if I rushed through this no one would notice me, I doubted it would work.

I unhooked the sling, slid my arm out, and grabbed the wheelchair arms to help ease myself from the chair to the floor in front of the lethe demon. The room still spun, but not nearly as much as before, and I tried to focus on that, not the fear thrumming through me.

He held out his hand. "Give me your hand."

"It's a very recent memory." The words blurted out before I could stop them from revealing my fear that this demon could see things I didn't want him to see.

"Marcus made that very clear." He extended his hand a little closer to me, and I could feel his demonic heat radiating from his skin.

Behind the demon, Marcus shifted on the bench. Now he looked uncomfortable on top of itching for a fight. I'd never seen him like that before. When I'd been his partner, he'd always been in control. His control hadn't been rigid like an angel's, but it had been there. I'd always felt like he'd be able to handle anything. At least until I'd screwed up and we'd ended up in a fight for our lives with four werewolves on a night of the full moon, when they were the most volatile. Now he looked like he was barely holding it together.

"Your hand."

I wrenched my attention back to Yadveer and took his too-warm hand before I could change my mind. His fingers clasped mine and heat trickled over my wrist and up my arm.

It seeped across my chest, up my neck, and into my head, soothing me. It wrapped around me like a blanket, soft and fuzzy, whispering into my soul and taking me to that warm, lazy place between awake and asleep. I lay on a blanket in my mom's backyard. Dappled sunlight, dancing among the leaves of the maple tree above, warmed me, and a gentle breeze caressed my cheeks and forearms. Beside me was a thin chapter book, the kind I had started reading in first grade, but the cover was out of focus. I couldn't tell what I was reading.

I frowned. Was that part of the concussion? It hadn't made anything else out of focus, and the leaves above and the weave of the blanket were perfectly clear.

So why the book—?

Because that detail had faded from memory.

I jerked up and my mom's backyard rippled, as if it were a reflection in water.

No. This wasn't right. The lethe demon was too far back. Way too far back.

"You don't get to take this one." And oh, God, in a few minutes my mother was going to walk onto the deck and tell me we were moving again. A team of angels hunting the last of the fallen angels had established a temporary base in our small town and we had to leave.

My pulse jerked into a rapid tattoo. I had to leave this memory. Now.

My mom had always been honest with me about who I was and why she did the things she did. My angelic nature had to have come up in that conversation. And I wasn't going to try to remember if it did or not and risk Yadveer seeing it.

"Get out." Think of something else.

I heard the back door slide open and my mom's foot-steps on the deck.

"I said get out!"

Everything went black. The room flickered into view, Yadveer clutching my hand, eyes closed and brow furrowed in concentration, and Marcus's cold rage stinging my skin. Then darkness jerked me back and I crashed into the alley wall. Blood was everywhere, more than what I was sure I'd seen that morning, as if my subconscious had glommed onto that detail and exaggerated it.

The robber screamed and the monster broke his neck and shattered his skull, the sound sickening, emphasized like the blood.

I jerked away to get the hell out of there, tripped, was grabbed, tossed, and slammed into the alley wall. Then the monster seized me, its viscous smoke thicker, stickier than I remembered, the darkness and power oozing evil. Its tentacles squeezed agony through my chest and it poured its essence into me, drowning me with its darkness. I fought to breathe, gasped a trickle of air, and choked on its smoke again.

Reliving that terrible moment crystallized the horror into sharp detail. I was on fire, but I couldn't tell if it was from pain or emotion or something else. My lungs screamed for air, my body grew heavy, unconsciousness threatening to take me.

It felt like an eternity before I wrenched the revolver up and fired, and another eternity before I fired again. I heaved in the monster's grasp. I had to get free and get it out of me. I had to get—

Something cracked against my cheek and pain stung my face. I opened my eyes and found myself lying on the floor. I must have collapsed and smacked my cheek on the black tiles and Yadveer hadn't tried to catch me. He clutched his throat as if he struggled to breathe and stared at me in horror. If he'd fed off my emotions, he was probably close to having a panic attack. Except I was still terrified, my pulse still racing, so the emotions were still in me. In fact, I think I was more scared now than I'd been before.

Two sets of booted feet hurried across the floor, but one set stopped before reaching me.

The other set drew close and Kol knelt beside me, placing a hand on my shoulder. Warmth slipped into me but it didn't ease the panic clutching my heart.

The stopped set of feet shifted away. That had to be Marcus. He'd been sitting beside Kol and had jumped up to help me, then had thought better of it. I couldn't blame him, but a small part of me was disappointed.

"Did you get his essence?" Gideon asked from behind me.

"It doesn't fit with what she saw." Yadveer's voice trembled. "I can't make sense of it."

"I'm not doing that again so you can figure it out." No way in hell.

"You shouldn't have to," Kol said, helping me sit.

"Shouldn't? That doesn't inspire confidence." And I didn't want to risk Yadveer seeing any of my other memories.

Gideon strode toward us. "Show me."

Yadveer pressed his palms to Gideon's temples. The angel's eyes rolled back and he gasped, coughed, choked on something, and gasped again.

I pushed away from Kol and stood, needing to get farther away from my memory even though I wasn't reliving it with Gideon. My stomach churned, the clinging thick smoke too fresh in my mind, and my buzz began to roar under my skin.

Gideon jerked away from Yadveer and his gaze jumped to me. His eyes were dark as if a cloud had passed over their summer-sky blue and dimmed their angelic glow, and his icy demeanor was arctic.

His intensity drilled into me and my pulse froze. I couldn't tell if he knew I was a nephilim or if the danger radiating from him was because the monster had tried to drown me with its essence.

I staggered back a step, needing to put more distance between us, but he jerked forward and his hand clamped around my biceps. Pain burned into my skin where he held me.

"What was that?"

I wrenched against his grip but he held tight and the burning intensified.

"You're hurting her," Marcus growled.

"I'm not holding her that tight."

And he wasn't. So why the hell did I feel like I was being branded with a hot poker?

"Why didn't that wraith possess you?" Gideon asked. "And why didn't it have a wraith's essence?"

"How the hell am I supposed to know?" I yanked at

his grip again. "For the love of God, if you don't let go I'm going to start screaming in pain or pass out."

"You shouldn't have an injury this painful," Jacob said. "Amiah can't pick and choose what she heals. Her magic heals the worst first, even if she doesn't complete the healing."

Gideon grabbed my wrist with his free hand, keeping hold of me, and yanked up the sleeve of my hospital gown. An angry red welt in the shape of a sigil looked like it had been burned on the inside of my left biceps, just above my elbow.

"What is that?" I asked, my voice cracking.

Kol's eyes widened. "Is that an angelic mating brand?"

"A mating what?" Oh, God. Was it something an angel got when they were ready to have a family? Did this give me away as a nephilim, since my essence clearly wasn't that of an angel?

"It's rare," Jacob said, drawing closer from his position at the door.

"It's a mark that binds an angel's soul to another soul, mating them. It's usually between angels, but it can be between an angel and a non-angel," Kol said.

My thoughts stuttered. I was already mated? How the hell was I already mated? And with who?

"The connection is deep," Kol said, "intimate. It can make an angel do crazy things to protect their mate."

"That's because their souls are so intertwined they're compelled to protect each other," Jacob said.

"It only looks like a compulsion to those who've had no experience with it." Gideon glared at Jacob. "If you're in the bond, you don't feel compelled at all. It's beautiful."

"We've seen differently during the war," Jacob said.

"That couldn't have been a true bond, or it had been so twisted with evil intent that it was permanently warped. But this..." Gideon's attention turned back to my arm. "I know it's a mating brand, I can sense it, but the magic feels wrong. It doesn't even feel like that twisted brand we came across during the war," he said to Jacob. "Not to mention a true mating brand would be gold, not red."

My gaze locked on the painful welt. I had to get rid of this. I couldn't be bonded with anyone. I couldn't have anything to do with the supernatural world.

"So what does this mean?" Marcus asked. "There wasn't anything in her chart indicating she had the brand before, and you," he said to Gideon, "are you branded?"

"I would have felt it if I was," Gideon said.

"The only other angel she's been in contact with is Amiah and Essie isn't her type. So does this mean our killer, this wraith, has an angel's magical essence?" Marcus asked. "And did he brand her?"

Gideon's gaze grew unfocused and he frowned. "According to Officer Shaw's memory, he did."

CHAPTER 5

"That thing branded me?" This wasn't happening. It couldn't be happening. The words whirled in my head over and over again. "It can't be true." I couldn't be caught up in a supernatural anything. I had to get out of there before Gideon realized what I was, before—

God, no. No no no no.

I staggered back a step, but Gideon's grip on my wrist tightened, keeping me captive.

"Just take a breath," he said. "We can protect you."

"Protect me?" From an intimate magical connection with a monster that would compel me to protect it? "I want you to get rid of it."

A shadow passed over Gideon's expression, just a flicker but I saw it and my throat tightened.

The racing, screaming panic inside me froze into icy fear. "You can't get rid of it."

"Of course we can get rid of it," Marcus said.

The muscles in Gideon's jaw flexed.

Jacob drew closer, but his attention wasn't locked on

the brand like everyone else's. It was on my face and the intensity of his gaze held me captive, as if he were trying to help me fight my panic. "It's not a true brand, so anything is possible."

"Don't give her false hope," Gideon said. "This is an angel brand. The only way this kind of soul bond is broken is when one member of the bond dies. And even then the remaining half usually dies soon after or goes insane. Our best bet to help her is to capture the wraith and magically put it in permanent forced hibernation. It would still have a connection to you, but you might be able to have a normal life with it."

"Might?" This was getting worse and worse. The freeze around my panic cracked, but I mentally clung to the ice. I wasn't sure if an angel's icy demeanor was genetic or not, but I was going to pretend it was. I couldn't let my fear continue to control me. I needed to think. And as much as I wanted to just run and scream and curl into a ball and hide, that wouldn't help me.

Jeez. Some cop I was, panicking the moment something terrifying happened.

Except that wasn't true. If I wasn't the victim, I'd still be calm and collected and working on a solution. Because that would have meant I would have been able to leave the supernatural world whenever I wanted to.

Now? I was pretty sure even if Gideon could capture this wraith and put it in hibernation, he was going to be watching me for the rest of my life.

Which could end sooner rather than later if Gideon's team found that monster and was forced to kill it.

"How hard is it to capture a wraith?" I asked, but I had a sneaking suspicion I wasn't going to like the answer.

"Challenging at the best of times," Kol said. "But this one has ripped apart two angels and a weretiger. That's more powerful than any wraith I've heard of."

"And his essence doesn't feel like a wraith's," Gideon said. "He's enhanced somehow."

"Yeah, with an angel's magic," Marcus said, his attention still locked on the brand.

"I'll be blunt with you," Jacob said, his voice a soft rumble. "It would be easier to kill it."

"We're not killing it," Marcus growled. "We just need a plan."

"We can't even find it," Kol said. "How are we going to *capture* it?"

"You said the brand creates an intimate connection." God, this was the stupidest thing I'd ever done, but I was in the middle of this whether I wanted to be or not, and I didn't do well just sitting on the sidelines. "Can the wraith use the connection to find me?" And I still wasn't convinced it was a wraith.

The temperature in the room turned frigid and Marcus jerked closer. "You're not using yourself as bait."

A hint of frost tickled the back of my hand and I tugged against Gideon's grasp, hoping he'd release me before he noticed it.

His grip remained firm. Shit. "I agree with Marcus. I can't endanger you like that."

"Except he's branded her for a reason," Jacob said. "He's going to come after her. We should use that to our advantage."

"We might do a lot of things, but we don't use humans as bait." Gideon shifted close to me, pulling me against him as if he wanted to protect me. Heat from his body warmed my back and the frost on my hand evaporated. His scent wrapped around me and for a moment I wanted to forget who I was and who he was and take comfort in his presence.

But that was just as terrible an idea as volunteering to be bait.

I turned to face him, forcing myself to put a few feet between us. "You saw that thing." A hint of panic shuddered in my chest. "You felt it. It's going to keep killing and it's going to come after me. The smart move is to pick the battleground and have the advantage."

"She's right," Jacob said. "And she's not completely helpless. She has some training."

"The Union City PD isn't trained to deal with a super like this," Gideon said. "She didn't even know it was a wraith."

"That's why I'm just the bait." I bit back a huff of frustration. "I'm not spending the rest of my life under this thing's influence. Come up with a better plan and I'll happily oblige."

Gideon glared at me and I refused to break eye contact. It was a dangerous game, but I was already on his radar and bonded with a monster. My situation couldn't get much worse.

Light radiated from his eyes, white, crystalline. Icy. A shiver swept over me and his gaze dipped to my arm, the brand covered again by the sleeve of the hospital gown. I had no idea what he was thinking and I had no idea what he saw when he looked at me.

Please let it be a normal, boring human.

But not quite so normal that he thought I couldn't handle this... as much as I worried that *I* couldn't handle this.

"Fine. But we're not doing this without protection." He released me and strode from the room.

"I'll, ah..." Kol shifted from foot to foot, looking at a loss for what to do and only knowing that he needed to take action. "I'll get a room made up."

"I'll arrange for proper clothes and your personal affects to be sent over from the hospital," Jacob said.

"I can go get my purse myself." I wasn't helpless. And I really needed a patch to ease the buzz.

"It's safer if you stay here for now," Jacob said. The intensity in his gaze softened. "This won't be for long. You'll get back to your normal life soon enough."

He, Kol, and Yadveer left. The moment the door clicked closed Marcus turned on me.

"Bait?" he growled, the room's temperature flickering between hot and cold. "Now I know you're crazy."

"I didn't see you coming up with a better idea." I turned to leave and catch up to Kol or Jacob. I wasn't going to be able to figure out what Marcus's emotions meant, and I didn't want to deal with hot flashes.

He grabbed my wrist and yanked me around to face him, but I jerked free and opened the door.

With a growl, he slapped his hand against the door and slammed it shut. I turned to face him and he leaned in and slapped his other hand against the door, capturing me with his body, his arms on either side of my head.

The temperature jumped to sweltering and stayed there, a stark contrast to the cold metal door pressing against the parts of my skin exposed by the hospital gown. His clear green gaze locked with mine and a shiver of desire slid down my spine. The sizzling attraction between us burned so hot it made my breath catch in my throat. My thoughts stuttered, going blank. All I could think about was his lithe-muscled body and how close he came to pressing it against me, closer than he'd ever done before. Jeez, something about Marcus Diaz made me lose all sense.

His breath caressed my cheeks, and I bit back a groan. I had no doubt he knew how he affected me. He wouldn't be standing so close if he wasn't trying to use it against me. Gideon had already agreed to the plan and left. I was pretty sure that meant the discussion was over. But that meant if Marcus wanted to get rid of me, the only way to do that was to get me to back out of the plan.

Except without the plan, the wraith was free to murder more supers and come after me.

"Why do you do that?" he said, his voice low, dangerous. His pupils dilated and a hint of humidity thickened the air. "Why do you throw yourself into the most dangerous situations?"

"I only did that once." Guilt twisted in my chest. Over four years, and I still hadn't forgiven myself for that. "I learned my lesson."

"It doesn't look like that to me."

"Do you honestly think I wanted this?"

"I think you don't consider the consequences." He leaned closer, his lips curling back in a snarl. "And now you're branded by a serial killer."

"Yeah, no shit." I needed to get out of this conversation. If he got any closer, I was going to scream or kiss him, and both would draw unwanted attention from the rest of the team.

I planted my hands on his sculpted chest and shoved.

He didn't move and his snarl deepened.

"God damn it, Marcus. What do you want?" And a tiny voice hoped he'd say me.

"For you to gain some sense of self-preservation." His breath came fast and he squeezed his eyes shut, as if struggling for control. But over what? I had no idea. "Let the team find the wraith. Don't use yourself as bait." His eyes opened and while his snarl was gone, the sense that there was something ferocious inside him remained and all that power was focused on me. "We can't protect you if you do."

"I know that."

"*I* can't protect you."

My pulse stuttered and a mix of emotions churned within me. I wanted that to mean he felt the same attraction to me as I did to him, but I also feared that. "Marcus—"

A phone rang and Marcus jerked away, turning his back to me and pulling his phone from his pocket. He answered, gave a grunt of affirmation, and hung up.

"Your room is ready," he said, the sense of ferocity vanishing, leaving him tense and suddenly cool toward me. He jerked his chin to the door. "I'll take you."

"Sure." I opened the door and stepped into the hall.

Marcus stalked past me and headed deeper into the building, his walk liquid and powerful, as if there were something dangerous inside him. His stride had always been confident, but there was something more to it now, something that matched the ferocity I'd just seen. If he'd transferred right away and became an agent of the Joined Parliament, then what I was seeing was four years of experience on a job that was seriously dangerous for a human.

We reached an elevator just past the threshold between the original warehouse and the new high rise addition, and took it up to the fifth floor. The door opened into a plain hall with a utilitarian gray carpet, cream-colored walls, and wooden doors stained a dark chestnut. Each door had a card reader like the kind found in hotels, and the third door down on the right had a card sitting in the holder.

Marcus used the card to unlock the door and strode inside. The room looked very much like a hotel room done in blue-grays, creams, and sky-blue accent pieces. It had a door leading to a bathroom, a queen-sized bed against the left wall—the T-shirt Kol had picked up for me lying at the foot—and a panel TV on the wall across from it. A small seating area—also against the left wall—of couch, chair, and coffee table lay beyond that. Behind the chair stood a massive window that took up almost the entire back wall the curtains drawn open revealing a spectacular view of the park ringing the Supers' Quarter.

"Jacob will be up in a bit with your purse and clean clothes." He tossed the keycard onto the bed. "There's a cafeteria on the first floor. Continue past the elevator and you won't miss it."

"Thank you."

His gaze jumped to me then jerked away and slid over the room, looking anywhere but at me. "Gideon doesn't like to drag things out, so be ready to go within the hour."

"Go?"

"If he means the kind of protection I think he means, you'll need to come with us. The witch who makes the best protection charms doesn't leave her apartment."

He left, the door clicking shut behind him and the temperature dropping to normal. Which now felt chilly.

I hugged myself, trying to fend off the cold and all my other churning emotions. The sun still sat high in the sky and the clock on the bedside table read just after 2 p.m., so I hadn't spent a lot of time having my memory read. My stomach growled, reminding me I hadn't eaten since that morning and I was more hungry than nauseous now.

I contemplated heading down to the cafeteria while still in my backless hospital gown and borrowed scrub pants. To hell with what anyone thought. I'd just had the shit beaten out of me by a wraith and now had the monster's brand on my arm. Marcus already thought I was crazy. It didn't matter if everyone else here thought I was, too.

Except I wasn't sure if Marcus really thought I was crazy or not. One minute he was yelling at me, the next he was so close the attraction, or whatever it was between us, set my nerves tingling... and he'd still been yelling at me.

This wasn't the same Marcus Diaz who'd been my

partner. He was more volatile now, more intense, and that turned a part of me on even more. Not that anything would or could ever come of that. It couldn't have happened before because we'd been partners and I'd almost gotten him killed. And it certainly couldn't happen now because he was fully immersed in all things supernatural, and I was going to get as far away from this as possible.

Once this thing with the wraith was dealt with.

If this thing with the wraith could ever be dealt with.

How the hell had things gone so wrong? One minute everything had been perfect, and now...

Now I was going to pull myself together and deal with the situation. Maybe if I focused on that, I'd be able to ignore the fear still whirling inside me. I couldn't do anything about what had happened. All I could do was try to fix it. And that meant I needed to clean up, put on proper clothes, and grab a bite to eat.

I didn't know how long Jacob would take getting my things, so I decided to have a shower first. If what Marcus had said was true, Gideon would want to head out soon and the angel didn't strike me as the kind of guy who'd wait for me to have a shower first.

The bathroom was decorated to match the bedroom with a mix of cream, gray, and blue tiles, plus chrome fixtures. The shower-tub combo took up one side, while the vanity and toilet took the other. It wasn't fancy, but it was better and fresher than the no-tub shower-stall-only bathroom in my one bedroom apartment.

Folded white towels in a variety of sizes sat on a rack on the back wall, between the toilet and the tub, and a full complement of toiletries were displayed on the vanity, including a toothbrush and toothpaste. Thank goodness, because while I'd been ignoring it, my mouth felt gross. In fact, my whole body felt gross.

And I looked gross. My long brown locks were disheveled and not in the sexy 'I just had sex' kind of disheveled. More in the 'I just went toe to toe with a wind storm and lost.' While pain didn't scream through me any more, I still looked like I'd lost a fight, except now it looked like I'd lost the fight a few days ago. A mottled purple and green bruise colored my cheek and jaw, and when I pulled off the hospital gown, I found more bruises. Most of the right side of my body where the wraith had slammed me into the alley wall was one giant bruise.

Bands of brighter purple wrapped around my chest and I shuddered. That was where the thing had squeezed me, so it could hold me while it poured into me.

Bile burned the back of my throat and my left inner biceps burned. It wanted me for something and I didn't doubt it knew I was a nephilim. How could it not when it had been inside me, flooding my cells with its essence? I didn't want to know what it wanted and I could only hope that this plan to win my freedom wouldn't expose my secret.

CHAPTER 6

I took a quick shower and avoided looking at my bruises in the misted mirror as I dried off. I pulled on the baggy T-shirt Kol had gotten for me, put the scrub pants back on, turned on the TV, and sat on the bed while I waited for the promised real clothes to arrive. There was nothing on any of the all-day news channels about the wraith, not even on the news ticker at the bottom of the screen. That surprised me, but I suspected Gideon had made it clear to my captain that the attack in the alley needed to be kept under wraps. That was what I'd do. Having a super who crushed people beyond recognition and was roaming beyond the Supers' Quarter would cause panic and most of the human population still feared supers, or at least were extremely uncomfortable with them.

The rest were split into those who welcomed the supers for a variety of reasons, and those who welcomed the supers because the angels had told them to.

The news story changed to protests in Rome outside

the Joined Parliament buildings. Like with all things, there was always a group that vehemently opposed those who were different even though, much to everyone's surprise—including myself—there wasn't a large difference in the crime statistics between humans and supers.

The current theory was that supers were so used to living in the shadows or hiding their true natures from humanity that they didn't want to screw this up—or were still really good at hiding their activities. I know many of the shifters loved that they didn't have to hide their packs. Vampires didn't have to hunt in the darkness for sustenance and cults had formed around most of the elder vampires made up of humans who were enthralled with the macabre or desperate for immortality and eternal youth. I couldn't see the appeal, but I wasn't going to judge. Not like the protestors on the TV.

Someone knocked on my door and I got up and answered it. Jacob stood in the hall holding my purse, a bulging bag—most likely the clothes he'd promised—and a sandwich on a plate.

"Gideon has contacted Zella and wants to be back before nightfall, so we're heading out as soon as you're ready." He held up his offerings. "You should probably eat before we go."

My stomach rumbled again and I stepped aside to let him enter. "Thanks."

"It would be best if you could eat while we head back to the garage." He set everything on the bed and stepped back into the hall.

"Copy that."

The door clicked shut and I opened the bag. Yep,

clothes. A pair of black cargo pants that had an elastic waist and a stretchy black long-sleeve T-shirt that was going to fit a lot better than Kol's baggy one. There was also a pair of black socks, a sports bra with a small fit that didn't require a specific cup size, and a package of simple white undies.

Oh, thank God.

Everything was picked to be more or less flexible in its size and had only required Jacob to guess whether I had a small or medium build. Smart man.

I changed into the new clothes, shoved my feet into my runners, and grabbed my purse to get my wallet and my phone. I didn't want to take the bag with me, but I did want my ID, money for a taxi if I needed to get the hell out of there, and my phone.

Inside, at the top, was an unopened box of nicotine patches.

Thank you, Pam. She must have tossed it in my purse when it'd been found in the store. Thank you, thank you, thank you.

I took out a patch, pulled up my shirt, and stuck it to my side. It would take a few minutes for the nicotine to kick in, but it would kick in, and the buzz gnawing at my body would finally ease the hell up.

I shoved my phone, wallet, and room card into my pant pockets, grabbed the plate with the sandwich, and joined Jacob in the hall. His intense gaze swept over me and he gave a nod of approval. I was pretty sure the approval wasn't of me but of how well he'd picked my clothes.

"Tell me about Zella and where we're going. Is she the

witch Marcus mentioned?" I asked, then bit into one half of the sandwich. Ham and cheese with tomato, lettuce, and mayo. Not my favorite but I wasn't going to complain.

Jacob hit the call button for the elevator. "Yes, and she's incredibly powerful. She fought with us during the war."

"Us?"

"Me and Gideon." He frowned. "Or is that Gideon and I? Gideon and me? I've been alive for well over a hundred years and I still can't remember which way is right."

I gasped and almost choked on my sandwich. "A hundred years?" I hadn't known shifters lived that long.

"I know. You'd think Gideon would have picked an older, more powerful vampire for his team. I'm still not sure why I was selected."

The elevator door opened and he stepped inside. He didn't look like a vampire at all. Of course, I hadn't seen many, only the few who made the news, and they were either young and had done something illegal, or very old and were a part of the Joined Parliament. Jacob, with his tanned skin, must have spent a lot of time outdoors before he was turned—

"If you're a vampire, how were you at the hospital in the daytime?"

The door started to slide shut and I realized I hadn't joined him. I scooted inside and the door shut, capturing me in the small space with his intense presence. It was like a physical thing with weight and thickness, pressing against my senses, but it didn't terrify me. No, the wraith had terrified me and nothing could compare to that.

Jacob being a vampire who worked for the JP was almost reassuring, since I doubted uptight 'following the rules of good even if it hurt someone' Gideon would let anyone malicious onto his team.

"I'm a JP agent, so I've been given a charm that protects me." He held up his wrist, showing me a thick silver bracelet with prongs digging into his skin every eighth of an inch.

"That looks like it hurts."

"Not nearly as much as sunlight."

Yeah. There was that.

The elevator dinged, announcing the first floor, and the door slid open. Gideon, Marcus, and Kol waited in the hall.

"Good. You're eating," Gideon said. "Let's go."

He turned on his heel and marched away. Marcus followed without making eye contact with me, and Kol flashed me a grin that made my pulse stutter with desire, but it seemed like he'd intended it more for encouragement than anything else, since my thoughts didn't completely stall out.

"We're going to Rouge," Gideon said over his shoulder. "It's in the heart of the Quarter, about as far away from humans as it can get, and caters to the less than virtuous supers."

"And your witch is there?" I was surprised someone who'd fought with Gideon would live in a place like that, let alone that he'd continue his association with her.

"I would have preferred if she'd picked a different place to call home, but she has her reasons."

"She always did," Jacob said.

"It's mid-afternoon, so there shouldn't be a lot of supers at Rouge, but you're human so you might still draw attention," Marcus said. His glower darted to Gideon and darkened even more, and I got the impression heated words had been exchanged between them. Then his gaze jumped back to me. "So don't draw attention. Keep your head down and don't be stupid."

Gee, thanks for the vote of confidence. "Copy that."

We piled back into the SUV and drove deeper into the Quarter. The buildings still looked the same, a mix of late 19th century to modern, and only a few reaching taller than ten stories. Fewer buildings had store fronts on the first level, and those that did weren't as welcoming as the ones on the main strip. Many windows had a purple hue, indicating they were UV blocking, and others had the windows completely covered up.

We stopped at a red light. The street ahead as well as the crossroad were narrower than the one we were on. Four seven-story buildings, all in the same white modern architecture, stood sentinel on each corner, and each were joined with a walking bridge crossing the streets four stories up. UV-blocking glass shimmered in all the windows, and I could see people inside on the second floor of the building closest to me, sitting around a conference table.

The light turned green and Marcus drove around a corner and into the shelter of a UV-blocking canopy. The canopy was built down to the rooftops to prevent even a small band of light inside and stretched to the end of the street. It even carried over to a covered park where the plants were kept alive with angelic magic. This street had a little more activity on it than the previous one, but it was mostly delivery men and shop owners gearing up for the evening's business.

We turned at the last intersection before the park and stopped in front of a converted bank or courthouse or something. Here the canopy had been built tight to the side of the building, creating a wall of purple glass that reached across the street—leaving an enspelled opening for traffic—and carried on into the park. The building was set back from the street with a dozen wide, shallow steps leading up to a dozen glass doors, the whole thing framed by two towering Roman columns. A neon sign hung above the doors, proclaiming it was Rouge, and more signs glowed from behind the glass panels on either side of the doors, one saying 'Open 24 Hours.'

"Remember to keep your head down," Gideon said as he got out of the SUV, this time waiting—much to my surprise—for everyone to join him on the sidewalk before striding up the stairs.

Inside, past the vestibule, the place looked like any other nightclub, with the walls, floor, and vaulted ceiling painted in a red so dark it was almost black—I guess that was why it was called Rouge—and the inner doors had been blacked out, so it could look like a dance club all day. Booths lined the wall on both sides, while standing tables were scattered along the edge of the dance floor. A long bar sat against the far wall, manned by a single demon with leathery red skin and tall horns twisting from his temples.

On either side of the bar sat an archway, each opening into what looked like different rooms. One had more light and I could see the edge of a pool table, while the other was just as dimly lit as the main room. Dance music thumped from the speakers in the main room but at a modest volume and there were only half a dozen patrons, all of which were sitting in the booths.

Gideon led us into the room with the pool table and pointed to a table in a dark corner. "Jacob, Kol, stay here with Ms. Shaw. I need to check in with Bane first. Marcus, you're with me."

The room was bigger than I'd expected, its width going beyond that of the first room. It had the same vaulted ceiling, and a wide staircase in the back corner that curved up to a second floor landing. It reminded me of a local pub, complete with pub-like wood furniture, brass accents, five pool tables, three dart boards, a big TV playing a baseball game, and a dozen beer taps at the bar.

There were two dozen people scattered throughout the room, not including the bartender—who looked like she was human until the light caught in her eyes and it reflected back like a cat's. Two of the patrons played pool at the farthest table, while two more groups, sitting far enough apart that they clearly weren't together, watched the game. There were a few more patrons in booths, and all of them had drinks or plates of food.

"Do we know how long Gideon is going to be?" I asked, pulling out a chair from the designated table and sitting. "We're going to stick out soon if we don't get something to drink. Or do you come here on business often?"

"We don't," Jacob said, joining me. "Gideon usually goes by himself."

"But he didn't want to bring you without the whole team, just in case—" Kol snapped his mouth shut.

"You can say it. In case the wraith decides to come after me."

"He didn't while you were at the hospital," Jacob said. "That would have been the easiest time to grab you, which tells me he's waiting for something."

Yeah, and I'd rather not find out what.

Jacob offered me a smile but it didn't reach his eyes. "The brand manifested less than an hour ago, so I suspect he won't be able to use it to locate you just yet."

"So we're just a precaution." Kol pulled out a chair but didn't sit. "You're right, though. I'll go get us drinks."

"You know, I'm not some fragile woman who's going to faint the moment the wraith appears," I said to Jacob. I hadn't fainted when Marcus and I had ended up in that fight with those werewolves, and that had been before I'd had the advanced training for dealing with supers. "You don't need to pussyfoot around the truth with me. In fact, I'd rather have the whole truth then have to figure out what's not being said."

He cocked an eyebrow. "You sure? You had a meltdown when you found out about the brand."

"And then I volunteered to be bait." I met his raised eyebrow with my own. "Any normal person would have a freak out when they learned their soul was permanently bonded to a monster." And I really didn't want to think about that, because I was sure I was going to start freaking out again. "Now I'm dealing with it."

This time the smile did reach his eyes, softening the

harsh intensity of his look and making him look more rugged instead of fierce. "That you are."

Movement out of the corner of my eye caught my attention, and a rake-thin man with sallow skin and stringy brown hair slid out of a six-person booth and headed toward us. Three more men of varying builds joined him. All moved like predators, their pace steady with the promise of powerful muscles ready to jump into action. Even rake-thin guy oozed danger. Just great.

The man reached our table and hooked his thumbs into the waistband of his low-riding jeans. His gaze, filled with a hint of the same intensity that was in Jacob's but not nearly as powerful, slid over me, drawing an involuntary shiver that made my pulse pick up and not in a good way. Vampires. I wasn't sure how I knew which of the supers they were—they could have been shifters or one of the few demons who looked human—but I knew with that look exactly what they were and that they were dangerous.

"Jacob Lockwood," he said, "have you finally decided to bring Victoria her tribute?"

"Victoria knows I'll never pay her tribute." Jacob shifted, letting his duster open a bit, revealing the sidearm holstered at his hip.

The thin man didn't seem to notice. Neither did his friends who were inching closer around me.

"Every vampire needs to pay tribute," the thin man said.

"Even one living with the angels," one of the men behind me said. He had a stockier build than rake-thin guy and looked like he'd had a bath in the last few months.

"*Especially* one living with the angels," another said, the tallest of the group, and he slapped a meaty hand on my shoulder.

Jacob stood, and a sense of barely contained violence radiated from him. "No vampire has to pay tribute," he said, his voice low.

He was taller and broader than all of them, but the thin man sneered instead of backing down. "You're not strong enough to take all of us. I can see it in your essence. The angels have you convinced you don't have to drink from the vein, that you can survive on the stale blood they keep in their blood banks."

The guy gripping my shoulder snickered and his hold on me tightened. "If you're not going to pay tribute with the pretty human, maybe I should. Victoria is gonna like her."

"You're aware feeding on someone without their consent is illegal," I said. Not that I expected this group to just give up because of that, but I was obligated as an officer of the law to give them fair warning.

The thin guy sneered at me. "Oh, you'll give your consent. You'll be begging for it."

Jacob pushed his duster open all the way, looking every bit like a Wild West gunslinger. His hand settled on the grip of his sidearm, but he didn't draw. "It's not consent if it's coerced."

"And you're not going to open fire in your sire's establishment," the thin man said.

"Try me," Jacob growled.

"Hey, guys," Kol said, approaching the table with three full pint glasses, his posture casual but with a hint of hellfire in his eyes. "What's all the commotion?"

"Oh, and you brought a pretty boy, too," the thin man said, with a wicked smile that promised violence. "How did you know it's my birthday?"

CHAPTER 7

ONE OF THE UP-UNTIL-NOW SILENT VAMPIRES SEIZED KOL and wrapped an arm around his neck. Kol dropped the glasses and wrenched against the guy's hold.

The guy squeezing my shoulder jerked me up. I twisted before he could choke me, but he grabbed my arm and yanked me toward him. I tripped on the chair, and he grabbed the front of my shirt and wrenched me off my feet.

Out of the corner of my eye, Jacob lunged at the thin man, who darted out of the way. Kol rammed his elbow into the guy holding him, and five more men from the back of the room hurried toward us.

The guy holding me shoved me chest first against the wall, capturing my body with his, and pressed his lips against my throat.

He sniffed and softly moaned in pleasure. "Victoria is going to enjoy you."

"Yeah, not going to happen." I bucked against him

and hissed the spell that summoned a blast of divine light.

The guy shoved me back against the wall. "That's not going to work. I'm stronger than you, human."

I bucked again and finished the spell. "That was just a distraction." I slapped my hand against the side of his face, and white light burst from my palm.

The vampire howled and wrenched back, and I mule-kicked him in the gut, shoving him farther away. He snarled at me, my handprint red and oozing on his cheek, one eye cloudy and blinded. He lunged for me and I side-stepped his grab, seizing his wrist, twisting, and slamming him against the table.

Another guy rushed at me and I snapped a kick into his groin, making him stumble, and another kick into his knee making him fall. With all my pent-up anger and fear from the wraith's attack, I wrenched the arm of the vampire I still held, dislocated his shoulder, and shoved him off the table to the floor.

The guy I'd kicked was back on his feet. He grabbed my shoulder and yanked me to face him. I used the movement to strengthen my punch and rammed my fist into his throat. Something crunched, and he gasped and released me to grab his neck. It wasn't enough to stop him, but it was enough for me to summon another divine light strike and slap my hand on his face, catching both eyes.

I turned to block the punch from someone else when a gunshot roared through the room. Everyone froze, searching for the source of the shot. Jacob hadn't drawn and Kol had been fighting without a sidearm as well.

"That's better," a stunningly beautiful woman at the top of the stairs said in a sultry alto. She looked like a stereotypical vampire, dark locks hanging artfully past her shoulders to frame her narrow face and porcelain complexion. Her red dress plunged low in the front and hugged voluptuous curves, promising sinful sex, and her dark eyes were filled with the same intensity that I saw in Jacob's, only a hundred times more powerful.

Gideon stood beside her, his posture perfect and icy. Behind them, a sallow-skinned man shoved a gun into the waistband of his pants and sneered—I didn't know where he'd fired but no one looked like they had a bullet wound—while Marcus stood beside him with his arms crossed, glowering at me. Just great.

"It's been a long time, Jacob," she said. "You should visit more often."

Jacob bowed his head. "Of course, Victoria."

"Gus, did you try to take what belongs to Jacob?"

"I doubt she's his. I doubt any human is," the rake-thin vampire said, wiping blood from his upper lip and shoving his broken nose back into place.

Victoria's dark gaze leveled on the thin vampire, Gus, and he shrank back. "Is this true, Gideon? Is this human unclaimed?"

"No human should be claimed," Jacob said.

Victoria's eyes narrowed. "In my establishment they are. If she's not yours, Gus has the right to take her and you'll be confined to the box for a week."

"That isn't necessary," Gideon said. "They're here on my command."

"And you know the rules." Victoria turned to Gideon

and traced her fingers over his sculpted chest. The temperature in the room warmed but I couldn't tell if it was with desire or anger. "Did you think you could just sneak her in?"

Wow, that was surprising. I thought angels abided by every rule, even when it didn't make sense.

"We're here to see Zella," Gideon said. "We won't be long."

"That doesn't make it better." Victoria raised a hand and made a fist.

Jacob gasped, grabbed his chest, and dropped to his knees, his face scrunched in pain, while Gus sneered in pleasure.

"That will be two weeks in the box for my offspring." Her fist tightened and Jacob screamed.

"Victoria, be reasonable," Gideon said.

"Reasonable?"

Jacob screamed again.

"You angels with your rules think you don't have to follow mine."

Another scream and the temperature turned sweltering.

"This is my house. My rules. The JP agreed to that." She glared at Gideon, and Jacob screamed a third time, collapsed on his side, and curled into a ball of agony. "You think you can disrespect me like that, angel? Think again."

She brought her other fist up and Jacob gasped and started gurgling.

For the love of God, just stop. I jerked a step forward. "I'm his."

"Essie—" Marcus barked.

"He's claimed me," I said, even knowing that my luck probably wasn't good enough for Victoria to just take my word for it.

Jeez, first an unwanted angel brand and now I was going to risk letting a vampire stake his claim to me. But I couldn't stand by and watch Victoria torture him. A vampire's claim entwined the vampire's essence with the human's in a way only vampires could sense. It signaled that the human had relinquished her free will and belonged to the vampire. I couldn't imagine why anyone would let someone else control them—and this control was complete, take-over-your-body-and-make-you-do-horrible-things-even-commit-suicide kind of control—but they did.

For whatever reason, some people didn't want control of their lives and some didn't care about that price tag to reap the benefits of being claimed, like enhanced senses and an extended lifespan. And there had been people willing to be claimed before the vampires had joined the cause and helped save humanity. It boggled the mind. Of course, maybe the rumors of sexual euphoria were true, that being claimed enhanced the already erotic sensations that came with a vampire feeding.

"She's lying," Gus said. "Give her to me."

"You can't just give her away," Marcus said. "There are laws."

"And there are laws in my house, too," Victoria said.

"She hasn't been claimed." Gus's tone sharpened. "His essence isn't in her."

"Well, either she's lying or it's been too long since he's

fed and wrapped his essence in her." Victoria's eyes narrowed. "You should rectify that, Jacob."

Gideon shifted, the only indication he was anything but icy calm. "Zella is expecting us."

"You should have thought of that before trying to sneak an unclaimed human into my establishment," Victoria said, her tone sickeningly sweet.

"She said she was claimed." Marcus tensed and looked like he was going to attack, but Gideon put a hand up and stopped him.

"So she's already submitted." Victoria raised her chin, daring Gideon to defy her in her house. "Wrapping his essence in her again shouldn't be a problem."

Gus shoved me toward Jacob and I dropped to my knees at his side.

"You don't have to do this," he gasped, his voice low so only I could hear him.

"I'm not going to let her torture you," I said just as quietly, and helped him sit up.

He leaned close, pressing his forehead to mine. "You don't know what this will mean."

"If you have a better plan, I'm all ears."

"I'm waiting," Victoria said in a singsong. "On your feet, vampire, and repossess your human."

"I don't just have to bite you," he said. "I have to touch you, my palm over your heart, flesh to flesh to bind my essence with yours. It's... intimate."

A nervous tremor swept through me. I'd expected it would be something overly personal, but I had hoped just drinking my blood would have been personal enough. I didn't know this guy. I didn't know any of them other than Marcus, and now I was in a position where I needed them to protect me from the wraith. I still wasn't sure I trusted them —including Marcus—but I couldn't see any other option.

"Unless you'd prefer to take her on the bar floor." Victoria flashed a dark smile. "Or I could just keep killing you." She made a fist and Jacob tensed. He clenched his jaw but a strangled cry still slipped out.

"You do whatever it takes." I met his gaze, letting him know I meant what I said, then pushed away from him and stood.

Gasping, he grabbed the chair beside him to help him rise and joined me.

"Atta boy," Victoria said.

With an apologetic look, Jacob stepped close, with his chest at my back, and turned us to face away from Victoria and the others. But the master vampire tsked, and Jacob gasped again, tensing against me as if an electric shock had surged through him.

"You don't get to be ashamed of what you are, Jacob. Turn around." Her tone promised more pain if he didn't obey. "I want to watch."

"I'm sorry," Jacob whispered against my temple, then turned us.

"Very good," Victoria hissed, her smile deepening as Jacob wrapped a bulky arm across my waist.

He drew me tight against his broad chest and I was hyperaware of just how big he was, the broad muscular planes of his chest and his arms nearly the size of my thighs. He was probably double my weight if not more of pure muscle, and with my head tucked under his chin, his embrace nearly engulfed me.

I shivered but wasn't sure if it was fear or the fear that I wasn't afraid of him. His free hand tipped my head to the side and back and held me there with a light pressure. The hand at my waist slid along my stomach and dipped under my shirt. I expected his hand to be cold, being undead and all, but it wasn't, merely chilled, which meant he'd eaten recently.

My mind latched on to that. That was good. He wasn't starving. He could just take a quick sip, entwine his essence into mine, and we'd be done.

His hand moved up my chest, close to my skin but not touching, a whisper of movement that made me shiver, then his fingers dipped inside the sports bra, sliding over the top of my breast, and made my breath hitch. His palm settled over my heart, and I tried to detach myself from his touch, but it was so intimate it made my body thrum, desire flickering through me.

He dipped his head down, his lips against my throat, and murmured, "Just relax."

Sharp pain bit my neck and I tensed, the realization that his teeth had plunged into my neck making panic surge through me and my pulse pound.

Victoria licked her lips. Her canines extended and a hunger burned in her eyes. Beside her Gideon was rigid, his expression pure ice while Marcus's was pure rage. He looked like he was going to go on a rampage. To my left, Gus looked like he was going to throw a fit, and Kol had gone pale, hellfire burning in his eyes.

Jacob sucked, drinking my blood with a tug on my

throat that pulled all the way down to my core. The tension that had seized me twisted into sudden aching need. My body grew limp, desperate to let him take me, overpower me, do whatever he wanted.

The boneless ecstasy seeped deeper, spreading over and into every nerve, making my breath shudder. Jacob held tight and his palm against my heart began to warm, adding a new pull, one that curled into me and made my head spin.

He took another pull, or was that his third or fourth? I couldn't tell, I couldn't feel his teeth in my neck anymore, only heat from his hand pressing against my heart and the aching pleasure coursing through me and gathering in my core.

I shuddered and Jacob groaned, the rumble in his chest vibrating through me, sending my cells into sympathetic vibration with his. The bliss swelled—I hadn't thought it could be possible, not without actually having sex—as if our aligned resonance allowed his essence to penetrate deeper into me, and every part of me turned its attention to him. There was no one else in the room, the city, the world. There was only Jacob and his desires. If he needed to drink me dry, I'd slit my throat for him. If he needed protection, finances, sex, whatever I had, it was his. I'd give it freely.

As soon as the thoughts rooted within me, a part of my mind started screaming. That wasn't right. He wasn't my everything. He couldn't be my everything. I barely knew him. A flicker of panic joined the screaming. He needed to let go. Release me. Stop. This wasn't right. It had to stop.

Please. Stop.

But if he stopped, Victoria would resume torturing him. I had the power to stop that so long as I let him finish his claim. That was the reason I'd become a cop: to have the power to help others.

He took another bone-melting pull on my neck that left me spinning and weak. His grip on me tightened and his body trembled, then with a growl he jerked his mouth away. A chill swept around me and the panic surged at his absence, while that other, small part of my mind screamed that feeling that way was wrong. Then his mouth was back again, his lips against the puncture wounds and a flicker of heat, the miniscule healing magic every vampire possessed, sealed the wounds shut. It would still be obvious for the next day or so that I'd let a vampire bite me, but at least I wouldn't bleed to death. The kiss was light, feathery, sending a shiver of desire down my spine, and he withdrew again, leaving me chilled even though I was still wrapped in his embrace.

"Satisfied?" he asked, his voice low, dark, and edged with hunger.

No, not even close.

"Until next time," Victoria said.

I tried to open my eyes to see her expression, tried to find strength in my legs to stand without help, but everything within me just kept whirling.

Jacob's hand slipped out from under my shirt and he hooked his arm under my legs, lifted me, and cradled me against his massive chest.

Just where I wanted to be...

Except I was pretty sure that wasn't right.

"It'll take you a minute to regain your bearings." He pressed his lips to my forehead and the part of me now connected to Jacob soared with pleasure at his attention.

"What the fuck is wrong with you?" Marcus growled, his voice suddenly close, not far away on the second-story landing.

I forced my eyes open. Marcus stood close, they all did, but he was the only one glaring at me. Behind him, the room spun around and around and around and—

Marcus's glare jumped above me to Jacob. "What the fuck is wrong with *you*?"

"Zella is waiting," Gideon said, his body language so cold I wouldn't have been surprised if frost formed on his sculpted cheekbones.

"You should have told me I wasn't supposed to come here," I said, my lips numb with pleasure, my words muddling in my mouth. "I'm sorry I got you in trouble."

"That wouldn't have stopped us from bringing you here," Jacob said. His intense gaze had turned sad and the muscles in his jaw tightened. "It's been nearly a hundred years since I've claimed someone. I'd forgotten how... intense it can be."

"And the claim will fade, eventually," Kol said, the fire and hunger still burning in his eyes.

"If I don't feed from you again, it'll be gone in a few months."

My warring thoughts cheered and wailed at that, but I was too dizzy to try to figure out which side I wanted to win so I just leaned my cheek against Jacob's chest instead.

"The first claiming is always the hardest on the

human." The angel glow in Gideon's eyes dimmed, more clouds passing over his summer sky. "We should get to Zella's apartment before anyone notices she's still stunned."

Marcus was hurrying toward a narrow door under the stairs before Gideon had finished talking. The others followed, with Jacob at the back still carrying me.

The room continued to spin and my muscles still felt like goo. At least this spinning was better than the concussion I'd had earlier. This time I didn't feel like throwing up.

"When will I stop being stunned?" I asked Jacob.

"Everyone reacts differently." His voice rumbled through me, making my essence vibrate again. "I tried to take as little as I could to keep the claim weak, but—" His grip on me tightened. "It's been a long time since I've fed from a human. The claim is stronger than I'd like."

Which meant he'd taken more than he'd intended. The sane part of me shuddered at that. The part that was possessed by him was thrilled.

And either way, there wasn't anything I could do about it.

"It's okay." I pressed my palm to his chest. The claim would pass, and there wasn't anything saying that once the wraith was apprehended I had to stick close to Gideon while I waited for Jacob's essence to work its way out of me. This was manageable. I could handle this. I *had* to handle this.

The door under the stairs led to a narrow, rickety set of stairs going into the basement. Marcus led the way into a narrow, dimly lit hall. Sparks of light flickered through the glow from the bare bulbs hanging at irregular intervals from the ceiling, but I had no idea what kind of magic was on them that made them do that. The walls were fitted fieldstone, telling me the building was old, or that it sat on an old foundation. Moisture glistened in the cracks between the stones and a runnel of water trickled along a shallow gutter on the floor into a small metal grate.

I couldn't imagine why anyone would want to live down here, but then I'd been assuming Zella was a human who'd made a demon-deal or had an ancestor who'd made a deal, and that was why she was a witch.

Perhaps she wasn't human at all and didn't want to live in areas frequented by humans. There were a few kinds of supers who could cast spells, primarily those who'd been born human and had been infected with lycanthropy or turned into a vampire. There were also a few angels who could cast spells beyond their one primary innate magical ability. But I couldn't imagine an angel wanting to live down here. Given that the bar above was a vampire den, I was guessing Zella was a vampire.

Except that didn't fully explain why she was in the basement when there was UV-blocking glass on the windows above as well as over the street outside.

We reached a wide, heavy wooden door at the end of the hall. Marcus knocked and the door creaked open an inch. He shot Gideon a wide-eyed, worried look and the temperature in the hall chilled.

Jacob set me on my feet and leaned me against the wall, my head still spinning. "Stay here," he said, and he drew his weapon.

Something twisted in my chest, but I didn't know what, and really, the unlocked door and the guys' fear was more important.

Marcus pushed the door open and froze. Frost rushed across my cheeks and a sense of powerful evil slammed into my chest. Gideon growled and Kol gasped.

The room was an underground chapel with a massive stained glass window against the back wall, impossibly illuminated—it had to be magic. An altar was positioned just before it and dead center above that was an angel, suspended in the air, her wings unfurled, mangled and bleeding, and her body ensnared in ice and wrapped in the wraith's writhing tentacles.

CHAPTER 8

THE ANGEL GURGLED AND WRENCHED AGAINST THE WRAITH, but its smoke had poured into her while its tentacles crushed her chest and sliced shallow, torturous cuts into her body. An angry red scar disfigured three quarters of her face and twisted over her bare forearms. The tentacle around her chest had hiked up her shirt, revealing more scars across her belly, as if she'd been flayed or set on fire and hadn't been magically healed. Blood seeped down her body and pooled onto the floor, and ice encased her hands.

Except the ice wasn't capturing any other part of her body. Instead, it held three tentacles and poured down the wraith's side, anchoring it to the floor. More ice swelled around her hands, and spears of ice shot from her palms and shattered against the wraith's chest, tearing into the smoke until I could almost see through it.

Another barrage of ice shot from the angel's hands, but there were fewer spears and they hit with less force.

None of them punctured the wraith this time. She was running out of strength.

The wraith's smoke shuddered and shrank, then billowed and the power radiating from it increased. The tentacle around her chest twisted tighter. Bones cracked and the angel screamed and convulsed with pain. The ice holding the other tentacles back started to crumble.

"Free Zella," Gideon said to his team and rushed into the room, his hands raised. A blast of divine light shot from each palm and slammed into the wraith, but didn't cut through it.

The wraith growled. Its form shuddered again, thinning and surging as if fighting a windstorm. One tentacle dissolved in a puff of smoke, but it wrenched another one free from the ice.

Kol unsheathed two daggers that he'd had hidden somewhere on his body and leaped into the room, while Jacob bolted around the corner faster than humanly possible and fired two rounds into a tentacle that was crushing the angel's leg. Marcus growled and barreled after them, claws extending from his fingertips.

My pulse tripped with horror.

He had claws.

I *had* ruined his life.

He dove for the wraith, jumping high, and dug his claws into its back. A tentacle snapped out, seized him, and tossed him against the wall. He hit the ground on his hands and knees but quickly stood. Kol sliced at the tentacles clutching Zella, but every time he cut one another would appear.

Light formed in Gideon's palms again as the ice

anchoring the wraith to the floor snapped. It whirled around with a roar and hurled Zella into Gideon before he could get off his shot. She crashed into him and they skidded across the floor, Gideon trying to protect Zella's broken body with his.

Jacob fired another shot, the bullet slicing through a tentacle, but a flurry of more tentacles exploded from the wraith's body. They swatted at Jacob and he dove out of the way, then they flung Kol into Marcus and shot toward me.

Marcus's eyes flashed wide. "Essie, move!"

I jerked to get out of the way, but my muscles seized and I couldn't move.

Marcus scrambled toward me but he was going to be too late. "Essie, go."

I jerked again. Nothing. "I can't." *God, why can't I leave this spot—?*

Ah, shit. Jacob had said to stay there. He'd given me a command.

The tentacle reached for me and I cast a divine light strike as fast as I could. Light streaked from my palms and sliced into the tentacle as it tried to grab me.

"Jacob," Gideon said.

"Shit." Jacob fired at the tentacle that was already reforming to continue coming after me and severed it from the wraith's body. It turned to smoke and vanished. "Essie, defend yourself."

My body lurched away from the wall and I twisted out of reach of the reformed tentacle, my pulse pounding.

Gideon blasted the wraith with more light and Marcus tore into it. The wraith screeched and shuddered, its smoke shredding away. With another cry, it bolted past me and disappeared in the darkness at the end of the hall.

"Get the car," Gideon said, pulling Zella into his arms, her body limp, one mangled wing half on his shoulder, the other dragging on the floor.

Jacob rushed away, the fastest of the group with his vampiric enhanced speed.

Blood poured down the front of Gideon's pants and his grip on Zella tightened as if just by holding tight enough he could save her. Except if his angel magic didn't involve healing—and since Amiah had healed my broken bones, so best guess was that it didn't—then there was nothing he could do.

Marcus ran ahead of us to clear the way, Gideon running after him, while Kol and I followed. The hall still threatened to turn into a vomit-inducing fun house from the effects of Jacob's claim, but I gritted my teeth and kept up. I was dizzy, but I was fine. Zella needed immediate medical attention and no way in hell was I going to slow the group down.

We barreled up the stairs, through the pub, across the dance floor, and out the doors. Jacob had the SUV turned around, the engine running, every door except the far middle one open, and his hands on the wheel ready to go.

Gideon climbed onto the middle bench, cradling Zella, blood oozing over the leather seats. Kol shut the door after him and jumped into the front passenger seat as Marcus and I piled into the back.

We peeled away from Rouge, our tires screeching

around the first corner, gunned it down the stretch under the UV-blocking canopy, and ran every red light to get to Operations. Thank goodness we weren't far. Marcus called Amiah and told her to have a team waiting for us in the garage, then glared out the window, pointedly refusing to look at me.

I, on the other hand, couldn't stop looking at him. I tried not to, but my gaze kept jumping back to his hands. His fingers had returned to normal, his claws gone, but the image of them filled my mind.

It was my fault. All my fault.

The SUV squealed to a stop in the parking garage where Amiah, two others—a man and a woman, I had no idea what kind of supers they were—and a gurney waited. Gideon set Zella on the gurney and they whisked her about twenty feet down the hall into whatever lay beyond the frosted-glass sliding door.

Marcus, Kol, and I got out and Jacob pulled into a parking spot.

Gideon stood rooted in the garage, staring through the glass doorway into the now empty hall. A blood trail, dark red against the pale gray floor, pointed the way they'd taken her.

Jacob placed a hand on Gideon's shoulder. "She's in good hands."

"I know," Gideon said.

Kol shoved his hands into his pockets, a hint of hell-fire still in his eyes. "We didn't know the wraith was going to be there."

The muscles in Gideon's jaw flexed. "I know."

"And we couldn't have killed him without endangering Essie," Marcus said, his voice low and rough, as if he didn't like what he'd said.

The temperature in the garage ping-ponged between hot and cold and I hugged myself, keeping back from the group. If it wasn't for me, they could have stopped the wraith this afternoon.

Which was ridiculous. If it wasn't for me, we wouldn't have been at that bar and stumbled across the wraith.

Still, the guys looked angry and exhausted, and I didn't want to remind them that I was a complication they didn't want.

Gideon drew in a ragged breath. "Jacob, mind what you say to Officer Shaw until your vampire claim on her diminishes. We can't have her stuck in one spot again."

Jacob gave a tight nod.

"Marcus, take the coalescence snare we bought from Bane to Summer to ensure it's the real deal," Gideon said. "Without Zella's protection charm, we need it to work without a hitch because this plan just got more dangerous."

"So we're going ahead with using Essie as bait without the protection charm?" Kol asked.

Gideon glanced at me, his summer-sky eyes frosted and hard. Of course he was going ahead with the plan. I could see it in his eyes. The wraith had almost—please let it be almost and not actually—killed another angel. One measly human was worth it to end the slaughter.

I squared my shoulders. "You pick the time and place and I'll be there."

Marcus growled, shoved open the glass door, and stormed away.

The temperature in the garage continued to lurch between hot and cold, Marcus's departure not giving me any relief.

Gideon followed him, his stride tight, restrained, every inch of him radiating frozen control.

The heat eased up, but I was still cold. Uncertain what to do or where to go, I hugged myself and brushed the brand, sending a spike of pain through my arm. They'd given me a room. I should use it. I needed another shower and I needed a bigger meal than just a sandwich. Except I didn't want to leave Jacob.

Which had to be his claim on me.

That was going to become a serious problem if I needed his permission to do everyday things like eat, shower, or sleep.

"I should..." Kol glanced at Jacob then at me. The hellfire had vanished from his eyes, but there was still an edge there. Of course, we'd just witnessed the wraith tear into Zella. I'm sure there was an edge in my eyes, too.

"I should..." Kol jerked his thumb at the door. "I'll—" He rushed inside as well.

The door clicked shut and Jacob turned to me. "You need my permission to go back to your room, don't you."

"Yeah." And I didn't like the feeling one bit... even if a part of me seemed to love it. That had to be the part claimed by Jacob.

"I was afraid of that." His hand slid to the butt of his gun, but I didn't get the sense he wanted to threaten me. Instead, it felt as if this was an instinct, something his body returned to over and over again when he wasn't thinking about it. "I took too much and the claim is too strong."

"So what does that mean?" Was I going to be like this for the entire time that his essence was entwined with mine? Jacob had said that would be months. I couldn't live like that. I had to deal with this wraith and get away from Gideon before he learned the truth.

"It means I need to be more careful what I say to you."

I barked a bitter laugh. "You think?" I hadn't been able to move more than an inch from that wall.

His gaze shifted to the garage behind me and the grip on his sidearm tightened. "I don't have a lot of experience with this. I've only claimed someone once before." The air in the garage turned thick, foggy—at least for me, since I doubted Jacob saw it—his grief manifesting as water suspended in the air around me. "I don't want to have that kind of mastery over someone's life again."

"Does that have something to do with why you think an angel bond is unhealthy?"

His fog misted my cheeks and he frowned, drawing closer.

Shit. I turned my head to hide the moisture, but he captured my chin and urged me to look up at him.

The sadness in his eyes deepened. "It'll be okay." He cupped my face and traced a thumb across my cheek, wiping the mist away and drawing a shiver of need into my heart.

Please let him think I'm crying.

"We can protect you. We'll put the wraith in hibernation." He brushed more moisture from my cheek. "My claim will fade. You'll get your life back. I promise."

I pursed my lips. I wanted to run screaming from him, from all of it. Except it wasn't because I thought his claim on me was wrong, but because the longer I remained here, the greater the odds I'd be discovered. A part of me was in shock that entwining our essences and drinking my blood hadn't revealed my angelic nature to him. While another part, a part that didn't care about discovery or self-preservation, wanted to lean into his touch and beg for a command, anything to please him.

I resisted all of that and made myself just stand there, trying to ignore the fog billowing between us that he couldn't see.

"The need to be told what to do short of breathing will pass soon."

"How long will that be?" *Please say soon. Please don't let my kneejerk reaction to protect him have completely screwed up my life.*

"It's different for everyone. Could be a few hours, could be a few days."

Swell. No good deed goes unpunished. But even if I hadn't known the specifics about what I'd gotten myself into, I'd known enough. And if I could go back and do it again, I'd make the same choice and save Jacob.

And that wasn't the claim talking.

"Once it passes, you'll have more autonomy. There's still a danger of me commanding you if I don't watch what I say, but if I don't give you an order, you'll be able to do your own thing."

"Okay." I could handle this. Except the things I needed to handle were piling on and it hadn't even been a full day.

Jacob slid his other hand to my cheek, capturing my face between his palms, and met my gaze, the look in his eyes still intense and still sad. "I hate that I have to say this. Go take care of yourself. If I need you, I'll find you wherever you are."

A pressure in my chest released, and I let out a breath I hadn't realized I'd been holding. Two sentences and I'd been freed... a bit. I could do whatever I wanted and go where I wanted... although I sensed there were limits to how far I could actually go from him. But for now I was no longer obligated to stay by his side and wait for a command.

"Thank you."

"No. Thank you. Victoria wasn't supposed to be at Rouge. All our intelligence said she was out of town."

"Which is why you thought you could sneak me in." The fog thinned, Jacob releasing his grief. "I'm surprised Gideon went ahead with it. From what I've heard, it's not like an angel to break the rules."

"This is an unusual situation."

Yeah, and it wasn't because I was involved. If the wraith had killed three cops, the entire police force would be doing everything to catch him. With an attack on three angels, I could see why Gideon was willing to do almost anything to stop him.

Jacob slid his hands from my face and gestured to the door. "I don't know when Gideon will reassemble the team to work out the details of capturing the wraith. You should—"

The pressure returned around my heart.

"Sorry. Go take care of yourself. If I need you I'll find you wherever you are," he said.

I rushed into the hall before he could say anything else to me while he waited in the garage, probably with the same goal. A few feet away, a janitor mopped up the blood trail. I hurried past him, keeping my head down, afraid to make eye contact, and went straight to the elevator.

My stomach grumbled. I ignored it. Yes, Marcus had said the cafeteria was straight into the new section, but right now I just wanted to avoid any other super. I needed to figure out the best options for the plan to use me as bait so I wasn't strong-armed into a bad idea. Not that I thought Gideon would have a bad plan. He and everyone else on the team probably had more experience with these things than I did.

In honesty, my nerves were shot from the fear of being discovered, the wraith attack, and learning my soul was permanently bonded with that monster. And I really wanted to be in a room with a steady temperature for more than a few minutes.

The elevator door opened and I rode it to the fifth floor. With a ding, the door opened and I stepped into the hall. Marcus leaned against the wall beside my door. His gaze lifted and locked onto me and the temperature shot up.

His anger was still hot, the air thick with humidity. I'd never experienced anything quite like it before. His piercing green gaze froze me in place, and now I knew why. He was a predator, his human nature twisted with a wolf's, and I was prey.

My chest tightened. He was a predator because of me. God, how did someone atone for that?

A person couldn't atone for something that terrible and permanent.

But I also didn't have the emotional fortitude right now to take whatever he wanted to throw at me. Even if I did deserve it. And jeez, my arm was stinging and I was sweltering.

The elevator closed, blocking off my escape. Not that leaving wouldn't have been blatantly obvious that I was avoiding him. I shoved up my sleeves—doing nothing to alleviate the heat—and forced myself toward him. *Please just make it quick.*

"No Jacob?" he asked, his voice low.

I stopped just out of arm's reach. I needed to get past him to unlock my door, but I was afraid that if I got too close, the attraction sizzling within me would keep me there. "I have permission to do my own thing."

His eyes narrowed.

"I don't like it, either, but Victoria was going to keep torturing him."

"He's a big boy. He could have handled it."

"Sure. And she would have detained him to continue torturing him and you'd be down one team member. You needed everyone to save Zella, which means you'll need everyone to trap the wraith."

His hands fisted at his sides and he jerked a step forward. "Don't pretend this is about protecting yourself. We both know you have no sense of self-preservation. You'd sacrifice yourself in a heartbeat if it meant saving someone."

"Hardly." I forced a huff of disdain, his words hitting too close to home.

"The fight with those shifters was because a child was in danger. The fight with the wraith, you were protecting the pharmacist and cashier." Tension radiated from his body and the temperature rose. Sweat beaded on my forehead and between my breasts.

"I get it. You're pissed. You have every right to be pissed. But please—" My throat tightened and I fought back tears. God damn it, I was stronger than this. And I could be, if I just had a moment to steady my nerves.

"I'm not pissed," he growled, sounding even more furious. "I'm terrified."

"You're what?" My brain stuttered over his words. That didn't fit with the temperature or his body language or his tone or anything else about him.

He jerked closer, captured my face between his palms, and crashed his lips against mine, stunning me. The kiss was hungry and wild, his stubble rough against my skin. Sultry heat with humidity pasted my T-shirt to my body, my pulse roared, and heat spiraled through me.

A growl rumbled in his throat and my breath stalled, not from fear, but from the desire that had instantly struck the moment we'd first met and had never let up, even with four and a half years apart.

I slid my hands over his chest, savoring his sculpted pecs, and melted against him, needing to be closer, to feel his body pressed against mine.

His fingers tangled in my hair and tilted my head back to deepen the kiss, his tongue plunging inside. His passion was ferocious, consuming.

I moaned with pleasure, and he froze, his body trembling, his breath fast.

"Essie." He breathed my name against my lips and pressed his forehead to mine. "You're not supposed to be a part of this world. I know you don't want to be." He jerked away from me, his gaze piercing into my soul. "I left so you wouldn't have to be."

Then he stormed away, past the elevator and around the corner, taking his ferocious energy and the humid temperature with him.

What the hell?

I pressed my fingers to my lips, stunned, as the return-to-normal temperature chilled the sweat slicking my body.

He'd left to protect me?

And then he'd kissed me.

I had no idea what that meant.

CHAPTER 9

FOR THE NEXT FEW HOURS I PACED MY ROOM, TRYING TO concentrate on devising a safe plan to use myself as bait to catch the wraith, finding a way out of this mess, or hell, just staying calm. But the pain in my biceps where I'd been branded was definitely growing stronger and my mind kept jumping back to Marcus's kiss.

God, he'd kissed me.

Sure, when we'd first been partnered together, I'd had fantasies about what that would be like. He was sexy and confident and there was a spark between us.

Boy, was there a spark.

My cheeks heated at the thought.

But I never thought it would actually happen. And that didn't mean it would happen again or that it should. He was right that I wanted nothing to do with the supernatural world. So why did it bother me that he'd disappeared from my life to protect me from it?

Maybe because he hadn't given me a choice? Or was it because he'd let me believe that I'd messed up his life?

Although I had screwed it up, and we hadn't been anything to each other when he'd left. We'd been partners. Nothing more.

And did I want it to be more?

More meant staying in contact with the supernatural world when this was all over. More meant possible continued encounters with Gideon and the risk of revealing my angelic nature.

My stomach rumbled and I checked the time. A little after six. Dinnertime. I should eat. Take care of myself.

But I resisted the urge to rush out of my room. Going in search of the cafeteria now was a terrible idea, no matter how much my body thought it agreed with Jacob's command. Yes, Gideon could want to initiate the plan to capture the wraith at any moment, but facing that monster hungry was better than walking into a room filled with angels. Yes, there was only one investigative team stationed in Union City, but this was also a research facility. I didn't know how many other people were stationed here and I had no idea how many of them were angels. I was willing to bet, however, there were more than the two I'd already met.

I pulled out my phone for a distraction and checked my messages. Only two. Thanks to a childhood of fearing everyone and constantly moving, I wasn't close enough to anyone to be missed right away.

The first message was from my captain, telling me Gideon had demanded I be put on temporary medical leave and was taking me into protective custody, and the other was from my partner, Hank, telling me to get better soon. Hank's message sounded awkward, which didn't surprise me. We hadn't gotten close in the four and a half years we'd been partners. Everyone had heard what had happened with Marcus and no one had wanted to get stuck with me, including Hank, and the new-partner-tension had never eased between us. The middle-aged, slightly overweight cop was probably glad I was out of his hair.

I managed to kill another hour and a half flicking aimlessly through the TV channels and doodling on the notepad I kept in my purse instead of brainstorming solutions to my problems. There wasn't any safe way to use myself as bait, not with how powerful the wraith was. The guys had worn him down trying to free Zella, which was the only reason I could think of as to why it had fled, but I was pretty sure Zella's fight before we'd gotten there had helped. Without her and without being able to use lethal force, the guys were at a serious disadvantage.

My stomach growled. Again. After eight. Here was hoping enough people had visited and left the cafeteria that I'd be able to get food without being noticed, and that the unpredictability of a JP agent's job meant food would still be available.

I left the room, took the elevator to the first floor, and headed deeper into the new section of the facility—as instructed—to find the cafeteria. Ahead, the hall opened into an area sunk a few steps down. Tables ranging from two-person to eight-person with chairs neatly pushed in filled the space. Natural-feeling light—since it couldn't actually be sunlight because it was after dark—illuminated the front half of the cafeteria with a comforting glow, while the back half of the cafeteria was in shadow, closed down for the night.

The far wall was a bank of windows and a door leading to a patio, and to the left, creating a separation between the cafeteria and a sunroom-style glassed-in section with tables and chairs, stood a wall made of massive rocks. They were stacked to create nooks and crannies that held lush verdant plants and pathways for miniature waterfalls. The waterfalls trickled into a pool at the bottom that wrapped from the front around to the back. To the right were the standard cafeteria stations with metal counters and two fridges at the end, closest to the stairs, with glass doors.

Near the back, almost out of the light, Amiah and the woman from the team who'd whisked Zella away sat huddled around a table eating, their voices hushed.

I turned around before hitting the steps and darted into a dimly lit hall, hoping they hadn't seen me. I didn't want to deal with Amiah. She had to have known Marcus was a werewolf because of me and I had no doubt that her anger over that said she had strong feelings for him.

Great. I had no idea what I was going to do now. I could wait in the hall for her to leave, except she could easily see me when she passed by and with my luck she'd have business in this direction. My best option was to go back to my room and wait half an hour or so. Surely she'd be done by then.

Footsteps squeaked on the tiled floor, coming from the cafeteria. I hurried further down the hall and around the corner into a wide band of soft light emanating from a large window. Beyond the glass was a hospital room

complete with high tech, beeping equipment. Zella lay
on the bed, her tattered, bloody wings in metal braces
extended and supported, holding them in place, and her
complexion gray. The scar on her face was mostly
covered with a bandage, while the other side of her face
was puffy and red with the formation of a massive
bruise. Both of her eyes were swollen shut so I couldn't
tell if she was awake, but from the slow steady beep of
the heart monitor, best guess was that she was heavily
sedated.

Beside her, Gideon sat holding her hand, her
knuckles pressed against his lips, his expression barren,
not even icy, just stunned and aching, as if he'd been
stripped raw and this was what remained. His clothes
were still covered in blood, and a wide streak painted the
side of his face into his hairline, as if at some point he'd
swiped his hand through his hair without realizing it was
covered in blood.

I shifted to sneak away, but his gaze lifted and locked
on me, and I found myself going forward instead of back
and opening the door.

"How is she?" I asked. The room was cold, but I
suspected that was Gideon's worry and not the actual
temperature.

"They've stabilized her, but she has to go back in for
surgery." His attention swung back to Zella, and he
lowered her hand to the bed but kept a hold of it. "She's
resistant to magic. It's part of her unusual ability to create
charms and what made her such an asset in the war. But
it's not selective, so Amiah's healing magic barely works
on her." He drew in a ragged breath. "She isn't certain if

she can save Zella's right leg or her wings." His voice choked on the last word.

"Oh, Gideon. I'm so sorry." The horror of that made my throat tighten.

"She didn't deserve this. She was already in self-imposed exile, so ashamed of what she— of what *we'd* done. Of what we'd had to do." The muscles in his jaw tightened. "She's already paid too much. She'd paid it all back in the war." His thumb traced the raised flesh on the back of her hand.

"Her scars?" Duh, of course her scars, but the question slipped out and I couldn't take it back.

"A nephilim with a powerful fire magic," he said, and heat flickered across my senses. "The animal nearly burned her alive."

The heat flickered again, Gideon trying to control his rage. But I didn't need my empathy to see how upset he was. It was clear in the disgust and anger hardening his expression. "Those abominations murdered too many. Angels, supers, humans. I couldn't protect nearly enough and I couldn't protect her." His grip on Zella's hand tightened. "Be glad you're too young to remember those times and you never have to face one of those monsters."

I nodded, forcing myself to stay put and not flee in the face of his barely controlled rage. He didn't know what I was and running would only make me look suspicious. But God, I needed to get as far away from him as soon as possible. "So you think this has something to do with the war?"

"Three members of my squad are dead and Zella

would have been next if we hadn't shown up," he said. "I wouldn't call that a coincidence."

Neither would I. "Who's left in your squad?"

"You mean should I warn them, Officer Shaw?" he asked, a hint of amusement in his tone.

"Sorry, I'm sure you did. I didn't mean to imply you didn't."

"I warned them after the first two and again while Amiah was working on Zella." His gaze lifted to mine and he studied me.

The hint of heat in the room vanished and ice returned to his eyes and posture. Not enough to eliminate the sense of soul-aching exhaustion radiating from him, but enough to make my nerves thrum with worry. Everything within me screamed to flee. Take care of myself. That's what Jacob had commanded. Risking discovery wasn't taking care of myself.

But neither was facing the wraith on my own.

The brand's burn was increasing and I knew that couldn't be good.

The immediate threat of the wraith's danger won out over the chance of discovery, and I stood my ground. I pressed a palm to the brand. God, would it just stop hurting for one minute?

Gideon's eyes narrowed, his attention on my biceps. "How bad is the pain?"

"Almost as bad as when it first appeared."

"He's using the unnatural connection to look for you. We don't have a lot of time." A hint of the ice melted in his eyes. "I'm sorry you're experiencing a perversion of an angelic brand. The connection is supposed to be pure, soul-deep."

"And compelling," I said, unable to keep the bitterness from my tone. How long would it take before the wraith found me? And how long after that before its brand made me do horrible things?

"Compelling because the bond is transformative for angels, attuning souls together in a connection closer than even a vampire's claim on a human. Mates, if they concentrate, can find each other, sometimes they can even communicate mentally with each other, on very rare occasions they can overhear each other's thoughts without trying," he said, with a hint of awe. "The bond is so strong, it even enhances an angel's magic."

I shuddered. Was that what the wraith was doing with me? Using me to somehow enhance his magic?

"The two souls belong together, have always been destined to be together, and the mating brand physically represents that knowing."

"I really hope I haven't always been fated to be mated with this wraith."

"If you were, your brand wouldn't hurt and it wouldn't look like it was infected."

I didn't want to check to see if the welt had gotten worse. It sure felt like it was worse.

"I have no doubt the brand was forced upon you."

"And that still doesn't mean you can get rid of it." A part of me hoped he'd correct me, say he'd been wrong when the mark had first been discovered, and tell me he could get rid of it.

But from his grim expression, I knew his answer hadn't changed.

"Which leaves us with catching him and putting him in hibernation."

Gideon's frown deepened and he pursed his lips. "Marcus thinks you'll be a liability."

Of course he does. "Marcus knew me when I was a rookie. I'm not a rookie any more." Although given the kiss, I was pretty sure me being a rookie had nothing to do with his fears. Regardless, we all knew, including Marcus, that using me as bait was the best, most expeditious plan.

"You're right, you're not a rookie, and you didn't have to step in and help Jacob, but you did."

"Yeah, about that—" I'd already gotten a dressing down from Marcus. I really didn't want another one.

"It was foolish but courageous," he said. "Still, you shouldn't have done it."

"I couldn't let Victoria torture him." Marcus hadn't really accepted that line, but I was still hoping Gideon might. Except his expression didn't change and I couldn't read it to tell what he was thinking. I shrugged, trying to look nonchalant. "I'm a cop. I serve and protect."

Still blank.

"We also need all hands on deck to capture the wraith."

He gave a tight nod that I took as agreement.

"We might need all hands just to kill it," I said.

The ice returned. "I told you killing it isn't an option."

"You saw what it did." I glanced at Zella, my body aching

just looking at her. "Killing it might be our only option." And I knew he already knew that. "I know I'm not reading this situation wrong. I understand the consequences." Yes, I didn't want to die or go insane, but I wasn't a fool, either. Gideon's squad might be safe and in hiding, but what would that make the wraith do? Start killing innocent people indiscriminately? That wasn't a price I was willing to pay.

His gaze slid back to Zella. "I'd hoped I was done with horrible choices."

Marcus hurried around the corner at the end of the hall, stumbled when he saw me, then growled and picked up his pace heading toward me. Heat and humidity warmed the air. It wasn't sweltering like it had been before and I prayed it would stay that way. My pulse picked up and a strange mix of emotions churned in my chest. Desire, embarrassment, confusion, fear. None of which were going to help me, so I gritted my teeth and ignored them.

"Summer confirms the coalescence snare spell is the real deal," he said to Gideon, without looking at me. "It'll solidify the wraith into its humanoid form so we can cuff it."

"Good. Tell Kol and Jacob to meet us in the cafeteria in ten. We can make our plans there while I eat. But first I need a change of clothes." Gideon stood and brushed his lips against Zella's forehead.

"Come on," Marcus said, before Gideon had straightened. "I'll show you to the cafeteria." Without even a glance at me, he stormed away and I scrambled to catch up.

We returned to the main hall and down the steps into

a thankfully empty cafeteria. Marcus pulled out a chair at a rectangular table with six chairs and sat, his arms crossed. I pulled out a chair opposite him.

He shifted, his gaze flickering to me, barely making eye contact before flickering away.

My lips tingled with the memory of our kiss. We should probably talk about what had happened. Except I had no idea what to say, and I had no idea what the kiss had meant.

He shifted again.

Come on. Just start a conversation. It couldn't be more awkward then sitting here. "So, ah—"

He jerked to his feet and paced to the rock wall.

So much for conversation. Fine. I still hadn't eaten anything and Jacob's compulsion to take care of myself was still gnawing at my insides. It was probably best anyway not to talk about what had happened. I'd screwed up his life, and he'd walked out on me without a word. Not that we'd had anything but a professional partnership to walk out on, so I had no right to be mad.

Jeez. Deal with the biggest problem at hand, then deal with Marcus. If things didn't go well with the wraith, Marcus's kiss would be the least of my worries.

I headed to the closest of the two fridges with glass doors and peered inside. It had packaged sandwiches, wraps, salads, sliced fruit, and yogurt. The fridge beside it was filled with an assortment of beverages including… was that blood? Well, the Joined Parliament did employ vampires. I grabbed a sandwich labeled turkey club and a bottle of water and returned to my seat as Kol sauntered down the stairs.

A panty-melting smile curled his lips and lit his eyes, making my pulse stutter, and he slid into the chair across from me, where Marcus had been sitting.

"How you holding up?" he asked, his voice sliding across my senses. He had to know the affect he had on a woman just by talking to her. It didn't even look like he was trying. Without his focus on the business at hand, this was his natural, sensual self, lounging in a fold-up metal chair, exuding sexual invitation.

"Well enough to get the job done," I said, my voice breathy.

He straightened in his chair, frowned, and the sense of sexual invitation eased. "Sorry, it's been a day. I usually have better control than that."

"Have you eaten, Kol?" Marcus growled from close behind me, making me jump. He dropped into the chair beside me, crowding into my personal space but not touching me.

"I have," Kol said.

"Good." Marcus pushed my unopened sandwich closer to me. "Pick your jaw off the table, Shaw, and eat."

"And you back the hell off, Diaz," I snapped back. If I wanted to drool over the sexy incubus—which I wasn't— I had every right to. Yelling at me, kissing me, and then storming off didn't give him the right to be mean.

Marcus glared at me. I glared back. Finally! I was done with being afraid and tearful. Now I was pissed. Now I could get something done.

Marcus snarled.

I stood my ground. Probably the stupidest thing I

could do with an angry werewolf, but I didn't care. He shouldn't have kissed and run.

"What the hell?" Gideon said. It sounded like he was near the stairs, but I wasn't going to look away from Marcus first.

Marcus snarled again, wrenched his gaze past my shoulder to the stairs, and shifted his chair away from mine.

"Oh, you made the angel swear," Kol said under his breath.

Gideon marched past our table to the fridge with the sandwiches. "I need you on this, Marcus. Don't make me bench you."

"By *this* you mean setting a human up as a sacrifice for a wraith?" Marcus asked.

For the love of—

"We've been over this." Gideon grabbed a sandwich and sat at the head of the table. "The decision has been made. You're either on board or off the team."

"Don't say I didn't warn you when that thing crushes her to death."

"Can we move on to actually coming up with a plan?" I didn't want to talk about my imminent death, because even if I survived, my soul was still bound to that monster. "He knows I'm with you, so it's going to be harder to lay a trap."

"I've been thinking about that," Jacob said as he hurried down the stairs and joined us, sitting beside Kol. "I know you want to keep as many civilians out of this as possible, but the best place to lay the trap is Essie's apartment."

I wasn't going to ask how Jacob knew I lived in an apartment. He'd probably read my file. They probably all had. Which meant they all knew I'd worked with Marcus before. Did all of them know I was the reason he was a shifter?

"Absolutely not," Gideon said. His attention jumped to my unopened sandwich. "You should eat that."

"The circle to cast the coalescence spell can only be about a five-foot radius," Jacob said. "If we set it in a room that's too big, that will give the wraith a chance to snag her with a tentacle without even getting close to the circle."

"And if the plan goes south, how many people in the building do you think it will kill?" Gideon asked.

I ripped open my sandwich's packaging and took a bite, but didn't really taste anything, trying to figure out whose argument was the best. That, and the pain from the brand was really becoming a distraction.

"Essie is right, it already knows she's with us," Kol said. "We won't get a second chance at this."

"Ensuring the circle encompasses as much space in the room as possible increases the likelihood of solidifying him," Marcus said.

Gideon shook his head. "It's bad enough we're endangering Officer Shaw's life. I can't endanger a whole building."

"Then force it up," I said. "It can fly and my unit is on the top floor. I have roof access and a skylight. If you can't capture or kill it, make it flee. If you block the way to the hall and the rest of the building, he'll take the path of least resistance."

I didn't like the idea of fighting this thing in my apartment, but Jacob's plan was good and no one had suggested anything better. This way, there wouldn't be any chance of it standing at the back of the room half a dozen feet away from the circle. The biggest problem would be close-quarter fighting.

That, and if we couldn't get it to solidify, all those tentacles were going to beat the shit out of the guys and it was going to take me.

CHAPTER 10

THE GUYS TOLD ME TO MEET THEM IN THE GARAGE AND left, returning changed into presumably work clothes, although I couldn't tell what made these work clothes and the others not. Gideon was the only one who'd noticeably changed his style, but he'd done that when he'd changed from his bloody slacks and button-down into black cargo pants and a black T-shirt. Jacob was the only one who'd added a weapon, and now had a 92 FS Beretta holstered at each hip, although I suspected Kol had hidden his daggers back on his person—if he'd ever taken them off. Marcus looked the same. Sexy as hell in his T-shirt and jeans and without a doubt dangerous.

Gideon tossed a half-stuffed duffle bag into the back of a different SUV than before—guess our earlier one still needed to be cleaned—and we left the Supers' Quarter and drove to my apartment building. It was a four-story walkup in a neighborhood of four-story walkups. My building sat at the back of the three-building complex, creating a small green space between the sidewalk and the entrances, and the superintendent's wife did an amazing job planting flowers and making the space bright and friendly. At this hour, the flowers and shrubs farthest from the lit path were mostly in shadow, and the maple, just off center beside the walkway, filtered the streetlight's illumination into uneven, shifting bands of light.

Marcus dropped us off out front then drove around back to park in the alley. He'd take the fire escape up to my place, so no one had to wait by the building's locked front door to let him in. The rest of the team followed me inside and up to my unit.

My place wasn't big and I didn't have a lot of things, but with just me, I didn't need big or lots of stuff. What I loved about it was that it had twelve-foot ceilings, sat at the back corner of the building, and had two walls of windows as well as a skylight. The living room-kitchen combo wasn't much bigger than the five-foot radius needed for the spell, and my bedroom, to the left, was even smaller, barely big enough for my bed and dresser. Beside that was a narrow bathroom with almost no counter space and a stand-up shower. No tub—the unit's biggest problem in my opinion.

I had a second-hand couch that sagged on one side, a second-hand coffee table that was still perfectly good, and an old twenty-inch TV on an old cherry-wood stand that had seen better days. Nothing I owned was new, with the exception of my laptop, clothing, towels, and sheets. There wasn't any point in spending that kind of money on something I might need to abandon at a moment's notice.

Not that I'd had to flee since I was seventeen, but I wasn't willing to give up that particular old habit.

The back of the couch marked the invisible line between living room and kitchen, which was a counter with a sink in the center and the fridge and stove at either end. Beside the fridge and along the wall separating the apartment from the outside hall were the stairs leading up to the roof.

Gideon's gaze lifted to the ceiling and the pyramid skylight, dead center above my living room. If the night had been clear and I'd had my lights off, moonlight would have filled the room.

Kol mumbled something about a minimalistic look, took the duffle from Gideon, and set it on the floor beside my coffee table, while Jacob headed to one of the two windows against the back wall and pushed it open.

Marcus climbed inside from the fire escape, his gaze sweeping over the room before landing on me. His expression was hard, but I couldn't tell if that was because he was still furious with me or terrified for me or whatever his heated emotion had meant, because the room's temperature didn't change. Whatever he was feeling, he'd locked it down. This was Marcus the agent of the Joined Parliament, not whatever he'd been before.

"So." The pain from the brand now radiated up to my shoulder and down to my elbow, and I shifted, keenly aware that I was in imminent danger but uncertain what to do or where to go. That, and I'd never been so aware of how small my place really was. Although perhaps it wasn't just the room's size, but the guys'. They were all taller than me and I wasn't a slouch at five foot eight.

Even Kol, the smallest of the group, had a few inches on me and a broader stature.

"Sit on the couch and stay out of the way," Marcus said.

Jacob pulled a compass from his pocket as Kol carefully withdrew four stone...? I had no idea what they were. They looked like squat miniature obelisks, about as big as both of my fists put together. Small glyphs were carved into each one, curling around and around from the bottom to the top, creating some kind of spell—I knew that from my enhanced supers training. The witches and spells session.

"Set the edge of the circle under the couch at the back, so we can catch most of the living room," Gideon said. "I don't think we can put it as far back as the cupboards, so we'll need to get smart about hiding the spell stones."

"You couldn't have had more stuff?" Kol asked. "It's not going to be easy hiding these."

Jacob turned to the couch, shifted, and pointed at an angle that hit the couch's back leg farthest from the door. "North is that way."

Kol placed the first stone. South required the TV stand to move a foot and a half, while the east stone was tucked behind the stairs. West was the hardest. I didn't have anything along the back wall. When I'd moved in, I'd fancied having a shelf with plants under the windows, but had never gotten around to setting that up.

"What are we going to do about this?" Kol stared at the stone on the floor, sitting in plain sight.

"We're going to pretend I'm a slob." I got off the

couch, grabbed a pile of clothes from my dresser, and dropped them over the stone. "The pile might clue him in to something, but hopefully he'll be standing in the circle by the time he notices it."

Marcus rearranged the pile, shaking out folded shirts and pants. "It should work."

"Good." Gideon knelt on the floor, the coffee table between him and me. "Officer Shaw, wait until the wraith is in the circle—the closer to the center the better, because there's a second or two delay on the spell's activation—then say *vade*."

"*Vade*. Got it." A simple word, easy to remember. I had this.

"And be ready to get the hell out of the circle," Marcus said.

"If you can't," Kol said, "I'll grab you."

"If I can't?" I didn't like the sound of that.

"The spell shouldn't affect you. You're human," Gideon said.

I really didn't like the sound of that.

"But if it does," he continued, "you might feel numb or disoriented."

Wonderful.

"Once the wraith is solidified, I'll run in and slap on the containment cuffs," Jacob said. "Simple and straight-forward."

I rolled my eyes at him. "In my experience, straight-forward is usually never simple."

Marcus snorted. "No shit."

"Do you see a problem with the plan?" Gideon asked Marcus.

"Only that Essie is involved." Marcus marched into my bedroom to lie in wait until the wraith showed up.

"He's normally not like this," Jacob said.

Kol shrugged. "Must be a super moon coming or something."

I forced myself to smile. "Or something."

Gideon cleared his throat, drawing my attention. "Repeat the activation word to me."

"*Vade.*"

"Good. I'm going to awaken the spell." He pressed his palms against the floor and closed his eyes. A hint of light seeped from beneath his hands and through the cracks between his fingers. Then four strands of light shot out, each connecting to a stone, and the buzz in my body burst to life, overwhelming the calming effects of the nicotine patch.

What the hell? I hadn't even had it on for twelve hours.

Gideon sat back on his heels. "Now we wait."

"Great." I gritted my teeth against the buzz. "Wild guess on how long?"

"How does the brand feel?"

"My whole arm hurts." And I feared the thing was getting bigger. God, that would be just my luck.

"I can't imagine it will be long now." He motioned to the guys to take their positions, Jacob in the bathroom and Kol in the bedroom with Marcus. "I can't promise I can protect you now," he said, his voice low so the others couldn't hear.

"You do what you have to do."

He gave a tight nod, stood, and headed into the

bedroom, leaving me alone in the living room while they watched me through partially open doors.

I turned my gaze to the skylight. I didn't know where the wraith would come from, but if it could see me before I could see it, I didn't want to give away the guys' locations. Not that staring up at the skylight wasn't odd with all the lights on.

This was the part I hated about stakeouts. The waiting. And I particularly hated it when my nicotine patch was running low, or out, or in this never-happened-before bizarre case where the buzz was stronger than the patch. I didn't like the idea that being in the center of this spell while it was awake but not activated set off the buzz. That was a new discovery I didn't need, not with an angel a few feet away in my bedroom. And I didn't want to think about what kind of effect the spell would have on me once it was turned on. At least Gideon had said it *shouldn't* affect me and not that it *wouldn't*. That still left the door open for them believing I was completely human.

I shifted, uncomfortable with the buzz and the growing burn from the brand. I contemplated turning on my TV. That would be a normal thing to do. More normal than the need to pace that was making me twitch.

Yeah, if I kept the volume low, I wouldn't look so obvious. I was professional enough to keep my attention on my surroundings. Why hadn't I thought of it in the first place?

But this was unlike anything I'd ever done before. I was a beat cop. I patrolled neighborhoods with my partner, answered calls for robberies, domestic disputes, shots fired, car accidents. I'd helped with a stakeout once when a witness needed twenty-four hour surveillance, and then I'd sat in an unmarked car with Hank watching the witness's house.

I grabbed the remote from the coffee table, turned the TV on, leaving it on the news channel I'd been watching when I'd had breakfast this morning, and set the volume low. They were no longer covering the protests in Rome. Now they were running a documentary on the Battle at Washington. The bloodiest fight between humans and nephilim during the war.

Grainy, shaking video from a body camera showed nephilim with brilliant white wings, just like angels, splattered with blood, tearing into a group of soldiers. All of the nephilim's eyes were wild, and many screamed or howled. They whipped bands of fire or shot bullets of ice or just pounded the soldiers to death with their fists. Fully automatic gunfire rattled over the TV's tinny speakers, nephilim staggered, some even went down, but it usually took a lot to kill a nephilim, more than just a regular angel. Weak flashes of light burst here and there as the soldiers who could cast combat spells, summoned divine light.

Then a flash of blazing white light blasted, the picture going blank for a second before returning to the horror. The camera panned away from the soldiers to the team of humans who had turned the battle in their favor. They each wore a ring imbued with divine light that could shoot multiple blasts, each blast as strong as the most powerful angels with combat light magic. So long as the human could cast a divine light strike, he could use a ring.

That had been one of the deciding factors in the war. We'd needed the supers to help fill out our ranks, but that hadn't been enough until angels had started filling rings with divine light.

The video jerked back to the fight as a nephilim lunged at the soldier wearing the camera and seized him. The camera caught the nephilim's face close up and there wasn't a hint of humanity in its eyes. It was a rabid beast, a monster, more horrific than the monsters who'd come out of hiding to help us.

The documentary paused for commercials, breaking the spell on me that had kept me watching even though I was horrified. It was like watching a car crash, except much much worse. It was no wonder everyone feared nephilim. Hell, I feared nephilim. They were the monsters Gideon had said they were.

Maybe it would be easy to convince everyone I wasn't that kind of nephilim. I didn't look insane. But I also knew from other videos taken during the war that when the nephilim hadn't been commanded into a fighting frenzy, they looked normal. If you couldn't sense essences and didn't get a good look in their eyes, you'd mistake them for a full angel.

I slid my gaze through my partially open bedroom door to the window beyond. Across the narrow side-street, light glowed from inside a few apartments, and work-out dude, as usual, had his blinds up—I wasn't sure he had blinds to cover his windows since they were never covered—and was shirtless, doing chin-ups on a bar secured on the frame of his bedroom door.

I turned my attention to the two tall windows on my back wall and the building across the alley. The light was on in the unit directly across from me, the shears drawn, but I could see the shadow of someone sitting close to them. Bookworm was in her window seat, staying up late reading again.

I sat up straighter to see to the unit two floors below Bookworm to see if the young couple with the newborn were awake. I hoped not. I'd come home late a few nights now after finishing an afternoon shift and grabbing a drink with a few fellow officers in an attempt to be social and not stick out by being a loner, and had seen them pacing back and forth with a red-faced, crying baby. The young couple's light was on, the curtains open. The guy paced into sight holding the infant as a billow of darkness swept past their window.

Was that the wraith?

My pulse picked up and I searched the darkness for confirmation that I'd seen the wraith.

Pain snapped through the brand on my arm and another billow of darkness swept past Bookworm's window. Was he heading for the roof? My mother had always said angels attack from above because most humans don't initially look up when searching for danger.

"Guys," I hissed. "We're on."

I drew in a steadying breath and concentrated on looking unaware. The trap only worked if he didn't think I was expecting him. I faced the TV but kept watch on the windows from the corner of my eye, but didn't see anything.

The buzz in my body made me jumpy, and the pain in the brand burned all the way to my wrist.

I glanced up. Nothing above the skylight.

Where the hell was he?

Darkness surged at the edge of my vision, and I jerked my attention down to the partially opened bedroom door as the wraith crashed through the bedroom window. The sense of malicious power filled the apartment, making my stomach churn.

"What the fuck?" That sounded like Marcus.

Blazing white light flashed—Gideon's divine light—and Kol dove into the living room and rolled to his feet, his daggers drawn.

Something crashed against the wall between the bedroom and the living room, drawing a grunt of pain. Someone growled—Marcus?—and the wraith howled.

Pain sliced into my arm, making my eyes water, and I jumped to my feet.

"Hey!" I shoved my coffee table toward the windows, hoping it was far enough out of the way that someone wouldn't trip over it.

Kol backed toward me, and I wasn't going to think too hard about what kind of effect the circle would have on him if he was caught inside it.

Another crash and the wall cracked. More light flashed.

Jacob glanced out the bathroom door but didn't rush out. He needed to be ready to secure the wraith with the magic containment cuffs as soon as it had solidified.

And I had to get that thing into the circle.

"I said hey!"

Someone roared. Another bone-crunching crash and Marcus smashed through the wall and hit the floor. Now visible through the hole in the wall, Gideon blasted more light at the wraith. It howled and a flurry of tentacles shot toward him. He twisted, trying to dodge the writhing mass of darkness. A dagger of light appeared in his hand, but the room was too small to avoid all the tentacles. There wasn't anywhere to go. The wraith seized his leg and hurled him at the hole in my wall. He crashed through, the throw so powerful that he flew over Marcus, slammed into the back of my couch, and knocked it over, revealing the spell stone.

Shit.

But the wraith either didn't care or didn't notice. It surged through the hole, its smoke smothering Marcus and flattening him to the floor, and shot a tentacle past me and seized Gideon's throat.

The angel gasped and slashed at it with his light dagger. Kol darted in with his blades, and Marcus thrashed on the floor, suffocating.

The activation word rushed to the tip of my tongue, but the wraith was at the edge of the circle and there was a chance it'd be able to escape.

"Come on." I hissed the combat spell at top speed and sent a small blast of light at it. My power was nothing compared to Gideon's but hopefully it was enough to get the wraith's attention. "Come on."

The smoke surged toward me and grew, the darkness fully obscuring Marcus. Tentacles seized Kol and Gideon.

It was a little closer, but was it close enough?

It was going to have to be.

"*Vade*," I yelled, as Kol was smashed against the ceiling with a sickening crunch and Gideon tossed out the window.

Magic exploded around and in me. The blaze from the brand seared through my body and the buzz kept the pain going as the world spun around me.

The wraith howled and the smoke whirled, caught in a tornado of power.

Marcus gasped and Kol shuddered. Both were prone, their eyes unfocused, but I didn't know if that was because of the spell or not.

Another surge of power made the two cry out and set my buzz into an inferno. The wraith screeched, and the darkness ripped from around him, revealing an angel with onyx devil's skin, fully extended black wings, and hellfire burning in its eyes.

Holy shit. It was an angel?

CHAPTER 11

THE WRAITH-ANGEL JERKED TOWARD ME. JACOB BOLTED from the bathroom, the magic containment cuffs in his hand, but the angel managed to yank his wrist up at the last minute and shoot darkness from his palms, like a reverse divine light blast. Jacob twisted out of the way, but the blast clipped his shoulder and sent him tumbling back toward the bathroom.

Marcus staggered to his feet. The wraith-angel sent another blast at him and lunged at me.

I tried to leap out of the way, move, do anything, but my muscles had locked and I could feel, barely, beneath the inferno of the buzz, the brand seizing my body.

The wraith-angel grabbed my arm, shot a blast of darkness above him, cracking the skylight's heavy glass, and took off. We crashed through the skylight, tearing metal and shattering glass. Something sliced my cheek and my shoulder, ripping my shirt.

We flew past the roof, straight up into the darkness. I twisted against his grip. I had to get him to let go before we were too high and the fall would kill me. I cast a light strike and slapped my free palm against his hand around my biceps.

My light stuttered. Weak. Ineffective. Crap. Was I out of juice? There were only so many times a human—or even an angel, for that matter—could summon divine light before needing to recover.

Panic seized my chest. If I was out of juice. I was dead. Or not dead. God, that thought was worse. I didn't know what it wanted me for, and I didn't want to find out.

I clawed at his fingers. A tentacle of darkness swept from his body and wrapped around my chest, squeezing tight while another blocked my nose, forcing me to open my mouth to breathe, then poured down my throat when I did.

Oh shit oh shit oh shit.

I clawed at the smoke on my face, choking on it, my stomach heaving but unable to expel it or my dinner.

Wind whipped my hair, pulling strands loose from my ponytail and stinging my cheeks, and my head spun with the nauseating churn of fear, lack of oxygen, and the buzz.

It was not going to take me. It couldn't take me. *God, don't let it take me.*

The words of the light strike raced in my head over and over again and the buzz exploded from my body.

Blinding white light erupted around me.

The wraith-angel howled. His tentacles burst, releasing me and dissolving from inside me, and his grip on my arm disappeared. Gravity seized me and I plummeted back to earth.

The wraith-angel dove toward me, but a blast of divine light shot past my head and sent it reeling. It glared at me, hellfire burning in its eyes. The brand shot agony through me and I convulsed, a clear reminder that it still possessed me, and it flew away.

Then strong arms caught me, cradling me. The scent of spring wrapped around me, and the stinging wind rushing past me stilled. I twitched and gasped with another convulsion from the brand, and Gideon hugged me closer to his firm chest.

We landed on the roof and the guys came storming out the door.

"You're never doing that again. Never," Marcus growled before he'd fully stepped onto the roof. "And I don't give a fuck what you think. It's not happening."

"Was that actually an angel?" Kol gasped, his face tight with pain, hugging himself as if his ribs hurt.

Gideon's pulse thudded where my ear pressed against his chest and a churning mix of hot and cold flashed over me. I didn't know what it meant. I couldn't make my mind focus enough to figure it out.

"I have no idea what that was," Gideon said, thankfully saying nothing about how powerful my divine blast had been. There was a chance—a slim chance—that the guys inside might not have seen it, but without a doubt Gideon had.

A whisper of a convulsion swept through me.

Marcus snarled. "It sure looked like a fucking angel."

The hot and cold grew stronger and my stomach churned.

"And a few minutes ago we thought it was a wraith," Jacob said.

Marcus jerked toward him, his hands fisted. "You guys are supposed to be the font of knowledge of this team. You're supposed to know what that was."

"Marcus, take a breath and calm down," Gideon said.

More hot and cold. More buzz burning my body, and my stomach heaved. "Put me down," I gasped.

"Calm down!" Marcus growled, claws extending from his fingers. "This is not the time for calm."

"Now more than ever," Gideon said, his tone frosty.

I pressed my palms against his chest, trying to get free from his hold, bile burning my throat. "Put me down."

His frozen gaze dropped to me and the fluctuating temperature made me dizzy. My stomach heaved again and I shoved out of his grip.

"Essie." Marcus reached for me, but I rushed past him. I had to get to the bathroom, hide until the world had stopped turning and burning. It was bad enough they were seeing me like this. If I couldn't pull my shit together fast, they'd agree with Marcus and I'd be locked in the Joined Parliament Operations Building until the wraith-angel was caught, or—and this was more likely—until I went insane and died.

I staggered down the stairs, barreled into the bathroom, and slammed the door shut. My stomach clenched and I threw up my measly dinner into the toilet.

Tremors raced through me and I sagged to the floor. The guys' nauseating mix of emotions still gave me hot and cold flashes, tears burned my eyes, and the buzz sliced into me stronger than ever before.

Come on, pull it together.

But I couldn't stop the shaking, or loosen the panic clutching my throat and chest. The tears released, streaming down my cheeks, and I bit back a sob, praying no one heard me.

It had almost had me. God. It had almost taken me. And there'd been nothing I could have done. The guys couldn't even protect me. There was no way out of this.

Someone knocked tentatively on the door.

"I'm fine. I just need a minute."

"Essie." Jacob's voice rumbled through the door.

"Don't you dare tell me to come out." I couldn't handle that. I wouldn't be able to resist his command and they'd all believe everything Marcus said about me if I came out looking like I was bawling my eyes out—even if I was.

Marcus said something, his voice dark, dangerous, but I couldn't make out what he said so he couldn't have been standing right outside the door with Jacob.

Gideon said something back.

"Do you need anything?" Jacob asked.

Yeah, for all of this to go away. A sob broke free.

"Essie?"

"A moment. I just need a moment," I said, my tone harsher than I'd intended. But what I really needed was a time machine so I could go back to this morning and... I don't know... wake early? Sleep in? Anything to change this horrible day.

Except if that had even been possible—which it wasn't—that would mean no one would have stopped the robbery and Abe could have been hurt or killed.

I sniffed and wiped at my tears.

So plan A hadn't worked. That didn't mean we couldn't come up with a plan B. We now knew more about the wraith. Knowledge was always good.

I spat a mouthful of bitter spit in the toilet, flushed, and used the edge of the sink to help me stand. My body still burned and shook, but at least my stomach had settled.

I gripped the counter and drew in a ragged breath, fighting to regain some control. The woman staring back at me in the mirror looked more stunned than she had when I'd caught glimpses of myself this afternoon, and I now had an ashen complexion and too-wide, puffy-red eyes. It was going to take more than a few minutes for that to clear up.

At least I could fix my ponytail. Maybe by then the shaking would have eased up enough so I could walk out of the bathroom without staggering.

Oh, wishful thinking.

I tugged the hair elastic from the mess, ran my comb through my dark locks, and retied it into a ponytail. I still looked like a disaster. I splashed water on my face and dried off with my bath towel. Nope, not any better. This was the best I was going to get.

My legs were still shaky, but I reached for the door-knob to leave anyway.

I grabbed for the knob and burning pain sliced through my arm. I gasped and clutched the counter, tears returning to my eyes. The agony seared like the wraith's brand, except it was now on the inside of my right forearm.

Another sob threatened to escape. It was making its claim on me stronger, adding another brand. It could find me with the first one. God, what would a second one do?

I shoved my sleeve up, revealing a complicated sigil made of delicate gold threads swirling through my skin.

Gideon's words jumped into my head. The wraith's brand wasn't a true mating brand because it wasn't gold.

My knees gave out and I crumpled to the floor.

Footsteps hurried to the door.

"Essie?" Jacob asked without opening it.

I couldn't tear my eyes away from the new brand. It was gold.

Gold. Real. Permanent.

This couldn't be happening. It was not happening. It was a nightmare. I'd wake up and everything would be back to normal. A real bond permanently tied me to an angel... or it revealed my angelic nature, if I wasn't bonded to another angel.

"What the—" Gideon said, his voice tight with pain.

Oh, no. Please, no.

"Dude, did you just get a mating brand?" Kol asked.

Not him. Anyone but him. He thinks I'm a monster, an animal, an abomination. God, please. Don't permanently bind me to him. Please. Another sob broke free.

"Essie," Jacob said. The doorknob turned and I jerked my sleeve down and hugged myself, my shaking returning with a vengeance. The door opened all the way and Jacob's gaze dropped to me, his eyes widening in fear, the room's temperature settling on frigid.

Behind him, Gideon grimaced in pain and held his forearm just below where my mark had manifested.

Divine light radiated from his eyes, accentuating his pain and shock.

"You said a real one was gold," Kol said. "Who is it?"

"I don't know," Gideon said with awe. His shifted and I caught a glimpse of his brand. I'd need a better look, but I'd bet it was identical to the one on my arm. Same spot. Same brand.

No, please. Another sob broke free.

Marcus hurried toward me as Jacob knelt to pick me up.

"I've got her," Marcus growled, pushing Jacob aside.

"How could you not know who it is?" Kol asked.

"The bond just happened. It needs to get stronger first. We don't have that kind of a connection yet, so it could be anyone. It could be Zella." He frowned, then hope flooded his expression and warmed his gaze into a perfect summer sky.

Heartache twisted in my chest. He thought his mate was Zella. He was going to be shattered when he learned the truth.

And then horrified when he learned the real truth.

CHAPTER 12

MARCUS PULLED ME INTO HIS ARMS AND STOOD. "WE NEED to get her back to Operations."

"It could be Zella," Gideon said. Now he looked even more stunned.

"Gideon," Marcus growled.

Gideon's attention jumped to us. "Right. I... I, ah..." Recognition of the situation flickered through his eyes, but it was like he couldn't think past the sudden appearance of the brand.

I couldn't blame him. I couldn't think past it either. My body shook so hard my teeth chattered with the shock of it. I hadn't had nearly as strong a reaction to the wraith's brand, and that only added to my horror that this one was the real deal.

His gaze landed on me, his eyes filled with apology, but it wasn't for binding my soul with his. It was because he needed to go to Zella, because he thought the brand was with her.

"Go," Jacob said to him. "We've got her."

"Thank you." Gideon extended his wings and flew out the shattered skylight.

Marcus growled again and hugged me closer. "You're freezing."

"Kol, go get the car," Jacob said.

"No." The muscles in Marcus's jaw twitched. "You've got the warmest body temperature. Have your broken ribs healed enough to take her?"

Kol gave a tight nod and Marcus handed me over to him, then hurried out the window to climb down to the SUV parked in the alley.

Kol's heat seeped into my skin, but my teeth kept chattering and my mind kept whirling. I was Gideon's destined mate. How the hell was I Gideon's destined mate?

Jacob and Kol hurried me out of my apartment, down the stairs, and out onto the street. Marcus drove the SUV up to the curb, and Jacob took the front passenger seat while Kol helped me onto the bench behind them, settled in beside me, and pulled me onto his lap.

I pressed my cheek against his shoulder and leaned my forehead against his neck, trying to get closer to him, desperate for more heat. This was a deeper cold than just my empathy. This went bone-deep, and I didn't know where the cold had come from.

A tear leaked from beneath my closed eyelids. I no longer had any control over my life. I couldn't even stop myself from crying.

"Hey," Kol murmured. "We can figure this out. We can fix this."

But they couldn't. There wasn't any fixing this.

My forearm ached with Gideon's brand, and my biceps with the wraith's. The buzz in my body was like a million bees stinging me over and over again, and I was clean out of emotional strength.

Please let me have seen it wrong. Let it be anyone else but Gideon.

Marcus drove us back to the Supers' Quarter and pulled up to the glass doors in the Operations Building's garage. He glanced back at me. "Is she still cold?"

"I can't get her to warm up," Kol said.

"We can't risk this being some kind of reaction to the wraith— angel— whatever the hell it is." His grip on the steering wheel tightened, turning his knuckles white. "Get her to her room and do whatever it takes to get her body temp up." He turned to Jacob. "We need a plan. There are wards on this building, but I have no idea if they will stop that thing."

"Agreed," Jacob said.

Kol climbed out of the SUV, still holding me, and carried me down the hall to the elevator and up to my room.

"Do you have your keycard?" he asked.

"Back pocket," I forced out.

He set me on my feet. The hall swayed and I was still shaking so hard I was having trouble standing. I pulled the card from my pocket and handed it over to him. No way was I going to be able to slide it into the reader.

He unlocked the door, carried me inside, and sat me on the bed. "Why don't I run you a bath," he said as he flicked on the bedside lamp and headed toward the bathroom, "see if we can't get your temperature to rise that way."

A bath? Panic seized me. There was no way he was going to let me bathe alone, not with how unsteady I was, but a bath equaled naked—or at least a lot less clothing. And while a part of me loved the idea of being scantily clothed with a drop-dead gorgeous man, scantily clothed risked revealing the new brand. And I just— I couldn't—

"No." I scrambled off the bed to stop him. My legs couldn't hold me and I dropped to the floor again, proving just how helpless I was right now.

Tears burned in my eyes. God, why couldn't I stop crying?

Kol knelt beside me, grabbed one of my hands, and rubbed it between his palms, his skin blazingly hot on my frozen fingers. "We need to get you warm."

"I know." I knew he wasn't going to leave me until I was, and honestly I didn't want him to. I didn't want to be alone with my thoughts, with the horror that I was mated with an angel. "Can you just hold me?"

His gaze captured mine and a hint of desire uncurled within me, then vanished as quickly as it formed—or at least some of it, but not all—and concentration pinched around his eyes. "I can do that."

He threw back the covers on my bed. I staggered into it, then he settled in behind me, both of us fully dressed, and pulled the covers back over top.

"It's going to be all right." He wrapped strong arms around me and tucked me tight against his body.

"Don't make promises you can't keep."

His warmth seeped deeper into my skin and for a

second my brain stalled, as if he was enthralling me. That was probably for the best. I needed to get a hold of myself, break through the panic, and I couldn't seem to do it on my own.

"Gideon will do whatever it takes," he said, his warm breath caressing the back of my neck, drawing a shiver of desire.

"Now you're making promises for Gideon."

"He said he'd protect you and he's an angel of his word."

Another shiver slid through me and that hint of desire uncurled a little more, but a convulsion quickly followed and sliced through it, consuming it and drawing a gasp.

Kol's arms around me tightened and my brain stalled again, caught between thoughts. There was only glorious nothing and Kol's warmth and embrace.

He murmured something into my hair, his breath caressing my neck again, but the words muddled before reaching my brain. It didn't matter, though. All that mattered was his body wrapped around me, his heat melting away the cold, and the room's temperature thankfully rising.

I floated in that warmth, weightless and without pain. The buzz was gone, the burn of the brand was gone, and the sudden changes in temperature were gone. There was only heat and darkness.

And Kol. It was wrong to be attracted to him now that I was destined to be Gideon's mate, even if that attraction to Kol probably wasn't more than a human's normal response to an incubus. He and Gideon were co-workers.

God, it was wrong to be mated with Gideon when it was clear he was in love with Zella and Marcus was attracted to me.

Except I didn't really know if Marcus was. Yeah, he'd kissed me, said he was terrified for me, but did that add up to a going-to-do-something-more-about-it attraction? Did I want it to?

And really, it didn't matter. Nothing was going to happen between me and Marcus, no matter what I'd fantasized about four and a half years ago, and nothing was going to happen with Kol.

And absolutely nothing was going to happen with Gideon. Whenever the brand's magic started to compel me to want to be with him, I would fight it. I would fight it with everything I had.

A laugh cut through the darkness. "You can't fight the brand," the darkness said, his voice low and sensual. A tendril of smoke slid across my belly and the buzz crackled under my skin. "I've marked you. You're mine. You will come when I call."

"If that was the case, you'd be calling me already."

The tendril broke apart, but another one slid up my leg, the buzz growing wherever it touched. "Give it time."

"Never going to happen."

The tendril broke apart again, and the darkness, or rather the wraith, growled. "They won't understand you."

"There's nothing to understand."

"Don't kid yourself. You're... complicated," the wraith said, and a tendril swept out of the darkness and curled over my wrist.

"Every woman is complicated." But I knew what he

was talking about and my words didn't dispel the tendril this time. Somehow he knew I wasn't completely human and knew none of the guys would accept me when they learned the truth.

God, if they didn't kill me, they'd lock me up for life, or worse, use me as a lab rat to figure out why I existed and was different from the monsters Michael had created. It was my mother's greatest fear. She'd spent her whole life— *given* her whole life to protect me. She'd said no one, human, angel, or super, would understand me, and when I was old enough, she'd shown me video clips of the war and just how monstrous the nephilim had been.

"They won't understand," the wraith hissed again, and another tendril rushed from the darkness and curled around my thigh.

The buzz in my body increased. The tendrils thinned then thickened again, as if struggling to maintain substance.

"They'll fear you. They'll sentence you without due process. You're an animal. You don't deserve the same rights as them."

They would be my monsters, like I was theirs. Except there were more of them. They were more powerful than me. I was a nephilim without magic. I could barely summon a blast of divine light. Most humans who could cast a light strike were more powerful than me.

"But I don't fear you."

Another tendril curled around my waist.

"I don't think you're an animal."

His words slid across my senses and his tendrils tightened. I could sense the promise of desire from him, but also deep-burning rage.

"I crave you, Essie. With me, you'll have unimaginable power. Power enough to protect yourself and to wreak vengeance on all the hurt they've forced on you." The tendril around my wrist slid up my arm and curled around the wraith's brand, framing it and drawing my attention to the red sigil seared into my skin. "I understand you."

The buzz in my body increased, and my muscles twitched as if zapped with electricity. I gritted my teeth against the pressure of the tendrils and the lure of his words. There might be truth in what he said, that the world would never accept or desire me. That they would always fear me and because of that I'd always live in fear. But I didn't want the vengeance he promised. It didn't even hold a hint of allure. I just wanted to live a normal human life.

"But you don't," the wraith said. "I can feel your true soul struggling to break free. Your angelic nature has imprisoned you. Your fear has imprisoned you. I'm trying to set you free."

"By branding me and permanently bonding our souls together?"

"Because I love you."

"I doubt you do." I could feel it in the smoke and darkness. What he felt wasn't love, it was madness, a need for power, and for some reason he saw power within me that he could possess and control.

"I do love you. I *need* you."

"Yeah, to fulfill your need for vengeance." His reason

for vengeance fluttered around in my head, but I couldn't grasp onto it. There was only his smoke and his hatred.

"You will give me what I want." More tendrils swept out of the darkness and wrapped around me. I jerked against them, but I couldn't break free. "We're the same," the wraith hissed. "You belong to me, your power belongs to me, and we will reap justice for the slaughter of our people."

A spear of smoke sliced into the ugly red brand on my arm, and the wraith's essence poured into me, flooding every cell, suffocating me from the inside out.

I screamed and thrashed. I had to get free. I couldn't let it control me, command me, possess me. I couldn't let it use me to do horrible things.

My elbow slammed into something solid and someone yelped, then a strong hand pinned my arm to my body.

"Essie," Kol gasped.

The darkness clung to my mind.

Get out. Get the fuck out, I screamed at the wraith, no— the nephilim.

"Essie, wake up."

I jerked into a sitting position and my eyes flew open. The darkness within me exploded into smoke and my mind swept it away with a ferocious wind. Nausea churned in my stomach and the buzz crackled under my skin at pre-nicotine levels. The wraith had been in my head, and I could feel its sickening darkness still clinging to me as if it had just poured down my throat.

"Essie."

I jerked my attention to Kol. He sat beside me, his

arms around me, hugging mine tight to my body. A red welt marked his cheek. I must have elbowed him in the face. Behind him, sunlight streamed through the window, the curtains having never been closed for the night, and the sky was beautiful and clear, like Gideon's eyes.

"It's okay," he said.

I shuddered at the memory of the wraith in my head. Then the weight of yesterday's events slammed into me and panic squeezed my chest. I struggled to breathe. It wasn't just the wraith. It was so much worse than that. I was mated for life. To an angel. It wasn't going to be okay.

I shoved that thought aside before my panic took over. I'd deal with it later, after I'd dealt with the wraith— because I doubted I'd be able to avoid it completely.

Kol's eyes narrowed and he frowned.

Yeah, no one could maintain a positive attitude in the face of everything that had happened, but then I realized his attention wasn't on my face, it was lower.

"Is that—?" His frown deepened and he grabbed my wrist, turning it to expose the inside of my forearm. "Is that Gideon's brand?"

Oh, shit.

I tried to jerk my arm away, but he held tight and shoved my sleeve up higher, exposing the whole brand. It glimmered as if it were real gold reflecting bright sunlight. The lines were crisp and delicate—the complete opposite to the wraith's brand—and they swirled in a complicated design from mid-forearm to my elbow. It was beautiful, and it made my breath hitch in awe and fear. Gideon had said the connection between branded mates was deep and pure. That it grew stronger with time, transforming each angel's soul, bringing them closer together than even a vampire's claim. At the root of it all was an attunement, fitting souls perfectly together and creating a yearning that they had to be together. That they belonged together.

"It's a mistake."

"A mating brand is never a mistake."

"This one is." I tugged at Kol's grip but he still refused to let go, his gaze locked on my arm.

"It's destiny."

"It's a disaster."

His attention jumped up to me, surprise in his eyes. "How could this possibly be a disaster? This is fate, the universe bringing you together."

"And did you see the way he looked when he thought the bond was with Zella?"

Kol pursed his lips. I could see he wanted to argue with me, but knew I was right.

"He'll be heartbroken when he realizes fate has mated him with me."

"I don't think he will." Kol raised a hand to caress my cheek but stopped before making contact, as if suddenly realizing I belonged to someone else.

God, that thought made me want to scream. I didn't *belong* to anyone. I didn't *want* to belong to anyone. And I sure as hell didn't want that *someone* to be an angel.

"I want my life back." My words came out small and soft.

"Being mated doesn't mean your life is over."

I was pretty sure it did.

Realization flashed in his eyes. "In fact, if your bond

with Gideon is stronger than the one with the wraith, I think it might actually save your life." He threw back the covers and hopped from the bed. "We have to tell Gideon, confirm if I'm right."

I scrambled from the bed and grabbed his hand, stopping him before he opened the door. "We're *not* telling Gideon."

"We have to tell him. He's going to find out soon enough. He said he'd know who his mate was as soon as the bond gets stronger."

"Kol, please." Yes, it was inevitable, but I wasn't going to be running around proclaiming it from the mountaintops just yet. Probably ever. "I need time to process this."

He pursed his lips.

"I need time to process everything." And make peace with how all of this was going to end. "It's all so complicated."

"It's your bond," he said, his tone soft, reluctant, then gave a tight nod. "It's your news to share."

I grabbed his hands and gently squeezed them. "Thank you."

He leaned toward me, as if he was going to hug me or kiss me or something, but pulled away before finishing the move. "We still need to figure out what to do about the wraith... angel... whatever it is. Are you up for that?"

"God, yes."

"Then let's go find the rest of the team."

I yanked my shirt sleeve down and opened the door. Marcus sat on the floor against the far wall, his knees up, arms across his knees, and forehead on his arms. His hair was tousled, making him look even sexier, and his clothes, the same as when we'd fought the wraith, were disheveled. He hadn't changed even though, unlike me, he'd had a chance to.

"Have you been here all night?" I asked.

His head jerked up. The agony in his eyes melted to complete, desperate relief, and he rushed to his feet and wrapped me in a tight embrace. "Oh, thank God."

His lean-muscled body pressed against mine, strong and sure and warm, and I melted into his hug. For a second I was going to pretend my life wasn't a complete mess.

"Thank God, thank God." His hands moved from my back to my head, his fingers tangled in my hair, and his lips captured mine in a fierce, possessive kiss, so intense it stole my breath.

Then he pulled back before it had really started and pressed his forehead to mine. "You're never doing that again. Please say you're never doing that again."

I cupped his cheeks in my palms and urged him to make eye contact. His fear licked cold across my skin and nearly broke my heart. "You know I can't make that promise."

A growl rumbled in his chest, but he swallowed it back. "I know. I just— God." He hugged me again, clutching me to him as if he was afraid to let me go.

Kol cleared his throat. "So I *am* into watching, but if I'm going to get a decent meal out of it, you guys need to be a little more... active."

"Shut up," Marcus growled without letting me go "And thank you."

"Sure," Kol said. "Ask me to spend all night with a pretty lady—"

Marcus's head jerked up. He glared over my shoulder at Kol and for the first time I truly saw the wolf within him, feral, protective, ferocious.

I slid my hands to his chiseled chest and gently pressed, easing a step back. "And, fully clothed, he helped me raise my body temperature."

Marcus's piercing green gaze slid back to me and the wolf released a soft rumble. I was safe. It was happy.

And I was seriously confused.

Guess kissing me yesterday *had* meant something.

"Now let's find Jacob and Gideon and figure out plan B," I said.

"When we left Gideon last night, he was with Zella. He's probably still there. I'll call Jacob and tell him to meet us in her room. Gideon won't be wanting to leave his mate right now." Marcus pulled his phone from his pocket and turned slightly away from me.

Kol stared at me with wide eyes and he mouthed the word *complicated* to me.

No shit, I mouthed back.

Marcus's free arm snaked across the back of my waist and tugged me closer to him, as if he couldn't stand to be away from me.

Jeez. Complicated didn't begin to explain the mess I was in.

CHAPTER 13

I SLIPPED BACK INTO MY ROOM, USING THE EXCUSE THAT I needed to visit the bathroom before heading down, and replaced my nicotine patch. I was going through them faster than I should, but these were extenuating circumstances. If I survived what was about to come and continued to burn through the nicotine at the same rate, then I'd start to worry.

The new patch brought the biting buzz back under control—or as under control as it ever got. I returned to the hall, and Marcus stepped close to me and stayed close as we got into the elevator and headed down to Zella's room.

If I was smart, I'd tell him right away about Gideon's brand. Letting him continue to hold me and kiss me like that could only lead to heartache for all of us. But if I was being honest with myself, I was thrilled at being held by him and the promise of satisfying the sizzling desire between us.

And maybe I was crazy. Fate said I belonged to

Gideon. If I stayed in Marcus's world, I'd be Gideon's whether I wanted to be or not, and even if I wasn't, constantly being with supers guaranteed that someone would notice the truth about me. Hell, it was a miracle no one had noticed so far.

It didn't matter how comfortable and safe and turned on I was in Marcus's embrace. As soon as the wraith, or rather nephilim— Nope, I couldn't think of him as the same kind of super as me. We weren't the same. Not even close. As soon as the *wraith-angel* was taken care of, I had to leave—barring, of course, being insane or dead, and if I was either, then being a nephilim in the world of supers was the least of my worries.

The elevator door slid open, and Marcus's phone rang. We stepped into the hall as he answered it, and he stiffened at whatever was said.

"Change of plans. We're meeting Gideon and Jacob in the garage. Union City PD has found another body."

"Shit," Kol said. "And we're going to the scene? Can't forensics confirm it was the wraith?"

"I thought they could, but apparently not," Marcus said. "And I have no idea why, so we're going."

Kol frowned. "So who's staying here with Essie?"

"No one." Marcus shoved his phone back into his pocket, not sounding happy about that. "Gideon doesn't want to separate the team until the wraith is dealt with and she's safest with us, so she's coming along."

Given how we'd had our asses handed to us last night, I wasn't certain I was safe with anyone, but I had to agree that I had a better chance of not being captured by the wraith-angel if I was with all of the guys instead of just one of them.

That, and I wasn't going to argue with Marcus right now. I could still sense his wolf, barely contained within him—now that I knew what the fury radiating from him actually was—and didn't want to push him.

"Okay," I said, "then let's go. I'm sure Gideon has his reasons for wanting to go to the scene."

I motioned and Kol headed down the hall. I followed.

"I think he can't just sit here, even with Zella, waiting to find out who's dead now." Marcus fell into step beside me. "And if it's a squad member, he and Jacob are the ones who'll be able to make the identification."

"Yeah, but he's endangering Essie by leaving the protective wards on Operations," Kol said.

"If our wards could even keep that thing out." Marcus shifted closer to me.

Kol huffed. "I still think Gideon is starting to lose his shit."

"I do, too, but investigating crimes committed by supers is also our job," Marcus said. "Maybe we'll stumble across a miracle and there'll be something at the crime scene to help us deal with the wraith."

Gideon was already in the garage when we arrived, standing just outside the glass doors, his expression still raw and haggard like when I'd seen him earlier at Zella's bedside. It didn't look as if things were going well with Zella, and I could only imagine his pain at thinking he could lose his destined mate before the mating brand had fully formed.

Kol opened the door from the hall to the garage, and

Gideon's attention jerked to us. Emotional ice swept over his face and through his posture, and the cold, emotionless angel I'd first met stared back at us. His attention jumped to the red mark on Kol's cheek—thankfully fading and it might not even bruise, so I mustn't have hit him that hard—and he frowned.

"Has forensics left for the scene already?" Marcus asked, still standing possessively close to me.

"Yes." Gideon's gaze slid to the space—or rather lack of space—between us. "The officer who called us said they hadn't managed to get an ID on the victim, but the scene looks like the other three. We're just waiting on—" His gaze shifted past my shoulder and Jacob stepped out of the hall into the garage.

His claim on my essence tugged in my chest, and I couldn't tear my gaze away from him. Every fiber of my being yearned to please him, begged for his touch and command.

I gritted my teeth and forced myself to stay where I was. Marcus bristled beside me, as if he could sense my need to go to Jacob. The tug squeezed tighter and I strained to draw a full breath. God, I couldn't wait for this compulsion to ease up, like he'd promised it would.

"As you were," Jacob said, his voice a low rumble, and the pressure in my chest evaporated.

Thank God.

"We good?" Gideon asked.

"Hardly," Marcus growled.

"Fine." It was as good as it was going to get.

Jacob gave a tight nod.

"All right," Gideon said. "Let's go. We're headed to Seventh and Foley." He tossed Marcus a set of keys.

Marcus caught them and glanced at me, as if trying to decide if he should decline driving to stay beside me, then squared his shoulders and hurried to one of the SUVs in the spot across from us. Thank goodness, because this whole situation was uncomfortable enough as it was.

Jacob fell into step beside me and pressed a hand to my back. "How are you feeling?" he asked in a low voice, his words just for me.

"I'm not going to start crying again, if that's what you're worried about." Although if something else monumental happened, I couldn't promise that I'd be able to keep holding it together.

"Given all that's happened, you have every right to still be crying."

"And what good would that do?" I climbed onto the middle bench with Kol, while Gideon took the front passenger seat and Jacob took the back. "We still need to figure out plan B."

"Ward you with everything we can find and keep you close," Marcus said, pulling out of the parking space.

"Unless I can wear those wards, no. I'm not spending the rest of my life trapped in a room somewhere."

Marcus shot a glare at me through the rear view mirror then drove onto the Quarter's main street and headed toward the human part of the city.

"I don't think we can try luring him again," Jacob said. "That didn't even work the first time."

"And what the hell is it?" Kol rubbed his face,

suddenly looking exhausted. I might have passed out and slept last night, but how much sleep had *he* gotten? "Is it a wraith or an angel?"

"I think he's both." A part of me screamed that I was going to regret pointing out that this thing was a nephilim, but not telling them only prolonged the inevitable. One of them would figure it out eventually. There was no point in pussyfooting around it.

Gideon glanced over his shoulder, his gaze jumping past me to Jacob. "I think she's right. One of them survived."

"Michael destroyed them all when we raided his laboratory," Jacob said. "None of them hatched in that blaze. You double-checked yourself."

"I know." The muscles in Gideon's jaw flexed. "But I've spent all night thinking about it and there's no other explanation."

"What explanation?" Marcus asked.

"An archnephilim, specifically half archangel and half demon," Gideon said.

"Are you shitting me?" Kol asked. "Demon and angel DNA doesn't mix."

Gideon turned his attention back to the road. "Angel DNA doesn't mix with any species."

"Not true," Jacob said. "A regular angel's DNA is compatible with an angel-touched human's. That's how Michael and Lucifer managed to get their nephilim creation spell to work in the first place. Demon DNA has to be powerful enough to withstand combining with an archangel's. We saw the partially formed demon-archangel hybrids ourselves. We know it's possible."

"Our DNA is only compatible because of unnatural magic," Gideon said.

"So you're saying Michael was creating even more powerful nephilim when the war ended?" I asked. God, if anything like the wraith-angel had joined the war, humanity would have lost. I shuddered. And that was what had branded me as his. A nephilim with the power of a demon and an archangel.

My thoughts stuttered and jumped back to something Gideon had said. "You said Michael destroyed them before they'd hatched."

"So we couldn't take them into custody," Jacob said. "We lost more than half the squad trying to take that facility."

"Could this archnephilim think you were responsible for Michael destroying his lab? That could be why he's murdering your remaining squad members." The wraith-angel had said he wanted vengeance, that I should want vengeance, too, for the slaughter of our people.

"So we have a guess what its motivation is," Marcus said. "Doesn't help us deal with it."

He had a point, but I wasn't willing to give up on that train of thought. "Maybe we can use that to make him make a mistake or something. In the very least, does knowing he's an archnephilim help?"

"It doesn't help you," Gideon said, his voice suddenly void of emotion, as if he didn't want to say what he had to say. "It's nearly impossible to win a fight with an archangel if you're not trying to kill him, and we'd need help from more than one archangel to do that—which, with the toll of the war being so recent, is never going to happen. The only sure way to stop this archnephilim is to kill it."

Marcus slammed on the brakes, stopping in the middle of the busy two-lane street, and growled at Gideon. "We are not killing it."

"If it's an archnephilim, there isn't any choice." A hint of Gideon's ice melted, revealing soul-rending pain. His gaze slid to mine and I could see he'd come to the horrible realization that he couldn't save me as he'd promised, and it was tearing him apart.

"What happened to not killing the human?" Marcus's wolf rose to the surface and his pupils turned to slits. "We don't kill humans."

"It might not kill her." Kol's gaze jumped to my arm.

Please, don't say it. Please. I'm not ready and there wasn't any guarantee Gideon's brand would save me.

He must have seen the panic in my face, because he opened his mouth to say more then snapped it shut.

"Sure," Marcus said. "She'll just go insane instead."

The temperature in the SUV dropped with Marcus's fear, and the driver in the sedan behind us leaned on his horn.

Marcus ignored him. "That's not acceptable. Essie gets out of this. She gets her life back. Free and clear of all of this."

More horns blared and someone started shouting.

"We all know that isn't going to happen," Gideon said.

"It God damn is gonna happen," Marcus growled, the temperature dropping even more.

The driver behind us jerked his sedan into an opening in the oncoming traffic and drove around us.

"If magic can create the impossible, maybe magic can capture the impossible," Jacob said. "Or break it. We have an archive of ancient texts and a handful of journals that we managed to confiscate from Michael's laboratory before it burned down. There might be something in them that can help."

His claim tugged in my chest. He wanted what he said to be true and, even without saying it, the claim needed me to help him. Now.

I dug my fingernails into my palms, hoping no one would notice, praying the urge to jump out of the SUV and go back to Operations would pass. Jacob wasn't rushing back. He was headed to the crime scene with the rest of the team. That was where I should be. Really. A hint of pressure eased, but not all, as if the claim only half agreed with my argument to stay.

Gideon shot Jacob a dark look, the warning clear: don't give false hope.

Jacob raised an eyebrow in response, *his* message clear: stop being an ass. "I'm not willing to give up on Essie. We're going to this crime scene then to the archives to find an answer."

The pressure vanished, but the temperature continued to drop until it was a struggle to keep my teeth from chattering.

More cars jerked around us, and people rolled down their windows and yelled at us.

I rubbed my arms, trying to get myself to warm up before my breath misted and frost formed on my skin. Now I could tell without a doubt that Marcus was terrified and he needed hope more than I did, if only to raise the temperature in the SUV. "We still don't know what to do about this archnephilim," I said. "Seeing if there's anything in these texts might help us to form a plan that won't get our asses kicked the next time we face off with it."

"*You're* not facing off with it again," Marcus growled.

"We've already been over this. I can't make any promises."

"I can," Gideon said. "Whatever we do, Officer Shaw is going to stay behind Operations' wards. With luck, their protection against malicious intent should be enough to prevent the archnephilim from entering."

But would they be enough for me to resist the pull of his brand? Gideon had said the brand drew mates together, and the archnephilim had said I'd give him what he wanted, that I belonged to him.

"Fine," Marcus said, his voice low.

"Now, can we get to the crime scene to secure it like we're supposed to?" Gideon asked. "If this perp is an archnephilim, this is my mess to clean up. Not the humans'. And it needs to be soon. Like yesterday."

Yeah, yesterday would have been great. Preferably before I'd gotten involved.

We arrived at a two-story motel on the outskirts of town, with exterior corridors, faded blue siding, and peeling gray accent paint. The parking lot was riddled with weeds growing out of the asphalt and if there'd been lines marking parking spaces, they were long gone. The neon sign at the front of the property wasn't on, since it was just after eight in the morning, but I suspected not all of it lit up, if any of it actually did.

Half a dozen cruisers were parked near the back of the lot, along with a black SUV—presumably the JP forensics team. Two uniformed officers were scouring the parking lot for evidence, while four more were in the field behind the motel. Another two stood outside the open door of a room on the second floor.

A young man with a rumpled dress shirt and glasses stood at the front of the building near a sign labeled OFFICE, talking with a man in a suit—probably the detective who'd caught the case before the JP agents took over.

Marcus parked halfway down the lot, putting us between the young guy being interviewed and the crime scene, and we piled out of the SUV.

"Marcus, talk to the detective and find out what he's learned," Gideon said. "Kol, Officer Shaw, you can wait with the officers outside the door while Jacob and I check in with Summer and her team. Let's make this fast."

Marcus stormed away toward the detective, while the rest of us took the stairs and headed to the room in question.

The two officers at the door frowned as Gideon approached, but he showed them his ID, and they waved him and Jacob inside. A flash of heat swept over me. Anger from Gideon or Jacob that was quickly contained under tight control. I didn't know if that meant they recognized the latest victim or if there was something else.

Kol leaned against the faded siding beside the closest officer, a woman with flecks of silver in her hair and a slightly green complexion. Her gaze swept over Kol and heat colored her cheeks as he settled in. The officer on the other side of the door, a man with a clean-shaven baby face who was probably in his thirties, cleared his throat, but the woman was too distracted by the incubus to notice.

I pulled my attention away from them and searched the horizon. Not that the wraith couldn't come from the other side of the building, but I couldn't help keeping an eye out. It was coming for me. Unless, of course, what he had said in my dream was true and I'd end up going to him because I wouldn't be able to resist the brand.

A shiver swept over me and I rubbed the sore spot on my biceps. It didn't hurt like it had last night, but it was still painful. Did that mean this was a temporary reprieve? Or had I just gotten used to it?

Gideon's brand, not even a day old, didn't hurt at all. In fact, I could almost pretend it didn't exist. God, I desperately wanted it to not exist.

I shoved that thought away. If the wraith-angel was really this archnephilim, as Gideon had said, and the only sure way to stop him was to kill him, then I *had* to pretend Gideon's brand didn't exist. If the mating brand made angels do crazy things to protect their mates, then there was a risk Gideon wouldn't be able to kill the nephilim for fear of hurting me. And this archnephilim had to be stopped. Gideon's team was just the beginning. He was going to go after every angel and every super who'd ever had anything to do with the destruction of Michael's nephilim laboratory. His thirst for vengeance would never be quenched.

So that left me with what? Lying to Gideon and

Marcus, and hell, everyone else on the team until I died or went crazy?

I glanced at Kol from the corner of my eye, hoping he wouldn't notice I was looking at him. I couldn't trust him to keep the brand a secret, not if he thought I was endangering myself, and not if he thought I was endangering Gideon. And if I died, Gideon would die or go insane.

Jeez, this was becoming a complicated mess. But I was pretty sure Gideon would be willing to sacrifice himself to protect everyone else.

Was that why fate had paired us together? We were both willing to do whatever it took to save lives?

Except if that was the case, then fate had royally screwed us both.

A Joined Parliament Medical Examiner's van pulled into the parking lot and two guys, one who looked human but could have been any number of supers, the other a demon with green skin, pulled a gurney out of the van and headed for the stairs.

I shifted to get out of the way, and the male officer across from me pushed the room's door open further, giving me a perfect view of the horror show inside.

The body of a demon with onyx skin lay on an unmade bed, like a discarded crushed doll. All of his limbs except one arm had been crushed and twisted, and half of his face had been smashed in. But what horrified me the most was the fist-sized hole in the middle of his chest.

Up until now, the archnephilim had crushed and sliced but not punctured. Now his smoke tentacles were powerful enough to stab straight through someone and I doubted that power had anything to do with natural development. Gideon had said the mating brand enhanced an angel's powers. I was enhancing the archnephilim's. That was why he'd wanted me.

I tore my gaze from the body, but my attention got stuck halfway up the wall, staring at a blood smear. Blood splattered everywhere, walls, floor, ceiling, but that smear looked like it had been done on purpose.

The medical examiner guys pushed the gurney inside, the demon going first and using his body to open the door even further.

That smear looked like a T and the smear beside it an H.

I stepped into the doorway to get a better look, and my pulse stuttered. The archnephilim had written in blood on the wall, 'thanks for the power,' confirming what I suspected. I was responsible for this new level of gore.

CHAPTER 14

WE RETURNED TO OPERATIONS, THE MOOD IN THE SUV grim. Gideon and Jacob had identified the victim as another squad member, which only made Gideon more brooding because the rest of his squad was supposed to be in hiding. Frustration and fear radiated from Marcus in snaps of hot and cold, and his fingers had elongated and narrowed, not fully forming into claws, but on the verge, while Jacob and Kol were on their phones, accessing the JP archives catalogue and searching for any document or recording that might offer a hint to capturing an archnephilim or severing an angelic mating brand.

Marcus pulled into the garage and parked in a spot near the door, and we piled out of the SUV.

"Show me where this archive is," I said to Jacob, the claim urging me to please him thankfully agreeing with my need to find answers. I hoped we'd be able to find a way to free me, but I was enough of a realist to know I shouldn't hold my breath on that. Knowledge, however, was power, and I was painfully short on any kind of information about archnephilim and angel brands, so learning as much as I could on this mess wasn't wasted time.

Except Gideon didn't think there'd be answers, let alone a solution. Even Jacob seemed doubtful.

God, I was going to die or go crazy, and I was going to take Gideon with me.

That thought burned the most. I couldn't even contain the casualties to myself. I was going to ruin someone else's life, just like I'd ruined Marcus's. The only way to save Gideon would be to give myself to the archnephilim and let him use me, but that would mean the deaths of others, many more than just me and Gideon.

A part of me wanted to scream and cry at the injustice. It wasn't fair. All I wanted was a normal human life. Why was that too much to ask for? I'd spent my childhood on the run, always afraid. I'd finally found balance and a purpose in my job. That balance had been slow in forming, but I had it, and I had no doubt the next stage, friends, maybe even a family, would also be— *have been* slow in coming, but it would have eventually come.

If I hadn't screwed it up by getting involved in the supernatural world.

And I'd tried. So damn hard. I'd had that one scare with Marcus where I'd realized I couldn't just pretend supers didn't exist, but I'd also managed to have nothing to do with supers since.

Until now.

And there hadn't been anything I could have done to

avoid it. If I went back in time, I would have done the same thing, interrupted the robbery then convinced the robber to go into the alley.

It was as if all those years I'd spent avoiding my supernatural nature had finally come crashing down on me in one horrible day, and fate had decided that even though I wasn't one of Michael's monstrous creations, my existence couldn't defy the natural order. Nephilim weren't supposed to exist.

I wasn't supposed to exist.

Perhaps this was why I'd been born. To help end this threat. Although why I also had to be mated to Gideon was beyond me.

And really, none of it mattered. Fate or not, it was what it was, and if I spent too much time thinking about how unfair and horrific the situation was, I'd curl into a ball and cry. That, and the part of me that knew being a cop was the only job for me wouldn't allow me to just give up.

If I was going to face my end, I was going to face it head on, and I was going to make sure the archnephilim didn't killed anyone else or any of the guys. That was the least I could do.

Which meant my main objective now was to join the guys in searching the archives to find a way to help kill the archnephilim and minimize casualties, since so far he'd kicked our asses.

And while I hoped the odds would be better now that lethal force was an option, the archnephilim was also now more powerful. Because of me.

"The archives is in the basement," Jacob said, and he

headed toward the glass doors leading into the main hall, Kol close behind.

"A word first, Officer Shaw," Gideon said, making Jacob and Kol pause and my heart skip a beat. Did he know about the brand? Had it already solidified enough for him to tell I was his mate instead of Zella? If he did, that could stop him from planning to kill the arch-nephilim and that would mean more people would die. That would mean some or all of the guys on the team would die. I couldn't let that happen. I wouldn't be responsible for that.

"You can meet me in the archives if you'd like," Jacob said, the command blessedly open-ended.

Marcus came around the back of the SUV and stepped possessively close to me again.

Gideon leveled a frozen glance at Marcus. "Alone, please."

Marcus's claws extended a little more from his fingers.

I brushed his arm, drawing his attention to me. "Get started without me. The more eyes, the greater the chance we find something." That, and if Marcus stayed, my chances decreased of convincing Gideon to go against the nature of the mating brand and keep his original plan to sacrifice me. If it was just us, I might be able to convince him to hold firm. But with Marcus arguing against it, there was a chance Gideon would break and give in to him.

Marcus—or was that his wolf?—huffed with displeasure, but he turned and marched after Jacob and Kol.

We waited in the garage as Gideon watched the

others leave, the temperature unnervingly steady as if the angel had managed to freeze over everything, expression, body language, and emotions, locking it all deep inside. That was good. That meant he'd hardened his heart to the inevitable.

Then a hint of mist unfurled in the air around me. Grief. Strong enough to manifest.

Shit. Where was the icy, hard angel when I needed him? I wouldn't be able to do this on my own, not against Marcus's ferocious protection.

"Can we talk at my mate's bedside? I—" He ran his hands through his hair. "I thought I could leave her and go to the crime scene, but the thought of her waking up alone is driving me crazy."

"Sure." Disappointment I wasn't supposed to have squeezed in my chest. He still thought Zella was his mate. That was supposed to be a good thing.

I shoved the emotion down deep, as far as it would go. It was an effect of the brand, nothing more. We didn't know each other, and he despised my species. Our joining wasn't wonderful, it was cruel.

He headed inside and I followed, giving my sleeve a tug even though the brand wasn't close to being revealed, unable to help myself. The mist followed me, growing stronger the closer we got to Zella's room.

"You said she's strong," I said, needing to say something, praying I could alleviate some of his grief before moisture collected on my cheeks. "She'll pull through this."

We reached the room's window and Gideon stopped,

pressed his hands to the glass, and stared inside. Her tattered wings had been cleaned but were still in braces, and her face was one big ugly bruise, although it looked like maybe some of the swelling had gone down. The blanket over her body, however, didn't look right, and I realized it dropped off above her right knee and lay flat where the rest of her leg should have been.

"Amiah still doesn't know if she can save her wings. I don't know if she'll survive losing them," he said, his voice low, raw, and the mist thickened, clouding my vision. He pressed his palm to his brand and heat seeped up my arm. "And with the scars on her arms and in her soul, the brand isn't visible and might not be noticeable for a long time. I won't be able to use it to save her. Losing them will finish the job the nephilim started during the war. It'll destroy her spirit completely."

"It won't, because she has you." Even if they weren't mated, his love for her was strong. And I really didn't want to think about what was going to happen to him if killing the archnephilim killed me or drove me crazy. Perhaps if we did it before the bond fully formed, that would save him. Perhaps his love for Zella would save him. I was sure it could save her. If I had someone who loved me that much, I could pull through anything. Well, anything except this.

My mind jumped to Marcus's breathtaking, confusing kiss in the hall this morning. He was going to be... I had no idea. Furious? Shattered? Broken?... when the inevitable happened.

I swallowed at the lump forming in my throat. "I need to ask you a favor."

"As much as Jacob thinks there's a way to save you, there isn't." Gideon pressed his forehead to the glass and the mist billowed around me. "I said I'd protect you, but I can't."

"I know you can't. What I need is for you to do whatever it takes to stay on mission."

Gideon glanced at me, clouds of grief and determination darkening his summer-sky eyes. "You don't have to ask that of me."

"Even when Marcus fights you over it." I met his gaze head on. "And he'll fight you over it." He'd been fighting to keep me out of this since he'd first yelled at me in the hospital. I just hadn't realized that was what he'd been doing until he'd kissed me.

"His file said you were partners about four and a half years ago. I didn't realize you two were still in touch."

I didn't ask if his file also said I was the reason he was a werewolf. "We aren't— weren't—" I didn't know how to explain it. "It's complicated."

"It didn't look that complicated when you met me in the garage this morning."

And if I wasn't Gideon's fated mate and about to die or go insane, it wouldn't have been.

"You two should talk about it." His attention slid back to Zella. "Soon. You have less time than I'd hoped. The archnephilim's brand isn't even a day old and the magic connecting you has already made it stronger. The longer we wait, the stronger it will get."

"And the harder it will be to kill him." Yeah, I'd already figured that out, too. Another thing I was trying not to think about.

"Have you tried sensing where it is?" he asked. "It found you last night, so the brand is strong enough. Even though you're human, your angel-touch is strong. I've only met a few other humans who could cast a light strike with as much power as you did last night."

Yeah, because I wasn't actually an angel-touched human.

"That's probably why the archnephilim branded you," Gideon said. "Which means there's a good chance you'll be able to use its brand to find it as well."

"How do I find him?"

"Close your eyes and concentrate on the brand and your connection to the archnephilim."

I closed my eyes and took a breath, hoping it would steady me and help me concentrate.

"Touching the brand might also help."

Without rolling my sleeves, I pressed my palm against the archnephilim's brand. It throbbed like a fresh burn. Not the searing pain when he'd been searching for me, but still painful.

"Flesh to flesh would be better."

I opened my eyes and gave him my driest look. "I'm not taking my shirt off."

"That's fair," Gideon said, his voice soft.

I closed my eyes again and concentrated on the pain in my biceps. The archnephilim had visited me in my dreams. He'd found me at my apartment. Whether I liked it or not, we were connected. I could sense his inky darkness, a noxious smoke under my skin, creeping thick tentacles out from the brand. My mind flinched away from it, but I forced it closer to the darkness, trying to find a way to connect to him, find him, but his essence wouldn't let me in.

"Just take a breath and relax," Gideon said, and heat from his brand curled up my other arm, drawing my essence like a moth to a flame. His brand was warmth and affection, determination and honor. I yearned to be wrapped in his confidence and take comfort in the heat of his spirit, but I knew if I let myself sink into our connection, it would solidify the bond and he'd know I was his mate. And that would make everything more complicated.

"Can you sense him?" he asked.

I pushed my concentration back to the darkness. It oozed between my mental fingers, making me shudder, twisted back around my mental hands, and tightened. Pain exploded from the brand, slicing into my mind and body, and a low, dark chuckle echoed in my head.

"Changed your mind already?" the archnephilim asked, his desire oozing through the pain. *"I thought you had more fight than that."*

"Isn't this what you want? Me?" I strained to sense anything about where he was.

"Except that isn't what you're doing." The archnephilim's desire spread across my chest, making my breath hitch. *"But it should be. Your wolf can't make you feel the way I can."*

Aching heat gathered low within me, my nerves thrumming with sudden consuming need. I yearned for his touch—

No. I gritted my teeth. I didn't want his touch. This was him messing with my mind. Where was he? He seemed close, but I wasn't sure if that was because he was in my head or actually somewhere close by.

"Not even your angel can make you feel like this."

More desire flooded me, drawing a gasp. If my eyes hadn't already been closed, I'm sure they would have rolled back, as the promise of a climax fluttered within me.

I jerked my hand from the brand and pressed my palms to the wall to keep standing. A foggy image fluttered across my vision. A concrete pillar with chunks chipped out of it. A band of weak hazy sunlight. A pool of murky water.

"Come to me." The archnephilim chuckled again, the sound racing through me. *"Come for me."*

The pain from the brand burned hotter, with a shocking mix of pain and pleasure. I struggled to fight it, to deny that his inky darkness and aching pain turned me on, and concentrate on where he was. The feelings weren't me. It was his connection to me, his control over my body. But my body didn't want to listen to my mind, and the image vanished, leaving me surrounded in a darkness that ratcheted up the sensations within me. My breath came fast, my need for release twisting tighter. Tears burned my eyes at the pain and pleasure and hopelessness.

"You're not hopeless, you're powerful. We're powerful," he said. *"I can give you pleasure and power beyond your wildest dreams. You never have to fear again. They will fear you."*

"I don't want them to fear me." I just wanted to live my life.

But that wasn't going to be.

"It can be if you join me."

"I don't want vengeance."

"You should." The pain burned brighter, slicing into the pleasure. "We're not animals. Our kind didn't deserve to be slaughtered before we were even born."

"You were made. You're not natural."

"You're not better than me," he snarled. More pain flooded me, consuming the rest of the pleasure. "And you're not as strong as me. You're mine. You belong to me. You'll give me your strength and power and do as I say until I'm done with you."

My hand fisted and I punched out, the archnephilim controlling my body. I jerked my eyes open as Gideon blocked my attack, shock flashing through his eyes. My other hand fisted and punched.

Gideon blocked my other strike, grabbed my wrist, twisted, and jerked me around. He captured my hand behind my back, wrapped his arm across my chest and held me tight, my back against his chest. "Officer Shaw."

My body wrenched against his grip as my mind struggled for control against the archnephilim.

He howled with laughter. "That's it, little nephilim. Struggle."

He made me heave against Gideon's grip, forcing the angel to yank my hand higher up my back, drawing a whimper of pain. A new pleasure swept into me, one thick with malice and delight at my suffering.

"Get out." I mentally shoved at the archnephilim's essence in my body.

His laugher increased.

"I said get out."

"*Make me,*" the archnephilim sneered.

I mentally twisted and clawed and shoved at his essence within me, but his sick pleasure kept growing. He was consuming me, his darkness oozing into my cells, clinging to my soul, and drowning me as if his smoke was pouring down my throat again, and there was nothing I could do.

CHAPTER 15

PANIC SQUEEZED MY CHEST AND I FOUGHT TO BREATHE against the archnephilim's control. I screamed at my body to stop writhing in Gideon's grasp, to stop obeying the archnephilim's commands, but it wouldn't listen. My body no longer belonged to me, nor did the sensation of dark pleasure and ferocious vengeance. I was trapped, a prisoner within myself, and his darkness was consuming me.

"Get out." Please get out get out get out.

The light strike spell flashed into my head, the words racing around and around, and tears burned my eyes.

The archnephilim's laugher increased, his certainty that he possessed me making my stomach churn. This was not supposed to happen. None of this was supposed to happen, and I wasn't going to die possessed by this monster.

"Get out!" The light strike released within me. Light flashed, turning the darkness inside my lids white, and the archnephilim screamed. The divine light seared through my being, consuming the darkness and driving him from my head.

My knees gave out and I sagged against Gideon.

"Officer Shaw?" He released my wrist and wrapped both arms around my waist, taking my weight and helping me stand. His scent and warmth enveloped me and all I wanted to do was stay in his embrace forever. It was where I belonged. Every fiber of my being thrummed with that knowledge while my mind screamed at the danger of even just being near him.

I pushed out of his embrace—he let me go easily—and clung to the wall to keep standing. "When were you going to tell me he could use the brand to control me?"

"He can what?" He sounded genuinely surprised.

"He can control me." I shuddered at the memory of everything the archnephilim had made me feel, the need, the desire, and the terror.

"That's not possible—" Realization rushed across his expression. "It must be because he's also a wraith. The brand connects you, gives him access to your soul, which is what a wraith needs to possess someone. Do you know where he is?"

"No. If he hadn't—" The memory of his pleasure and the need he'd made me feel shuddered through me. "If he hadn't—" Another shudder and I gasped back a moan.

Gideon shifted to grab my shoulders, probably to steady me, but the thought of his hands on me made my pulse race faster.

God, what was wrong with me?

I jerked back and raised a hand, stopping him from

holding me. "I'm all right. I started to get a sense of where he might be, then he took over."

A hint of mist billowed around me with Gideon's grief... or maybe this was regret, and I knew what he was going to say next.

"You want me to try again." If we were going to hunt down the archnephilim, it was the only way, but the thought of doing that again made my pulse race and not in a good way.

"Yes, but I'll need to arrange for some precautions first, so hopefully it won't be able to possess you again." The mist thickened. "Or you'll be contained when it does."

"Wonderful."

"In the meantime, you should say what you have to say to Marcus." He glanced through the window at Zella, his message clear: before it was too late. "Take the elevator to the basement. The archives is right there."

"Right." I couldn't tear my gaze away from him as he stared at Zella. My emotions were a mess, the desire from the archnephilim making me yearn for something I couldn't have and didn't want with Gideon.

"Right." I forced myself to turn and head away. I didn't know how much time I had left, but I wasn't sure I wanted to have a conversation with Marcus. What could I say when I couldn't tell him Gideon's plan was the only one that would work?

And even then, with the archnephilim able to possess me, that had the potential to make everything more complicated.

Except I had managed to break free. By the skin of my

teeth, but I had. Perhaps there was an angle there I could use, a way to help the guys. Maybe if I could distract him, Gideon would be able to strike a killing blow? And maybe I could do more than just distract him, but I needed to learn a hell of a lot more about angelic mating brands to figure out if that was even a possibility.

I hit the call button for the elevator as Amiah came down the main hall toward me, and I prayed she'd just glare at me and head down the stairs to the cafeteria. But she joined me, waiting for the elevator, her hard gaze locked on the closed door.

The temperature around me rose.

I shifted, waiting for her to hit the up button. She didn't, which meant I was going to be trapped in the elevator with her and her hot fury. Wonderful.

"I think you're reckless," she said, her tone filled with ice and the temperature rising a few more degrees.

"You don't even know me."

She slid her icy gaze to me. "I know enough."

Right. One fuck-up before I knew what I was doing, and I was forever reckless. Except that wasn't true. Marcus was right. I was still taking chances, letting Jacob claim me to protect him and using myself as bait before we knew anything about the archnephilim.

"I also know if it wasn't for you, Zella would be dead."

The elevator dinged, the door opened, and I hit the only basement button.

"Gideon will eventually get past his shock and thank you," she said, her tone softening and a hint of the heat diminishing. "But until he does, on his behalf, thank you. You brought her back to us."

In the most horrific way possible. "I wish it had been under better circumstances."

"And I wish," she said, her voice icy again, "whatever happens next, you think before you act and don't do something that gets any of the guys killed."

The door opened and she strode out, heading down a narrow hall to the right, taking her heat with her. A chill settled around me, the actual temperature of the basement, filled with a hint of musty air and the smell of old books.

Ahead of me, Jacob sat at a wide wooden table that was piled with books, looking at me, while Kol sat behind him on a couch watching his phone, listening to the video flashing on his screen with earphones and not disturbing the quiet. Two fluorescent lights hung from the ceiling, offering stark illumination, and beyond stood shelves and shelves of books creating long passages. Across from the table, opposite the couch, was a metal door secured by a lock with a fingerprint scanner, and through the thick security glass I could see a neatly stacked row of rifles. The archives and the armory.

"Find anything?" I asked, not that I'd expected anything to be found in the fifteen minutes I'd been talking with Gideon... not that I expected them to find anything at all.

"Not yet. I'm going through the journals and records confiscated from Michael's facilities. Kol is watching the videos we recovered. If Michael was making archnephilim, he had to have a way to control them. He may have thought humanity was a parasite on the planet, but he wasn't a fool. An archnephilim is too powerful a weapon to create without having a guaranteed means of controlling it."

I sure hoped he was right, but I couldn't place all my bets on that one hope. Michael might not have had a plan to control the archnephilim. Perhaps he was just planning on letting them wreak havoc until the archnephilim were dead or the humans and the supers were.

"I should learn more about the mating brand. Maybe there's a way I can use it to influence the archnephilim, give you guys a chance to subdue him."

"Or weaken or sever the bond completely," Jacob said. "Gideon says it's not a true brand. There's still a chance we could find a way to remove it."

Except Gideon had been adamant from the beginning that once a brand formed, the bond could never be severed, and I really didn't want to get my hopes up because if there was a way to sever the bond between me and the archnephilim, then there was a way to sever the bond with Gideon. And then I could leave all this insanity behind.

"I really hope you're right. I would give just about anything to remove the brand."

Kol's gaze jumped to me then slid down my arm to where Gideon's brand was hidden beneath my shirtsleeve.

Both of the brands.

Except a part of me didn't want to sever the bond with Gideon. It was crazy. God, it had to be the influence of the true mating brand. Staying with Gideon, who didn't even know me let alone love me, was a disaster waiting to happen.

But even if I didn't stay for Gideon, there was still Marcus. Confusing, frustrating Marcus. I still had no idea what to make of him or his ferocious protectiveness, and I really wanted to kiss him again and let his wild passion make me forget everything that was happening.

Jeez. This was a mess. I was a mess.

"Marcus is in the stacks toward the back left corner of the archives, looking for books on the angelic mating brand. You can join him or he can point you in the direction of books on archangels," Jacob said. "Maybe there's a way to capture them and we can go back to plan A."

For a moment, I considered asking Jacob to point me in the direction of the books on archangels so I could avoid Marcus entirely, but I really needed to know if I could use the archnephilim's brand against him. Everything else—finding a way to control him or capture him —sounded lovely, but that wasn't anything I could control or probably even help with. Using the brand, though? That was something I could do.

I headed down a long aisle, the shelves reaching all the way to a ceiling with long fluorescent lights running down the center. The aisle ended in a T-intersection and between the uneven top of the books and the books of the closest shelf, I could see more shelves beyond. I couldn't tell if the library took up the entire basement, but I wouldn't have been surprised if it had.

I wove my way through the shelves, always going toward the back and the left, until I rounded a corner and found Marcus sitting on the floor, an open book in his lap, more books piled on the floor around him. His piercing green gaze, filled with a need more powerful than I'd ever seen from him before, rose to meet mine. My pulse stuttered. Sultry heat fluttered around me, tentative and uncertain, but while I hoped it meant he desired me, I didn't know for sure. I didn't know what anything with Marcus meant. I didn't understand this man at all. He'd acted professionally when we'd been partners, even with the chemistry sizzling between us, and had never said he was interested in me, no matter what the temperature around him had told me.

And then I'd messed up.

"I thought you were mad at me."

"I was mad— *am* mad. You keep taking risks, putting your life in danger when you're not supposed to have anything to do with the supernatural world." The desire in his eyes hardened. "My world."

"That doesn't make any sense." He had no right to be mad at me now. This was my life, my decision, and this time it had nothing to do with him. "Why would you care? I'm the reason you're in this world in the first place. I'm the one who messed up and ruined your life. You have every right to be mad at me for that, but this—" I gestured to the library around me, meaning the supernatural world and not just the library. "—this has nothing to do with you."

"It has everything to do with me," he said, his voice low, and for a moment it seemed it wasn't him talking but his wolf.

"Bullshit. You haven't talked to me since that night. No call, no email, nothing. You didn't even clean out your locker. You just left. You made your point absolutely clear." My throat tightened with guilt that I'd never managed to get rid of, only gotten better at ignoring.

"And what point was that?" His grip on the sides of the book tightened.

"That you were furious. That you didn't even want to accidentally run into me when you emptied your locker. That I'd destroyed your life." And there wasn't any way I could make it up to him. The only thing I could do now was ensure my new mess didn't get him or any of the other guys hurt or killed—and with Gideon's brand on my arm now, at least one of them was going to get hurt.

"I didn't come back to clean out my locker because I started turning right away. I barely managed to get to the hospital in the Quarter in time." His gaze dropped to the book in his lap and he took in a breath that did little to ease the tension in his body. "And then I was angry."

A hint of mist curled around me, and I realized the flickering heat had vanished. His anger or whatever it was I'd felt before was gone, replaced with grief or regret.

"I was angry for a long time, but not at you. You were a rookie. You had less than six months on the job," he said. "I was angry at myself for letting you put yourself in danger. I should have done whatever it took to stop you."

"I shouldn't have rushed in. We should have waited for backup."

Marcus shrugged, but the action looked forced. "We should have. But every time I think about that night, I know Ariel Cromer would have died if we had."

"We don't know that." Except I knew he was right... or was it that I hoped he was right? I'd panicked. She'd been screaming and I'd rushed in to save her. And Marcus had been bitten. I had no idea how we hadn't been killed that night.

His gaze lifted back to me, stalling my pulse again with the desire in his eyes. God, with just one look he could control me, steal my breath, and he didn't need to use a mating brand. "But most of all I was angry because I couldn't stop thinking about you. There was something about you, Essie. There still is. I can't explain it. I'm drawn to you—" He huffed a sad laugh. "My wolf is really drawn to you. That's why I had to stay away."

"That still doesn't make sense." If he was drawn to me, why would he have had to stay away? Why say nothing about it for the six months we worked together? He had to know the attraction went both ways. You didn't have that kind of chemistry with someone when it only went one way.

"Come on, Essie. We'd had enough conversations while on patrol for me to know you wanted nothing to do with supers. Every time I brought the conversation up, you'd get this scared look in your eyes and change the topic." He flicked the tip of the pages with his thumb and the muscles in his jaw twitched. "It took me over a year to get through my transition, to feel right in my skin again. Thank God for Amiah. She was working at Mercy Memorial then. If it hadn't been for her, I wouldn't have gotten through it. But when I finally had my head on straight, I knew no matter what I'd felt about you, I had to stay away. You wouldn't have accepted my wolf and my wolf wouldn't have accepted that."

I opened my mouth to protest that, but couldn't say the words. Up until a day ago, everything he said about me had been true. I was afraid of supers and wanted nothing to do with their world. I still didn't want anything to do with them.

"So now what?"

"Now I tell my wolf to shut the fuck up, keep my distance from you, and get you your life back."

"Gee, when you put it that way it sounds so easy," I said, unable to keep the sarcasm from my tone. "How's that working for you?"

"Not well," he growled, the heat in his eyes making my pulse race. "I shouldn't have kissed you."

Pain flickered through the archnephilim's brand, reminding me that as much as Marcus wanted me to get my life back, it wasn't going to happen.

I pressed my palm to the brand—as if that would do something to ease the pain—and sat on the floor across from him. "I think you're also going to have to accept that this isn't going to turn out well."

His attention dipped to where I held my biceps and his expression darkened. "What happened to the rookie who thought she could run into a room with four were-wolves and get out alive?"

"She learned a hard lesson that night." I picked up the book closest to me. "And I never thought about me. I always thought about the girl. Right now I'm in a position to save a lot of girls. Don't fight Gideon on this, help me end this."

"I'm not losing you."

"I don't think you have much of a choice in the matter." Because even if I survived, Gideon's brand said I belonged with him.

CHAPTER 16

WE READ IN AWKWARD SILENCE, A STRANGE MIX OF attraction and regret and anger crackling between us that I didn't need my not-very-helpful empathy to sense, until Marcus's phone rang and he left. I wasn't sure what I thought about his revelation that he'd disappeared to protect me, that he wasn't angry at me for ruining his life, and I didn't want to think about it. It was complicated and I didn't want to spend my last days, hell, maybe even my last hours, worrying about that. I also didn't want to completely break his heart, so I didn't act on the desire to kiss him again, even if that would have been a much better way of spending my remaining time.

The first three books I flipped through were different texts of pretty much the same information, long-winded explanations of what Gideon had already told me about angelic mating brands. They were rare—sometimes centuries would pass between mated pairs—and they were unique to the angels involved. Not just the sigil etched into the angel's body, but how it connected their souls and how long it took to form. Sometimes it enhanced magic. Sometimes it didn't. Sometimes an angel developed new magic. A branded pair could almost always find each other, and the mating bond was never ignored—although I wasn't sure if anyone had ever tried. It was always seen as beautiful and sacred and couldn't be broken, ever, in death. The death of one killed the other or drove him or her insane, either raving mad, catatonic, or sobbing uncontrollably all the time. The soul-deep connection between mated angels was stronger than any other connection known to man or super and was seen with awe and respect among the angel community.

Yeah, because they'd never had an angel mated to a nephilim before. I was pretty sure all that *sacred brand* stuff would get thrown out the window the minute Gideon knew what I really was. He'd probably say it was a fake brand, like the one the archnephilim had given me. Except his brand didn't look anything like the arch-nephilim's and he wasn't behaving as if he even suspected it was fake—although that might be because he thought the bond was with Zella.

Of course none of that stopped him from changing his mind once all was revealed. And none of that really mattered. The hope I'd found in those books had been a paragraph in one of them about the bond not being completed if something happened to one of the angels before the brand had fully formed. That, at least, confirmed my theory that the sooner we dealt with the archnephilim, the better Gideon's chances were at surviving this mess.

The next book was more biographical than textbook,

and I wasn't certain how much was truth and how much legend. The first few chapters were the histories of the first recorded mating brands with an account that matched everything I'd learned in the previous books. The next chapter was about a branded trio which surprised me and yet didn't surprise me.

When angels had first revealed themselves to humanity, they'd been clear that they were beings of energy who existed in the Realm of Celestial Light—while demons existed in the Realm of Celestial Darkness—and that while they claimed to be divine, they predated all human religions. Angels were the law to the demons' chaos. Or at least they were supposed to be, until Michael decided humans were a plague that wasn't just draining the life of our planet but the life of the Realm of Celestial Light as well.

No one human religion ruled angelic behavior, so while a lot of the human population felt polyamory was taboo, that didn't mean angels did—and I doubted anyone had tried asking them about it. Most angels didn't leave their celestial realm, and those who did didn't socialize with humans. Given Gideon's insistence that angel DNA wasn't compatible with any other DNA, I suspected very few if any angels dated outside of their species.

The three stories after that were back to the usual pattern of perfect soul bonds and all the unconditional love that went with it—heterosexual and homosexual bondings, so I guessed the brand didn't mean *mating* in the sense of species reproduction—but the story after that was different.

This one started the same as the others, but the man was captured during an assault into the Realm of Celestial Darkness in an attempt to correct an imbalance between the two energies. His soul had been damaged, allowing him to be infected with dark energy and driving him insane. Not even the mating brand had been able to help him, and with the combination of both light and dark energy, he was more powerful than before, killing indiscriminately: angel, demon, human, whoever stood in his way.

After many failed attempts to save him, his mate gathered all the divine power within her—and according to the record she was a powerhouse when it came to summoning divine light—and blasted it through their brand, using their connection to reach and destroy his soul unobstructed.

The record wasn't clear if the blast had burned away both of their souls, killing them, or if her heart had stopped killing her because they were bonded and he'd died.

I'd found my answer.

I sat back and cracked my neck, feeling the weight of everything that had happened since I'd walked into Pam and Abe's pharmacy yesterday. Even though I'd slept last night, I was back to being exhausted. Maybe I wasn't back to anything. Maybe I was *still* exhausted. I couldn't tell. Or maybe it was the story that made me feel like I was carrying an enormous weight.

There was a way to end this, but it meant I was going to have to ask Gideon for help, since there was no way I'd be able to summon enough divine light to burn into the archnephilim's soul. I wasn't a magical powerhouse—even if it seemed as if my blasts had grown stronger the last two times I'd used them. It hadn't been enough to kill the archnephilim then, and it wouldn't be enough now.

So long as Gideon didn't know about *his* brand, I was pretty sure I could convince him of the plan. I doubted I'd be able to convince any of the guys, not until all other avenues had been exhausted, and if I wanted any chance of saving Gideon, using the archnephilim's brand to kill him had to be done right away before our connection solidified.

I was about to stand when Kol rounded the corner, carrying a bottle of water and a sandwich on a plate.

My brain stalled. Just for a second. He really was breathtaking. Every step radiated power and sensuality, and a hint of desire darkened his eyes. I was pretty sure he wasn't even aware of his movement or expression. This was just Kol, a demon who survived on sexual energy with a body that ensured he never went hungry.

"How goes it?" he asked.

My stomach rumbled in response.

"Thought so," he said, a tired smile tugging on his lips and softening his demonic look to almost boy-next-door, if the boy next door had horns. "You strike me as the kind of person who works through meals, so I figured—" He sat across from me, where Marcus had sat, and passed me the plate and water bottle.

I set the book aside and accepted the food and water. "How long have I been down here?"

It hadn't occurred to me to check the time and even if I'd wanted to, I'd left my phone in my room.

"It's almost seven. You've missed lunch and dinner."

And breakfast. No wonder I was so hungry. The last time I'd eaten had been yesterday evening, before the disastrous attempt to capture the archnephilim.

"Have you and Jacob found anything?" I took a bite of the sandwich. Ham and cheese again, but I was too hungry to care.

The smile melted from Kol's face. "No. All I've learned is that Michael was a nasty piece of work. I mean, I knew he was nasty. I was manifested into the human realm by him and forced to enthrall his victims into complacency until they were used to conceive his nephilim, but the video of his actual laboratory—" He shuddered. "He documented his experiments and didn't use demons to conceive his angel-demon hybrids."

"How could he not—?" Horrified realization swept through me. "He used human women as surrogates for those, too?"

"Humans are easier to control than angels or supers. The hybrids were carried to term, if the surrogate survived—which according to his records didn't usually happen—then put in tanks to rapidly mature, just like his regular nephilim." The muscles in his jaw tightened. "The human body wasn't made to give birth to that kind of monster. I know because I've now watched more than enough of Michael's videos."

I started to take another bite of my sandwich but didn't know if it would stay down, and instead set it back on the plate. "And Jacob hasn't found anything in the journals or records about how to control one of these monsters?"

"No, but he's only a quarter of the way through."

Well, damn. I knew they wouldn't find anything, at least not in the time I needed, but a small part of me had hoped a miracle would show up. Sure, I knew what needed to be done, but that didn't mean I liked it. "I'm not sure how much longer we can spend searching."

"It hasn't even been a day."

"And by tomorrow, someone else from Gideon's old squad could be dead."

Kol rubbed his face, looking as exhausted as I felt. "Well, we can't do anything about that until the arch-nephilim attacks or we have a way to find it, so we might as well keep looking."

"Actually, we can." I pulled out the book that had mentioned the risks before a mating brand had fully formed and offered it to Kol. "I think I can locate the archnephilim through his brand, and there's a chance Gideon can get out of this mess unscathed if we deal with the archnephilim before my bond with him solidifies."

"That would have to happen soon." Kol didn't open the book I'd given him. "We wouldn't have a chance to get through all of Michael's journals."

"I know." I met Kol's gaze. There wasn't any hint of desire smoldering in his dark eyes now, only worry and exhaustion. "I'm not willing to sacrifice anyone else on the slim chance that there's a way to save me."

"I'm sure if Gideon knew the truth, he'd disagree." Kol broke eye contact and studied the cover of the book I'd given him. "You have to tell him. You have to tell both of them. It's going to come out whether you want it to or not. Who do you think Marcus would rather hear it from? You or Gideon?"

"You're assuming there's actually something between me and Marcus."

Kol's gaze rose back to me and a hint of seductive hellfire burned in his eyes. "I felt that kiss. I *know* there's something between you and Marcus."

"Jeez." I took a swig of water as heat flushed my face. "Can't hide anything from an incubus."

"Well, you can't hide *that*. Although next time, if you want to hold my hand or let me... I don't know, touch your back, flesh to flesh would be ideal if we're not talking actual sex...' He batted his eyelashes at me, doing nothing to look innocent, then dropped his act, his expression serious... and strained. "Honestly, though, I could use a meal too, but I don't want to waste time going out."

I had no idea what to say to that. There were probably rules about seducing co-workers and while it had looked like the cafeteria catered to those supers with human dietary needs as well as vampires, I doubt it catered to incubi. And it didn't sound like he was willing to order in. "How about hanging out near Gideon and Zella?"

He rolled his eyes at me. "Wrong emotion. I need sex, not love, and what they have isn't going to turn into sex. At least it won't until she's healed up, which is going to be days longer than I can hold out and even then it probably won't turn into anything because of... well..." He waved at my arm.

"Because of this." I moved to press my palm to

Gideon's brand, but thought better of it and took another sip of water.

Kol pursed his lips, his expression tight, the strain even more obvious and, now that I knew what I was looking for, so was his hunger. When was the last time he'd eaten? I knew many demons who sustained themselves on humans—be it memories or emotions or something else—didn't need three meals a day. Some could go days without *eating* unless they sustained injuries or expended more then their usual amount of energy.

Kol had been going since I'd met him in the hospital yesterday. There might have been a time after rescuing Zella and before trying to capture the archnephilim that he'd had an opportunity for a meal, but then he'd broken his ribs and healing that had probably expended a lot of the magic that sustained him.

"You should make time sooner rather than later to replenish your magic." He'd gotten up just fine after last night's fight, but if he didn't replenish his magical essence, another fight could seriously injure or kill him.

He flashed me a wicked grin that made my pulse stutter and heat flood me. "Are you making an offer?"

"I... ah..." He was low because of me, and if he could replenish some of his magic by riding along on someone else's kiss, then I could help him out by kissing him. I didn't actually need to have sex with him. And really, I doubted kissing him would be a serious hardship. "How hungry are you?"

Surprise flashed across his expression. "You can't be serious. I must have slipped with my enthrall and I'm influencing you. You don't mean that."

"I'm not talking sex." I really couldn't believe I was saying this, and I knew—if all the stories about incubi were true—that while in the moment I'd beg for sex and I'd have to trust him to keep his word. "But I can offer you a kiss."

"That's not a good idea."

"If the archnephilim attacks, will you survive the fight?" I asked. "How hungry are you?"

"Hungry." The hellfire in his eyes burned brighter and the muscles in his jaw twitched. "But you're Gideon's mate. So not *that* hungry."

"So you won't kiss me because of Gideon even though I'm offering, but you'd ride along if I wanted to make out with Marcus?"

"You and Marcus clearly had a thing before all this started. That could be forgiven," Kol said.

"And I don't get a say in any of this?" I really didn't like the implications of this *belonging to Gideon* thing. What if I'd wanted to have sex with Kol or Marcus or anyone else before the archnephilim killed me? I didn't ask to be mated with Gideon. I didn't even know him.

"I owe Gideon my life. I won't do something that I know will hurt him."

And that was the crux of it. I didn't really *belong* to Gideon. I probably could have sex with anyone I wanted except his teammates, because they were standup guys and didn't do that kind of thing to their friends.

"Then you should slip out now before Gideon assembles the team and asks me to find the archneph—"

Pain lanced through the archnephilim's brand. The

plate slipped from my suddenly numb fingers, dumping the sandwich on the floor, and a fire alarm began to wail.

"He's here." I could feel his inky darkness sliding against my mind, trying to find a way into my soul.

Kol leaped to his feet. I scrambled to stand as well.

"Stay here."

"Do you really think leaving me alone in the archives is a good idea?" That, and I needed to get to Gideon to have him blast divine light into the archnephilim's brand.

"Fine," he said, and we darted down the aisle, back to the front of the archives where the table and couch were.

Books still covered the table but Jacob was gone. I didn't know if he'd been gone before the alarm had started or if he'd just left.

Kol ignored the elevator and headed to a door a little ways down and around a corner. He jerked it open, revealing a plain metal and concrete stairwell, and ran up the stairs, taking them three at a time with his long legs.

I followed, but with my slightly shorter legs I could only safely manage two at a time.

Kol wrenched open the door at the first floor landing and someone screamed. He drew his daggers, hidden in sheaths under his shirt and strapped to his back, and rushed out.

I reached the doorway and stopped. I didn't have a weapon, and while I was sure the archnephilim knew where I was, I wasn't going to make it easy to grab me by running headlong into danger.

The doorway opened into the cafeteria near the shallow steps. In the center of the room was the arch-nephilim in his wraith form. Zella writhed in his tentacled grip, gasping against the smoke crushing her chest. Her hospital gown had ridden high, exposing the bandaged stump of her right leg. One wing was still captured in a brace and stuck straight out, while the other hung limp at her side, bumping into a knocked-over table.

More knocked-over tables and chairs littered the area, along with two that had crashed into the fridges holding food and drinks for when the kitchen was closed. Dark liquid, thick like blood, oozed across the floor beneath them.

Gideon stood at least ten feet back, his expression desperate. He yelled for Zella, swinging a massive sword of divine light and slicing through tentacle after tentacle but not gaining any ground.

The archnephilim threw a table at him. He dove out of the way as it crashed to the floor, but another tentacle swept up and slammed him across the room. Gideon's temple cracked against the step and his sword vanished. His eyes rolled back for a second, then he gasped and his gaze locked onto me.

"Stay back." He shoved to his feet and his sword returned.

"I know how to stop him," I said.

His eyes widened, but Zella screamed, jerking his attention away from me.

The archnephilim slammed her against the ceiling, drawing a strangled cry. Kol dove in, slashing at the tentacles near her but couldn't get close enough to free her.

Jacob and Marcus ran onto the half dozen shallow

steps leading down to the cafeteria, and Gideon leaped back toward the nephilim.

"Get the hell out of here," Marcus said to me, his fingers extending into claws.

Jacob drew both of his sidearms and fired four shots as fast as the weapons would allow. The bullets slammed into what was probably the archnephilim's chest.

"Stop trying to kill Essie," Marcus growled, and he raced after Gideon.

The archnephilim swept a tentacle at Kol, who twisted out of the way and sliced it off, as more of its smoke wrapped around Zella.

"This blood is on your hands, angel," the arch-nephilim said, his voice booming more in my head than in the room, and he ripped off Zella's dangling wing.

CHAPTER 17

ZELLA SCREAMED, HER BLOOD SPRAYING ACROSS THE ROOM and rushing onto the floor. Gideon yelled her name and staggered, his face a mask of utter horror.

The world froze. I couldn't look away as the horrific image burned into my mind. Zella, bleeding, broken, her face locked in agony and eyes wide with terror, captured in the archnephilim's smoke. Her arms were wrenched taut and tentacles crushed her chest and choked her.

Then the world snapped back into action, and the archnephilim shot a tentacle at Gideon. He tried to twist out of the way, but wasn't fast enough. The tentacle swept around his neck and wrenched him up to Zella's level.

"This is for me and mine," the archnephilim said and speared a massive tentacle through Zella's chest.

I jerked my hand out, too late to do anything—not that I could stop him—and screamed. Gideon's grief and rage burst around me like a steamy sauna.

Zella sputtered and convulsed, and the archnephilim tossed her against the rock wall. She fell, tearing plants from their crannies and splashing into the water, her head and torso submerged.

Gideon howled and light exploded from his hands, consuming the tentacle around his neck. He hit the floor, barely kept his balance, and rushed to Zella as Marcus slashed through a tentacle and raced to her as well.

Marcus got to her first and dragged her out of the water, but she didn't move, her body limp. Gideon dropped to his knees, grabbed her from Marcus, and wrapped his arms around her. Blood pooled around them, but his gaze was frozen on Zella. His whole body was frozen, as if his whole essence had stalled, unable to get past holding Zella's lifeless form. His grief burned stronger than his rage and the steam thickened, obscuring the room, but his emotions also cut into me, squeezing my chest and making me gasp for breath.

"Now I'm taking what's mine," the archnephilim said. "Essie. Come."

Searing agony exploded in the archnephilim's brand and my body jerked forward a step.

Panic, my panic, sliced through Gideon's grief, giving me a jagged breath and evaporating the steam. I clenched every muscle within me, squeezing as tight as I could, and forced myself to not take another step.

"*I said come,*" the archnephilim hissed, his voice in my head screeching across my nerves like nails on a chalkboard.

More agony blazed through the brand, and the buzz burst past the nicotine from the patch and snapped under my skin. I staggered forward two more steps.

No. Please, no. I gritted my teeth and mentally heaved at the archnephilim's command.

"Essie." Marcus jerked away from Gideon and Zella and barreled toward the archnephilim.

Jacob fired another four rounds, center of mass again.

"Jacob, please," Marcus begged, slashing at tentacle after tentacle.

Kol also dove in, ramming his blades into what was probably the archnephilim's shoulder. The archnephilim seized Kol and flung him out the cafeteria entrance, sending him tumbling into the hall near the elevator.

I took another staggering step forward.

Come on. No. This was my body. I had to be stronger than him. *Please, let me be stronger than him.*

The fire from the brand screamed through me, and my breath came in ragged gasps. I tried to drop to my knees but my muscles wouldn't obey. I tried to fall, to step back, to do anything, but I could only clench everything within me and force myself still. Except the buzz was chewing away at my concentration and I didn't know how long I could resist him.

"You're taking too long," the archnephilim growled, and an inferno, a hundred times more ferocious than anything I'd felt before, erupted from the brand and devoured every other sensation within me. It rushed up my arm, across my chest, and crushed around my heart. I was burning up, being consumed from the inside out. Every breath I took burned, every thought evaporated the moment I thought it. I shuddered and broke into a run. Toward the archnephilim.

My mind screamed at me, cold panic fighting through

the fire, but I couldn't get my thoughts out of my head and into my body enough to just slow down. I hurdled over a fallen table and a flicker of control seized my muscles. I staggered, but caught my balance and kept running.

Jacob jerked toward me. "Essie." He locked gazes with me, the dark intensity in his eyes capturing my essence. "Stop."

I jerked to a stop, lost my balance, and fell, cracking my knees against the linoleum floor. Jacob's command flash-froze through the archnephilim's fire, and everything within me trembled with the need to obey both Jacob and the archnephilim. I pressed my palms to the floor and locked my gaze on the tile beneath them.

Just stay. All I have to do is stay where I am.

But the contrary commands ripped at my will, and the buzz had returned, threatening to steal my concentration.

The archnephilim's power jerked my head up as Marcus roared and dove at the archnephilim, his claws slicing through tentacles. Jacob fired at the center of the archnephilim's mass, making Marcus roar again, this time with desperation. But no matter what Marcus wanted, it was the right call. The guys were barely making a dent against the archnephilim. It would be a miracle if they managed to kill it. No way were they going to be able to capture it.

My trembling grew stronger, making my teeth chatter as I fought to keep my jaw locked.

"Marcus, you have to kill it," I gasped.

"I'm not killing you."

"Please." The warring commands ripped deeper, tearing into my soul, and then the fire from the archnephilim's brand exploded again, consuming Jacob's ice and the buzz.

I staggered to my feet, my attention locked on the archnephilim, and I couldn't look away as if I were a passenger in my own body.

Marcus barked my name, and Jacob commanded me to stop again, but his ice didn't blast through the archnephilim's fire and I heaved forward one step... two steps.

Someone swore. I didn't know who.

The archnephilim howled with pleasure, his satisfaction oozing inky darkness into the flames within me. My stomach heaved. He didn't have to pour a tentacle down my throat any more to control me. He was already inside me, ripping into my soul.

A sob tightened my throat and my eyes burned.

"Gideon, I can stop him," I said, but my words were a gasp, I wasn't even sure if they came out, and I couldn't look to see if Gideon was still locked in shock, holding Zella.

A tentacle swept toward me and out of the corner of my eye, Kol rushed forward and tackled me. We crashed to the floor, sliding into the side of a knocked-over table.

Thank God.

The archnephilim surged toward us, his tentacles tossed the table aside, and a massive tentacle grabbed for me. Kol seized the back of my shirt and wrenched me out of reach while Marcus tore through the tentacle with his claws. My body jerked, trying to break free from Kol's grip and stand.

The tentacle reformed and Marcus tore through that one, too, his lips curled in a snarl revealing his wolf's teeth. He swiped as the tentacle reformed again, and another one seized his leg. It jerked him off his feet and slammed him against the rock wall, then down onto the stairs.

I screamed. Blood rushed onto the steps around his head and he lay still, too still.

I heaved in Kol's grip, but I wasn't sure if it was to run to the archnephilim or Marcus. He was hurt because of me. Again. And this time I might have killed him.

A sob broke free. *Please don't let him be dead. Please, God.* If someone was supposed to die, it should have been me. Me. No one else. And certainly not Marcus.

"Gideon." This had to end now. He had to blast divine light into the archnephilim's brand and stop this. "Please, I can stop him."

Marcus moaned and his eyes fluttered open.

Relief flooded me, but the archnephilim surged toward him and a flurry of tentacles swarmed around the rock wall.

I screamed for him to get up, get out of the way, for Jacob, for anyone, to help him, but the archnephilim was too fast. He yanked the wall down, the stones crashing onto Marcus. Gideon dove out of the way, dragging Zella's body with him, and Jacob wrenched to the side, narrowly dodging another block.

"Marcus!" I twisted harder against Kol's grip. His hold slipped, and I scrambled to my feet and headed toward the archnephilim. *Shit. No.*

Kol snagged my shirt again, yanking me off my feet.

My butt hit the floor, the impact jarring up my spine and making my teeth snap. The force sliced through some of the archnephilim's power and I seized control of my muscles and fought to stay with Kol. I wanted to go to Marcus, somehow find the strength to heave those stones away and save him, but there was no guarantee that if I got free, I'd head to him. All I could see beneath the pile on top of him that now blocked the entrance to the cafeteria was his arm and half of his head. His eyes were closed and I couldn't tell if he was breathing.

"Essie," the archnephilim said, and his fire consumed all but the smallest voice screaming about Marcus.

My body wrenched to face Kol, twisting my shirt in his grip and using that hold to slip out of it, leaving me in my sports bra, then stood. Kol seized my arm and jerked me close, capturing me in a bear hug.

"Keep her away," Gideon yelled at Kol, his gaze filled with an icy fury, and with a scream, he charged at the archnephilim, his sword of light forming in his hand as he ran.

The archnephilim tossed another table at Gideon. He sliced it in half with his sword, without losing stride, and swung at the middle of the archnephilim's form. The blade sank into the archnephilim's smoke and jerked to a stop. The smoke burst apart, revealing the archnephilim in his angel form, blocking Gideon's blade with one made of darkness.

"Your mate makes me stronger than you," the archnephilim said with a sneer.

"And you killed her." Gideon leaned in, his blade

grinding against the archnephilim's until they were hilt to hilt.

"Not yet."

My body wrenched against Kol's grip but he held tight.

Jacob grabbed Kol's daggers, discarded on the floor by our feet, and lunged at the archnephilim. The archnephilim shoved Gideon's blade from his and blocked Jacob's attack, then swung back at Gideon before he could strike. Gideon blocked the attack and Jacob jabbed at the archnephilim's torso, but a tentacle seized Jacob's wrist and wrenched the blow off target.

More tentacles swept from the archnephilim, like extra arms, working in conjunction with his sword strikes, yanking at wrists and ankles, forcing the guys to slice at the tentacles before they could strike his body.

I twisted and heaved against Kol, my mind screaming to go to the archnephilim and not to go, my insides burning and buzzing.

Gideon sliced through two tentacles and twisted his attack, slipping it past the archnephilim's blade. His sword of divine light sliced into the archnephilim's side, drawing a yell. The tentacles dipped and Jacob leaped close, jabbing both daggers into the archnephilim's other side.

The archnephilim howled and the agony of his brand burned hotter.

"Essie!" he roared and power, not just fire, exploded under my skin, fiery, dark, consuming. Divine light blazed from my hands without me summoning it, more powerful than anything I'd ever manifested before, and my body slapped my palms against Kol's thighs.

He screamed. His grip on me loosened and I wrenched free, but instead of rushing to the arch-nephilim, my body slammed a blast of divine light into Kol's chest, making him stagger, then grabbed his head between my hands and shot another searing blast into his face.

Time slowed and bile burned my throat at what I'd just done.

Kol screamed with heartrending agony, his face and neck horribly burned and bleeding, his skin blackened and red, his features almost unrecognizable, his eyes barely open, unfocused. He wrenched back, but his legs, also with bleeding burns, gave out and he dropped to the floor.

Get up. Please get up.

Blood oozed from his chest, his T-shirt seared away, and he clutched his head, his body shuddering, wracked with pain, his breath shallow and desperate.

My body jerked toward him, divine light blazing from my palms again, and my mind screamed. *Take control. Stop this. Save him.* One more blast and I could kill him. I'd already—

My throat tightened. God, I'd already horribly disfig-ured him, probably blinded him. *I couldn't. Please, God, don't let me.*

The archnephilim's power made my hand rise.

No.

I wouldn't. I. Would. Not.

I wrenched my hand even higher and sent the divine

light into the ceiling, the blast ripping through the ceiling tiles and showering the bits down on me.

Surprise and fear swept cold around and through me. The archnephilim hadn't expected me to resist him. Bully for me. Except I had no idea if I could do it again.

"Enough," the archnephilim growled. "Essie."

My body started to step toward him. I wrenched my foot back. "No."

"Essie."

His fire squeezed tighter around my heart and I trembled with the effort to stay put.

"I said no."

Jacob rammed one of Kol's daggers into the archnephilim's back. Gideon swept his sword at the archnephilim's legs, and the archnephilim exploded into his wraith form of writhing smoke. He whipped a tentacle at Gideon, who sliced it in half, then surged toward Jacob.

Jacob sliced at the archnephilim, his hands a whirl of movement, but the archnephilim's flurry of tentacles slashed and twisted, and one shot past Jacob's guard and slammed into his body. He staggered, just for a second, but it was enough for the archnephilim to ram a massive tentacle through his chest.

The vampire screamed and the archnephilim tossed him at Gideon, who half caught him and half slowed his fall—his sword vanishing between one second and the next. Jacob sagged against Gideon, as lifeless as Zella had been. Gideon let him slide to the floor and leaped at the archnephilim, his sword reforming.

The archnephilim sent a barrage of tentacles at Gideon, jabbing and slicing into him. Nothing cut deep enough to stop him but he was starting to slow down. Blood splattered the cafeteria floor, making the footing slick, sweat glistened on his face, and his breath was ragged.

He twisted, dodging a tentacle, took another one in his right shoulder, and lunged, driving his sword in the center of the archnephilim's form.

The archnephilim howled again and his fire within me shuddered, weakening, and I seized control of my body. I yelled the light strike spell and sent a blast of divine light at him, not nearly as powerful as what I'd hit Kol with, but it didn't matter. I had to do any little thing I could to help Gideon. The blast slammed into the arch-nephilim, drawing a grunt of pain.

His fire flickered, and for a moment he had control of me again, but I forced him out with another yell of the spell and sent another blast at him while Gideon sliced a huge chunk out of his smoke.

The archnephilim roared and a massive barrage of thin, spear-like tentacles shot toward Gideon.

Gideon wrenched his sword up, slicing through four or five, but seven more impaled him, drawing a scream and jerking him off his feet. He swept his sword down to cut the smoke impaling him, but the archnephilim surged around him, completely covering him.

The archnephilim's form writhed, the edges tearing free, forming and reforming as if caught in a ferocious wind. A hint of light sliced out of the top, and Gideon's head emerged from the smoke. He gasped a desperate breath and heaved against the archnephilim's grip.

I shot another blast of divine light at the archnephilim, but this one was weaker than all the others. I was running out of juice. Still, it hit him and his inky fire within me shuddered, weakening even more.

All I could hope was that I could find another blast within me and that it would be enough for Gideon to break free. I yelled the spell again, using the cry to strengthen my will against the archnephilim's fire and the buzz within me, but the archnephilim surged back and crashed through the bank of windows at the back of the cafeteria.

I scrambled after them, everything within me now screaming that I couldn't let him take Gideon, couldn't let him die. Energy like sizzling electricity raced up my right arm from Gideon's brand and light gathered in my palms, stronger than my last few blasts.

The archnephilim swept to the end of the small patio enclosed by the buildings behind the Joined Parliament Operations Building.

I let a blast fly. It sliced through the archnephilim, nicking Gideon's shoulder and drawing a scream of pain, and erupted out of the back of the archnephilim's smoke.

"Do that again," the archnephilim sneered, a hint of his fire making my body twitch. "Next time I'll make sure you hit your mate."

"He'd be willing to make the sacrifice," I said, fighting his power and concentrating on Gideon's electricity to strengthen my will.

"But are you?"

The archnephilim's smoke curled away from Gideon's head, revealing the angel twisting and heaving to break free. Smoke poured down his nose and throat, and he gasped and coughed, desperate for air. Hints of divine light sliced through the darkness, but were quickly devoured.

"If I just squeeze, he'll be dead."

"Go ahead and squeeze." My pulse pounded, fear clutching my chest. I was going to kill Gideon, my mate, the mate who'd hate me the moment he knew the truth about me, and every cell in my body howled that I had to save him.

If he died, the archnephilim would still be allowed to slaughter supers.

Really. That was the only reason I had to save him.

The archnephilim's smoke contracted around Gideon, making him moan in pain.

I flinched and jerked forward a step.

"Are you sure?" he said with a dark laugh.

No. Not at all. Please, don't.

"I'm in your head. I know what you're feeling."

A flicker of divine light burst from the middle of the archnephilim. He shuddered, physically and in my head, weakening for a moment, and his smoke peeled farther away from Gideon's head. Then the archnephilim regained strength and twisted a tentacle around Gideon's neck and squeezed, drawing another strangled moan from Gideon.

"Give yourself to me," the archnephilim said.

Gideon's pale eyes, bright with angel glow, locked on me. I could see his desperation and feel it in the brand. If I gave in, the archnephilim would win.

Black misty angel wings pulled out of the archnephilim's smoke and he rose a few feet off the ground.

"Give yourself to me and I'll let your mate live."

Confusion flickered over Gideon's expression. His attention dipped to my arm then shot back to my gaze, his eyes now filled with realization and horror.

"Tick tock, tick tock."

Gideon's struggles grew desperate. He thrashed against the smoke, and shot feeble blasts of divine light from his palms. The archnephilim's form shuddered, weakening even more.

With a snarl he swept into the air and bolted away. "You have one hour. You know where to find me." The image of a warehouse and the knowledge of its location flashed in my mind. "Come alone."

CHAPTER 18

I raced to the edge of the patio, fear ripping into my soul, tearing at my heart. "Come back. I'll trade."

"*Come alone,*" the archnephilim said in my head. "*I see anyone else and your mate dies. Slowly.*"

"You kill him and I die. I die and you die."

The archnephilim laughed. "Your essence isn't strong enough to shatter mine, but his is definitely strong enough to shatter yours."

Pain bled through the electricity of Gideon's brand and I gasped for breath. I couldn't let him die. It didn't make sense. I didn't know him, didn't love him, and we weren't anything to each other, but the bond between us twisted deep within me.

I clenched my jaw and fought to draw a breath deeper than a shallow gasp. I needed to think, but with the archnephilim's fire gone, the buzz had taken over, screaming through me and making it hard to focus. Rushing off without a plan would get both of us killed. I needed a way to make sure Gideon lived—

My thoughts stuttered.

Jacob. Kol. Marcus.

I scrambled back into the cafeteria. The massive rocks from the wall still crushed Marcus, Jacob lay, his eyes closed, in an alarmingly large pool of blood, and Kol lay a few feet away, drawing ragged gasps that were coming too far apart.

I didn't know if Marcus was alive—

My chest tightened at the thought. But if he was, I wasn't strong enough to uncover him. I needed Jacob, probably Kol as well.

Vampires could take deadly blows and lose massive amounts of blood and still live. So long as he had his heart and his head, I could save him. He just needed blood.

I glanced at the shattered fridge, where the blood had been stored. There was no guarantee any of the blood bags survived, and if I wanted to help Kol—who'd been magically depleted before the fight had even begun and was probably unable to heal himself—my best bet was to let Jacob bite me. I already knew the sexual euphoria that came with a vampire feeding was strong, and if rumor was true, it would be even stronger now that he'd claimed me. I just hoped it was enough to help Kol if I was only holding his hand.

That, and I had to hope that Jacob would break free of the feeding frenzy that came with such a serious injury and come to his senses before he killed me. Of course, if the archnephilim had completely destroyed his heart, there would be no coming back from that, but I couldn't think about that possibility because I didn't have a plan B.

I grabbed the closest of Kol's daggers, set it on Jacob's chest—because I needed both hands to move him—and hauled him to Kol's side. Then I dropped between them, praying that this would work.

Before I could lose my nerve, I sliced the dagger against my forearm. The blade was sharper than I expected and cut deep. Blood rushed from the wound and I pressed it to Jacob's parted lips.

My pulse pounded, but Jacob didn't move, didn't even draw breath.

Blood leaked over his lips and oozed down his cheeks, and the buzz set my nerves on edge, making me tremble.

"Come on." I pressed my arm harder against his lips. "Please." This had to work. It had to. If it didn't, I didn't know if I'd be able to help Kol, not with his face—and God, his hands, too—so badly burned.

Then Jacob snarled, his eyes still closed. He seized my arm in a vise-like grip and bit hard, tearing at my flesh. I screamed and jerked, my body instinctually trying to stop the pain, but he held tight and sucked, the pain excruciating.

A whimper escaped my clenched jaw, but I had to keep going. Even if the sexual euphoria didn't come and I couldn't help Kol, Jacob might still be able to uncover Marcus.

Please, God, let him be alive.

Jacob's teeth dug deeper, and I sobbed. Tears leaked from my eyes, the agony more than I could bear. I had made a mistake. A horrible mistake. He wasn't going to come to his senses before he killed me and if I died, the archnephilim was guaranteed to kill Gideon.

I tried to pry his fingers from my arm but couldn't make them budge. "Jacob, wake up." I wrenched against his grip, making the room spin, proving just how much blood I'd already lost. "Wake up."

His eyes flashed open and his dark, intense gaze locked with mine.

"Essie." He breathed my name against my skin, sending a shiver of desire sweeping through me. One little word, and it was as if a switch had flipped and the pain melted into yearning. Even the buzz was muted.

I shuddered and grabbed Kol's closest wrist, trying to avoid the bleeding, oozing burns on his hand.

Jacob glanced at the connection then recaptured my gaze with his. His grip on my arm, both hand and teeth, loosened a bit, and the heat from his lips threaded into the ragged wound, staunching most of the bleeding but not all of it with a whisper of his healing magic. He took a long pull on my vein and another shiver swept over me.

The desire low within me erupted, hot and needy and insistent, and I focused on that. Not the pain. My pulse sped up, my breath suddenly ragged, and my whole essence throbbed. Need teased, taunted, strained within my skin and across my lips, and my thoughts jumped to the kiss with Marcus and his ferocious passion. The ache swelled low within me, tightening, trembling. I concentrated on the memory of Marcus's hands capturing my face, his lips forceful, commanding, taking control of me, body and soul. Just like Gideon was doing with his brand. Just like every cell in me craved from Jacob, *right now, please, God.*

I let a moan of pleasure escape my lips, not trying to

fight it, not that I could. I needed to embrace all of it and not hide from any of it if I wanted to help Kol, but I also didn't want to give myself fully over to Jacob. If I did, I knew I'd rip the clothes from my body and beg him to take me. I was barely resisting the urge as it was, but I knew neither of us would be happy once the moment was over... well, I had a feeling I'd be incredibly satisfied, but Jacob wasn't the one I wanted to have a relationship with.

My pulse stuttered. Did I actually want a relationship with Marcus?

Jacob sucked on my arm and all thoughts of relationships melted into a need for Jacob. I needed him inside me, needed to please him, needed—

No. Focus on Marcus. Just hold out. Think about his kiss. I shuddered. His kiss had been everything I'd thought it would be and so much more. I yearned to be back in his arms, to have his powerful body moving against mine. To hell with having Gideon's brand. The thing between Marcus and me had been sizzling long before Gideon, and time away hadn't changed it. Whatever lay between us, I wanted more, craved more. If he was alive—

I jerked, my eyes opening. A chill swept away my aching desire, and the buzz flared back to life. The room darkened and spun and I blinked, trying to get my eyes to focus.

Kol had broken free from my grip and now held my knuckles to his cracked lips. His face still looked burnt and painful, but his skin no longer bled or oozed, and his eyes were blazing with hellfire. Jacob had stopped feeding and stared at the partially healed wound he'd ripped through Gideon's brand, his expression stunned.

"Can you stand?" I asked him. He needed to touch me, satisfy me— Jeez. He needed to help Marcus... who had to be alive. He just had to be.

Jacob's piercing gaze shifted to me and my heart lurched.

Tell me what to do. Anything. Please.

"Essie." His low voice rumbled through me, sending my essence into sympathetic vibration with his.

"Yes," I said, my voice breathy. *Anything.*

Footsteps pounded behind me, and I was suddenly struck by the fact that someone had turned off the fire alarm because I could hear footsteps. But I couldn't tear my gaze away from Jacob to see who'd arrived. Out of the corner of my eye, I saw Amiah kneel by Kol's head. She said something to him, and his grip on my hand tightened, keeping it pressed to his lips.

More people rushed past, heading toward the cafeteria steps and Marcus. I still couldn't tear my gaze from Jacob.

Someone called out, but the words muddled in my head.

Jacob groaned and sat up, his attention turning to the pile of massive rocks.

By looking away, the pressure of Jacob's claim squeezing in my chest eased just enough for me to notice the hint of desire curling from Kol's lips and trailing up my arm.

A panicked conversation with raised voices erupted from the rock pile. Was Marcus still alive? *Please let him be alive.* But the room kept spinning and my essence was trapped between Jacob and Kol and I couldn't concentrate on looking for Marcus.

"Save him," I gasped to Jacob. "Please." Except I wasn't sure if I was begging for Marcus or Gideon.

"I'll try." Jacob stood, my attention locked on him as he headed to the rock pile.

Then Amiah shifted in front of me and my mind stuttered before my gaze slid past her shoulder back to Jacob. Behind her, Jacob and another man—an angel by the glow of his eyes—heaved a stone aside, revealing more of Marcus's body.

"Is he dead?" I asked, my voice too small for Jacob to hear across the cafeteria. *Please don't be dead.* I couldn't handle it if he was dead.

"Essie." Amiah gripped my shoulders. "Where's Gideon?"

I couldn't tear my attention from Marcus and Jacob. *Please be alive. Please.*

Jacob and the angel lifted the stone pinning Marcus's legs and another man and a woman pulled him free, smearing his blood, too much blood, on the floor.

"Essie!" Amiah shook me, making the room whirl. "Where's Gideon?"

"He's alive," one of them said.

The fear clutching me shot me to my feet to rush to him, but the world heaved and darkened and I stumbled.

Amiah grabbed me, sliding me back to the floor.

"Amiah, we need you," Jacob said, his tone urgent. My pulse pounded and the buzz burned through me. Jacob needed help. No. Marcus did. No—

Amiah captured my chin and forced me to look at her. "Where's Gideon?"

"Taken," I gasped.

Fear snapped frozen across my skin, but my thoughts were too muddled to figure out who it had come from. Best guess was Amiah.

"By that monster?" Amiah asked, the cold fear bleeding from her fingers onto my cheeks. "Why would he take him?"

"Torture," Kol said, his hand snaking out to capture mine again.

Horror widened Amiah's eyes and the cold deepened.

"But that means he's still alive," I said, and while the archnephilim might torture Gideon, his main target was me.

And it was torture. Even with the dizzying blood loss, the ache for Jacob, and the shiver of desire from Kol's enthrallment, my soul screamed to go to Gideon. Nothing else mattered.

"Amiah," Jacob barked.

Her expression hardened. "We're not done here."

"Amiah." Jacob sounded desperate.

My heart clenched and I fought to rise, but Amiah shoved me back onto my butt.

"Jacob, tell her to stay," Amiah said as she hurried to him and Marcus.

Jacob frowned. Guess someone had told her about Jacob's claim on me.

"How much blood did you take from her?" Amiah shot him a dark glare and knelt beside Marcus. "How much life force did Kol? She'll hurt herself if she moves."

"Fine." Jacob locked gazes with me and his claim sang with joy at the attention. "Stay there until someone helps you."

The compulsion swept through me and a part of me was grateful. There wasn't anything I could do to save Marcus, no matter how much I wanted to be by his side. That, and the need to save Gideon was twisting tighter and tighter within me. I didn't know how much longer I could hold out, not with the buzz tearing at my concentration. Jacob's command gave me time to pull myself together and think.

Except that was the hardest thing in the world to do at the moment. I was dizzy and exhausted. I didn't know if that was because of healing Jacob and Kol or something else. Maybe it was from resisting the archnephilim's possession. I was also cold with Amiah's fear.

"He'll be okay," Kol said, squeezing my hand and sending desire shivering through me. "Amiah is the best."

My throat tightened and I forced myself to look at him and at the damage I'd done. Hellfire still burned in his eyes, although the fire was banked to a low glow. He looked like he'd been set on fire and ugly red scars covered most of his face. But they looked like scars, not fresh or even partially healed wounds like they'd been moments before.

"Are you going to be okay?" I asked.

"It was smart of you to use Jacob's bite to help me."

"I can give you more if you need." I'd give him everything, but not even that would make up for what I'd done.

His gaze dipped to Gideon's brand on my arm and he release my hand. "I've got enough to get me through."

Light flared, dragging my attention back to the steps. Amiah sat at Marcus's head, her palms pressed to his temples, and the power of her healing magic radiated around her, growing brighter and brighter, forcing me to look away.

Then it vanished and Amiah sagged back onto her heels, her shoulders slumping forward.

Marcus groaned and his eyelids fluttered open. His face was still tight with pain and his breath a little too short, but he was alive. *Thank God, he was alive.*

"You have to finish the rest by shifting," Amiah said. "Cassey, help him undress so the shift doesn't destroy his clothes."

"Let's clear the room and give him some privacy," Jacob said. "Reassemble in the triage waiting room."

"We won't be long," Amiah said, sounding exhausted.

With the exception of a woman, who I recognized from the team that had taken care of Zella, the others headed back to the patio and around the side of the building.

Kol staggered to his feet and offered me a hand to help stand. I gingerly took it, afraid I'd hurt him, and rose. The room twisted, and he stepped close, wrapping his arms around me and holding me up. His body was almost too hot for comfort, but I leaned into his embrace anyway, hoping his heat would melt some of the cold. I still couldn't stop shaking, but most of that wasn't the chill. My legs were weak, and I throbbed with pain and unsatisfied sexual desire.

"Jeez, Essie. You're freezing." Kol's embrace tightened as if he could hug the cold out of me.

My throat constricted. How was I going to help Gideon when I could barely stand? Even if I was going to go to the warehouse to make the trade, I was too weak to walk. I'd need help getting there, certainly within my one-hour time limit, but if I asked, the guys would refuse to help me.

"I can take her," Jacob said as he approached.

Kol opened his arms, and Jacob swept me off my feet and cradled me against his chest. His shirt was sticky with blood, but there wasn't a hole in his chest any more. His claim soared through me. He was touching me. He wanted me. And I didn't try to fight it because it was stronger than the buzz and the pull to Gideon. The sensation was a lot stronger than before. Before I'd needed him to tell me what to do. Now I outright needed him, to think, to breathe, to live. I could only hope Jacob wouldn't take advantage of that and I could control myself long enough for the effects to ease off. Except I had no idea when that would be now that he'd bitten me twice.

"We need a plan," Jacob said, his voice rumbling through me, making the claim thrill at the sensation.

Have sex—

No, save Gideon.

That's right. I had to save Gideon. But that wasn't a plan, that was a desire born from a mating brand I didn't want to have.

Kol grabbed the vampire's shoulder to help keep his balance, and we left the cafeteria, stepping onto the patio and heading around the side to a plain metal door.

"We need to go down to the armory and grab that ring imbued with divine light from the war that still has its charge," Kol said.

"You said the archnephilim took Gideon," Jacob said, and I realized—thank God—he, Kol, and Marcus had probably been unconscious for the archnephilim's ultimatum. That meant if I could find the strength to move, I could go to Gideon and kill the archnephilim without having to fight the guys about it. "Why wouldn't it kill him outright like it had with the rest of the squad?"

I pressed my hand to Jacob's chest. His skin was cool, which meant we were far enough from Amiah's fear for me to warm up, but I couldn't feel a heartbeat. Of course, he was undead. He didn't have a heartbeat. But that didn't mean he wasn't alive in a magical sense or couldn't be killed. God, they all could have been killed. And now I had less than an hour to meet the archnephilim's demand.

"Gideon was the squad leader," Kol said. "The archnephilim also made a point of killing Zella in front of him. He wants Gideon to suffer."

We entered the side door and stepped into a narrow hall that looked like all the other halls in the building—white walls, gray floor—except this one was about two feet narrower and only had one door in the middle of the left-hand side.

"Except Zella wasn't his mate." Jacob's grip on me tightened.

"But he didn't know that at the time," I said.

Jacob shook his head and sighed. "He would have known once the bond had gained more strength. You wouldn't have been able to hide it forever. Why didn't you tell him?"

The compulsion to answer him twisted in my chest and the buzz ate away at my willpower, but I couldn't just tell Jacob it was because I didn't want the bond with Gideon to be real and I didn't want to break his heart. He loved Zella and knew her. She's been a member of his squad during the war, and she was an angel like him. I was, as far as everyone believed, just a powerless human he didn't know.

"Our wolf makes it complicated," Kol said.

Among other things.

The claim twisted tighter. I needed to say something but I couldn't tell the whole truth, that I was the thing Gideon and everyone else hated and feared the most.

And I needed to save Gideon. Save him.

"I'd hoped we could kill the archnephilim before my bond with Gideon fully formed," I said, the words blurting out, easing the compulsion from Jacob's claim. "If he didn't know the truth, my death might not have killed him or driven him insane."

Except it was too late now. The electricity from his bond tingled up my arm, told me he was alive, and that we were permanently connected.

Jacob led us around a corner into a wider hall with more doors, which I soon discovered was the main hall. We reached the sliding frosted-glass doors where Amiah and her team had taken Zella when we'd first brought her in and entered. To the right was a waiting area with a padded leather couch, two matching armchairs, and a TV —currently not on. To the left was a miniature version of a hospital emergency room, packed with equipment and three beds, while the hall continued straight ahead with more doorways leading to other areas of the miniature hospital.

The others who'd rushed into the cafeteria to help— one girl and four guys—sat on the couch and chairs. They'd been talking when we entered but had fallen silent.

"I've lifted the lockdown, sent the research team home, and called in Chris and Jasmine to help us with clean up," the angel who'd helped Jacob move the rocks said as he stood and offered his chair.

"Good." Jacob sat me in the chair and Kol perched on the wide arm. "Grab a body bag for Zella and go help Amiah."

The angel jerked his thumb. The three other guys stood and they left.

"Summer," Jacob said, and turned his attention to the petite woman with a hint of divine glow in her soft brown eyes. Her brown hair was cut into a short bob, accentuating her cherub-like face, but her expression was anything but innocent and childlike. "Call in a specialist to reinforce the wards, and then take stock of what we have in the armory that can kill a wraith or an archangel."

Summer's eyes widened, but she nodded and hurried out the door as well.

"So that leaves us with what?" Kol asked, still sitting beside me even though the rest of the seats had opened up.

Jacob eased onto the couch across from me, easily

taking up half the space with his massive frame and making me lean forward, the claim urging me to move and join him.

He ran his hands over his face, looking exhausted. "I have no idea. Now if we kill the archnephilim, we not only kill Essie but Gideon as well."

Not if I kill him before—

Fear squeezed around my heart. The bond was fully formed. Jacob was right. How the hell was I supposed to save Gideon now?

"Can we please stop talking about killing the arch-nephilim?" Marcus said from the doorway. Blood stained his gray T-shirt and blue jeans, but other than that I wouldn't have known he'd almost been crushed to death. His gaze slid from Kol, sitting close to me, to Gideon's brand on my right forearm. His expression darkened and he took the seat beside Jacob on the couch, facing me but farther away than the armchair beside me. His churning mix of hot and cold emotions fluttered through me, adding nausea to my spinning head and grating buzz.

"You need to call in backup," Amiah said, entering after him. She dropped my shirt in my lap and sagged into the empty armchair, her complexion gray, the skin around her eyes pinched with tension.

"The closest team that's bigger than two people is over four hours away in Los Angeles," Kol said. "Do we think he'll let Gideon live that long?"

Jacob sighed. "We're going to have to hope he will, because we nearly got slaughtered."

Except Gideon didn't have four hours and time was slipping away. And if the archnephilim killed him, that would kill me and ruin any chance of using his unnatural bond with me to stop him. I already knew he was willing to give up the extra power I gave him. Killing Gideon was part of his vengeance. I'd only been a surprise bonus in all this. He didn't need me, hadn't wanted me, but was more than happy to use me to achieve his goals.

I had to trade myself for Gideon. I had no doubt the archnephilim would go against his word and try to kill Gideon, but if I could get him free long enough to blast the brand, we could finish this.

The other guys, however, couldn't come. The archnephilim had said to come alone and if they showed up, he'd kill them this time. I doubted Kol could fully recover all of his magical strength within the hour, especially if he wasn't going to go out and replenish it, and while Marcus looked fine, I could still see a hint of tightness in his jaw that said he wasn't completely healed. Even Jacob, while no longer physically hurt, looked exhausted. It was a miracle they were all alive, and I suspected that was exactly what the archnephilim had wanted.

I clenched my jaw to keep from saying something stupid. If Jacob even suspected I was going to face the archnephilim, he'd command me not to go, and with his claim on me strengthened, I wouldn't be able to resist him.

Going alone was the only answer. It was the only way to protect them. Too many people had already died, and I wasn't going to add the guys to the list.

That, and no matter what I wanted or how foolish it was, I couldn't ignore the twisting need to save Gideon.

CHAPTER 19

"ALL RIGHT," MARCUS SAID, HIS VOICE LOW, DANGEROUS, his gaze locked on me as if daring me to argue with him. "We call in backup and capture the archnephilim."

Sadness crept into Jacob's eyes. He offered me a bitter smile and a hint of mist curled around me. "You've got to accept the truth, Marcus."

"My wolf is making that difficult," Marcus growled.

"Then you should sit this out," Kol said. "When we go out with the other team, stay here with Essie."

Amiah turned to me, making the leather creak. "How strong is your bond with Gideon?"

"I don't know. I know he's alive." But now that I thought about it, the electricity had shifted from a steady hum—kind of like the buzz, but at a gentler, lower vibration, and almost imperceptible against my grating buzz—to something more jagged, painful. He was in pain. Every fiber of my being knew it. The archnephilim might have said he'd let Gideon live, but he hadn't said in what condition.

Panic seized my heart as the image of the arch-nephilim ripping off Zella's wing flashed through me, making my throat burn with bile. I had to fight past my weakness and get to the archnephilim's warehouse before the damage done to Gideon was irrevocable.

Except my dying still meant Gideon would die. And yet I couldn't convince the need coming from the brand that my only plan was doomed, that it was impossible to save him.

"Can you sense anything else? His pain, his essence?" Amiah asked.

"I can't feel his pain like it's my own, but I know he's in pain." *God, so much pain.*

"We might be able to sustain him through Essie." Amiah eased from the chair and knelt beside me. The glow in her eyes was feeble, allowing me to see her exhaustion. "Right now you're weak, so the mating brand won't let him use your essence. You might even be draining him."

Marcus sat forward. "Amiah, don't hurt yourself. Gideon is strong. He can last at least an hour, long enough for you to partially recover your magic before you heal her."

Heal me? *She was going to heal me?* If she did, I'd be able to satisfy the compulsion from the brand and go ahead with my plan. And while Gideon could technically survive the archnephilim's torture for an hour, if I didn't show up, that would be all the time he'd get—

I forced a hint of a sob—I didn't want to overdo it— and dropped my gaze to my hands. I didn't want any of the guys to read my expression, for fear they'd be able to see the lie. "I don't know if he can survive an hour."

"Essie, he's strong," Kol said, brushing his hand across my shoulder, but not maintaining contact as if he wanted, but didn't want, to touch me.

"But he was hurt when the archnephilim took him." For all I knew, the archnephilim wasn't doing anything to him and he was just bleeding out from all the holes in his body. His pain could be the emotional agony from seeing Zella murdered. And finding out he was mated with me.

"She's low on blood and life essence. It's not like I'm fixing broken bones again," Amiah said, and she grabbed my hand.

I flinched, expecting the same agony from Amiah's healing as before, but instead a tingling warmth swept up my arm, mingling with Gideon's electric hum before spreading into my chest. I closed my eyes and let myself float on the sensation, wrapped in its warmth. There were no fears or worries, no heartache for Gideon's loss or my own. There was just peace and heat... and my God damned buzz. I could have stayed there forever, but that wouldn't save Gideon... not that I could actually save him... but I had to try.

Then the tingle vanished and Amiah sagged back onto her heels like she had when she'd healed Marcus, her eyes unfocused. My dizziness, exhaustion, and churning stomach were gone. Even the nasty, partially healed wound Jacob had gnawed into my arm was only a pale patch of pink over the top of the perfect golden swirls of Gideon's delicate mating brand. The buzz, however, remained.

Marcus left the couch and helped Amiah back into the armchair. "You shouldn't have done that," he said to her.

She brushed her fingers along his jaw, trailing them through his stubble, the tender move speaking of a familiarity between them that went deeper than just physician and patient.

"I bought Gideon time," she said. "Now go call in backup. He's mated with a human. There's a good chance he'll survive her death and a certainty he'll survive if she just goes insane."

The muscles in Marcus's jaw twitched and he shifted away from Amiah, closer to me.

"Is that true?" I asked her. Maybe Gideon *could* get out of this alive. Maybe only I had to be the archnephilim's last victim. Which sucked, but was the best of a lot of horrible choices.

"I've successfully treated the angel half of a broken angel-human bond."

"It wasn't in any of the books I read in the archives downstairs."

"Those books are older than the war," Amiah said. "A lot of things happened during the war, along with at least one human marked with an angelic mating brand."

Which meant there was hope. I had hope. I was half human. That had to be human enough to save him. Now I just needed to figure out how to get Gideon to blast light into my brand—since light magic was surprisingly rare among angels and I doubted there'd be another angel stationed here who could summon light. Would he even risk my life to do it? I was willing to do anything to save him. Was that because my human half wasn't strong enough to withstand the compulsion from the brand or was that just what the brand did? If Gideon felt what I felt, there was a chance he wouldn't be willing to kill me to stop the arch-nephilim. Better to not even go there. Kol had said there was a divine light ring in the armory. I needed to get my hands on that.

Yes, get the ring. That was a good plan. If I went soon, I might be able to catch Summer still doing inventory, so I wouldn't have to figure out how to get past the fingerprint scanner on the door. I'd either have to lie to her or steal it when she wasn't looking, but that was my best option. Then I'd go to the archnephilim. Sure, I could try to kill him from afar, but there was a risk he'd kill Gideon before the blast burned him up since I didn't know how long it would take. I needed to get him to let Gideon go, just long enough to kill him.

My stomach churned with hope and fear, all while my mind cheered that I could free Gideon. I could free my mate.

But I had to get away from everyone first. I could say I wanted to go to my room—and replacing my nicotine patch would be awesome—but I suspected someone would go and keep an eye on me.

"Okay." Amiah took in a deep breath and straight-ened. "Jacob, go into triage and grab a blood bag from the fridge, Kol, you need to eat."

"Can you get it done in thirty minutes?" Jacob asked, heading into the triage area and opening a small fridge under a stainless steel counter.

Kol shrugged. "I'm fine enough. I'd rather not leave you guys shorthanded."

Amiah huffed. "You're hardly fine. Every bit of magic you have is going to be diverted to healing your injuries and you know it. You're going to be weaker, slower, and less nimble. That makes you a liability and not an asset."

"She's right." Jacob pulled out a blood bag.

"Fine." Kol stood and marched out the sliding glass door.

"Marcus, can you be on Essie duty?" Jacob asked. "I should call the head office and request backup."

Shit. I wasn't going to be able to slip away, let alone snatch the divine light ring if I had Marcus shadowing me.

And I still needed a reason to go to the basement.

"I... I'm going to continue looking through Michael's research. Maybe there's a way to control the arch-nephilim and limit casualties the next time we— *you* go up against him."

"My phone call might take a bit," Jacob said, "but I'll join you when I'm done."

"And I need to change clothes." Marcus stood and tugged on his bloody T-shirt. "I'll meet you down there."

"Great." Fantastic! If I hurried, I could grab the ring and get out of there before Marcus returned.

Marcus held out his hand to help me stand, the action fast, easy, as if it was instinct, and I took it with the same thoughtless ease. But his attention jumped from our joined hands up my arm to Gideon's brand, and my chest squeezed. None of this was fair to Marcus. He'd said his wolf made it hard for him to stay away from me, but that he'd stayed away so I wouldn't get caught up in the super-natural world. Now I was, couldn't be his, and was prob-ably going to die. All in a matter of days.

And above all that, I ached for Jacob to give me a command, and was terrified that Gideon would die.

"I'll meet you down there," I said, slipping my hand from his and pulling on my shirt.

This situation was impossible. No matter what I did I couldn't win, so I had to focus on what I could do. Get the ring, go to the warehouse, and kill the archnephilim.

I strode out the sliding doors as fast as I could without looking like I was running, and hurried to the elevator and hit the down button. It dinged immediately, the door slid open, and I got inside and took it to the basement.

The large reading table was still covered in books, some half open, others with scraps of paper sticking out of them marking a spot Jacob wanted to return to. Had it really only been a few hours? Hell, it probably had barely been an hour. Most fights didn't last long and the arch-nephilim had been ferocious in his attack.

The armory door was open and the light was on. Summer stood at a small standup desk just inside the door, staring at a computer screen.

"Any luck finding anything that can kill a wraith or an archangel?" I asked.

She jerked her thumb to a long narrow table in the center of the room. On it were two rings—not placed together—and an HK416 assault rifle beside three boxes of ammunition. "You tell me. We've got two divine light rings but only one that's charged, and Gideon is the only angel in town able to summon divine light to put in the ring. And we have the rifle with ammunition enchanted to take down a greater demon, but I have no idea if that would work on a wraith since wraiths are insubstantial."

I had no idea either. My education on demons from the advanced combat training involved those I'd most likely run into while walking the beat, and most of those could be taken down by a Taser on its highest setting— added special for supers—or a few of the department-issued enchanted bullets. But the highest Taser setting and the enchanted ammunition wouldn't take down anything like a master vampire or an alpha were-anything. We'd also been told it wouldn't affect the more powerful greater demons. I didn't know where a wraith stood on the scale of a lesser demon with almost no magic and a greater demon with lots of magic.

I did know the ring would work. Just not in the way everyone thought it would.

"Not surprising," Summer said, waving at the computer screen, "we have nothing in our inventory that can kill an archangel. The only weapon made to stop Michael and Rafael is with Gabriel in the Realm of Celestial Light, and no one has been able to contact him since he killed his brothers."

"Well," I said, trying to keep my tone even, "I'll take the ring up to Jacob so he's prepared for anything, and you keep looking."

Summer stared at me, her eyes a little too wide. "You honestly think the archnephilim will attack again so soon?"

"We're hurt and disorganized. That's a serious advantage for him. I wouldn't put it past him." Save for the fact that I knew he was waiting for me to come to him. Which meant perhaps the fight had taken almost as much out of him as it had out of the guys. They'd gotten in some good strikes and by the end, his power over me had weakened enough that I could resist him. Maybe he was licking his wounds just like we were. Hopefully that meant I was guaranteed to kill him by blasting divine light into his brand.

"It's the one closest to us," Summer said, and she turned back to the computer screen.

"Thanks." I picked up the ring. It was heavy and masculine, too big for any of my fingers, but would probably fit my thumb. Power radiated from it, crackling over my hand, so much like the electricity coming from Gideon's brand. The compulsion to save him twisted inside me, my soul chanting, *save him, save him, save him,* and I turned to leave.

"The guys will get Gideon back to you," she said, her voice soft, making me pause. "You should have told him about the brand."

Jeez, did everyone know I hadn't told Gideon that I was his fated mate? Of course, a mating brand was rare, and Gideon had been certain Zella had been his mate. With a workplace this small, I shouldn't be surprised if everyone knew about Gideon's brand. And yeah, the odds were good everyone also knew about my kiss with Marcus.

"Just keep looking," I said, and hurried back to the elevator. If my plan didn't work, the guys would need every advantage they had to stop the archnephilim.

I pressed the call button and shoved the ring in my

pocket while I waited. I could have taken the stairs but they would have put me in the cafeteria with everyone cleaning up the mess from the fight.

Except each second waiting for the elevator felt like an eternity.

I had the means to save Gideon, to protect the guys, and to end this nightmare. I couldn't make myself see the situation as a good thing, but I could keep telling myself this was the best of many horrible options. If I died with the archnephilim and Gideon survived, he'd never have to find out what I really was. I wouldn't be imprisoned or sentenced to death or studied like a lab rat. I also wouldn't completely break Marcus's heart. He wouldn't have to live seeing me being Gideon's mate and not his. We wouldn't have to figure out how to deal with or ignore the sizzling attraction between us, because I knew Marcus was like Kol. A friend didn't get in the way of another friend's relationship, apparently even if that relationship was forced on both parties.

The elevator door slid open, revealing Marcus leaning against the back wall. He'd changed into a clean T-shirt that pulled tight over his deliciously muscled chest and jeans that hugged his hips and thighs.

He raised his piercing green gaze to mine and my pulse stuttered. Even with Gideon's brand fully formed, the attraction still burned between us. My heart raced and my breath came a little too fast just at the sight of him, while a hint of heat caressed my skin, telling me he felt the connection, too.

The door began to slide shut and we both jerked forward. Marcus caught it with his arm and it reopened, but now we stood so close his breath tickled my cheeks. If I took a deep breath, my breasts might brush his chest. God, how I wanted my breasts to brush his chest.

A hunger burned in his eyes and more warmth curled over and under my skin. I had to touch him, give in to the power between us, or I'd combust. But I couldn't be his. I wasn't going to survive past the next hour and that wasn't fair to him.

He must have seen something in my eyes, because the heat of his desire chilled with a hint of fear.

"Essie." He growled my name, tugging on something primal within me, and I leaned closer. Now barely a breath stood between us and I could feel the heat of his body, sense the power of his wolf, ferocious and passionate, curled tight within him.

I pressed my hand against his chest before I fully realized what I was doing, then jerked back when common sense kicked in a second later, but Marcus grabbed my wrist. The door started to shut, and he pulled me inside, turned, and backed me against the back of the elevator. He captured me with his body, his hands pressed to the wall on either side of me, and kissed me.

The kiss was soft, quick, tentative, as if Marcus was uncertain of his reception, but it sent a shudder sliding through me, making me moan with desire. Even just a brush of lips sent me trembling, aching for him.

I ran my fingers through his stubble, up into his hair, and pulled his lips back to me. He didn't need any more of an invitation. Heat swept around me and he claimed my mouth with his. The ferocity of the kiss left me breathless. His tongue invaded me, fueled the fire of my desire for him, and sent me spiraling.

His hands pushed under my shirt, a sizzling shock of flesh against flesh. One hand slid around my back, securing me—which was good, my mind was spinning and I wasn't sure if I'd be able to keep standing—and the other dipped into my sports bra and kneaded my breast. There wasn't anything delicate or slow or drawn out about it. This was ferocious, pent-up desire, released without control, and it made my blood sing, made me crave all of him. And it had nothing to do with being unsatisfied after Jacob's bite. It was all Marcus, all the desire between us that I thought was impossible, that I shouldn't be feeling, that I wanted to lose myself in.

He shoved my shirt and bra up, the heat of his desire building around me, and dropped his mouth to my breast, sucking my nipple into a tight bud and drawing a gasp. His hand that had been on my breast swept under the waistband of both my cargo pants and underwear. He found my slick heat, and plunged two fingers inside of me, sending a shock of pleasure zinging through me.

I gasped and he smiled against my breast.

"Mine," he growled, his voice low, dangerous, and so damned hot.

His lips returned to mine, capturing my ragged breaths, as his fingers worked inside me. The pleasure built fast, this whole moment fast and ferocious. The attraction between us couldn't be denied. It felt as fated, *more* fated than my brand with Gideon. Our desire for each other had nothing to do with a magical connection. It was pure, hot need.

The first tremor of a climax swept through me. I moaned, trying to keep my cry of pleasure in, but I couldn't, and cried out his name as ecstasy roared through me. He growled again, a noise of pure masculine satisfaction, and held me tight as I rode the wave, my legs wobbly, my whole body wobbly and satiated.

He pressed his forehead to mine, his breath fast and ragged like mine even though he hadn't come. "I don't care what marks your arm. You're mine."

CHAPTER 20

I SHUDDERED WITH DESIRE AT HIS WORDS AND AN aftershock of my climax rushed through me.

He hit the basement button and the elevator door slid open right away. We hadn't pressed a button when we entered and I guess no one had hit a button on another floor.

"You're mine," he said with a growl, "and I will move heaven and earth to get you your life back."

I didn't know what to say to that. A primal part of me thrilled at how much he wanted me, while the rest of me cried. There wasn't any way I could make this end well. "I... ah... I'll be back down in a minute."

He frowned. Yeah, not the response I'd expect either, but I couldn't stay no matter how much I wanted to.

"I was on my way to the bathroom when you... when we..." Desire flamed my cheeks, a mix of mine and his, inside and out.

He grabbed the door before it closed again and flashed me a heated smile. "When we...?"

"Yeah. When we." Another aftershock shook me, drawing a gasp. God, how I wanted to stay with him, satisfy him like he'd satisfied me, forget about everything.

But I couldn't forget. The buzz still crackled under my skin, reminding me that even if everything hadn't gone sideways, being with Marcus, living in the supernatural world, put me in danger. As well, the need to save Gideon twisted in my chest, reminding me destiny had shoved me to someone else, someone I didn't even know. Marcus had given me a temporary reprieve from the madness. Nothing more. Still, I was grateful for the gift.

"I really do need to go."

His smile softened. "There's a bathroom in the triage waiting room. You don't have to go all the way to your room."

He stepped away from the door and it slid closed.

God, this was a mess. Such a big, heartaching mess.

And there wasn't a damned thing I could do about it.

My shirt had fallen down, but the sports bra was still shoved above my breasts. I tugged it down and hit the button for the first floor. If I had the time, I'd go all the way back to my room and replace my nicotine patch, but I couldn't afford to run into anyone else. I had to leave now.

And please, God, don't let me run into Jacob and have him tell me to do something, whether he intended it as a command or not.

The door slid open to the first floor. No one was around, but I could hear people working in the cafeteria, the massive rocks still covering the entrance.

I hurried to the main hall and down to the garage.

Raised voices, coming from behind the door to the building's emergency room, made me pause, my pulse racing. It sounded like Amiah and Jacob, her voice shrill with distress and Jacob's a firm rumble.

"There's nothing to think through," Amiah said.

Jacob said something back, but I couldn't make out his words.

"Well, that's not my problem," Amiah said.

I hurried past the door and into the garage. Jacob and Amiah arguing wasn't my problem, either. Saving Gideon. Stopping the archnephilim from murdering any more people in his mission for vengeance. That was all that mattered.

First up, I needed transportation. All of the JP vehicles were too modern to easily hotwire, but I was pretty sure I'd seen a late model minivan and a late model compact hatchback at the back of the garage, most likely personal vehicles of people who worked here.

The minivan was gone, but the tan hatchback was still there. I hurried to it and tried the door. No point in breaking a window if it was unlocked. And in an enclosed parking garage belonging to the JP, I was hoping the owner wasn't security-conscious.

The door was unlocked. I checked the middle console and the sun visor for a key, but didn't find one. Guess that was too much to ask for, so I leaned down under the steering column and pulled out the wires I needed.

When I was in my late-teens, just before my mom had died from cancer, she'd taught me how to hotwire a car in the event I had nothing on me and needed to flee. I don't think she'd ever expected me to use the knowledge to head straight to an angel instead of away from one. I know I hadn't.

Never in my wildest imagination or even my nightmares did I ever imagine I'd find myself in a situation like this. My entire goal in life had been to be unnoticed, fly under the radar, and nothing about this was flying under the radar.

I stripped the wires with my teeth, twisted the ends together with my fingers, and got the car to start. My pulse racing with a mix of fear I'd be caught and what I was headed to, I put the car in gear and pulled out of the garage.

The archnephilim's warehouse wasn't in the Supers' Quarter, but close on the outskirts of town. I didn't recognize it as anywhere I'd been before, but I *knew* exactly where it was. I could also feel the pull of both Gideon and the archnephilim drawing me in its direction. Even if the archnephilim hadn't slapped the warehouse's location in my mind, I probably would have been able to find him.

Which only made me more nervous. My connection with both of them was growing stronger. I could feel their essences, the archnephilim's fire and Gideon's electricity under my skin. Gideon's pain hadn't increased, but it hadn't decreased either. His electricity was still jagged, and now I could feel a pull on my soul draining strength from me to him.

The archnephilim's fire, however, flared and banked without rhyme or reason, as if his fire was being battered within me by a ferocious wind. His brand also tore strength from me, ragged spurts cleaving chunks off my essence. I hoped that meant he was still weak from his fight with the guys and that I could manage to keep him from controlling me long enough to release Gideon and sear the brand with divine light. But I feared with both of them consuming my essence, I'd be too weak to withstand much of a mental assault from the archnephilim.

That only meant I needed to get to the warehouse as soon as possible.

I drove through the park ring separating the Supers' Quarter from the rest of the city, the need to hurry making my nerves thrum, but I managed to hold it together and not speed. Getting pulled over without a license and no key in the ignition was a surefire way to screw everything up.

I headed south toward the highway, but instead of getting on, I took a side road that, while it wasn't dirt, hadn't been maintained in a long time and only a third of the streetlights were working. The road headed into an old industrial section with the shells of factories and warehouses lining the street all the way to the end. It was a perfect spot for a business, close to the city for employees but also less than a mile from the interstate onramp. Most of the buildings, however, were barely standing and abandoned. Only a few had cars in their parking lots and half of those lots weren't full—although given that it was after suppertime, those businesses might be shut down for the night and not running twenty-four-hour shifts.

While Michael hadn't managed to exterminate all of humankind, he'd sure been determined to try, and even with the influx of supers coming out of hiding and those

—mostly demons—coming from the realms of light and darkness, the world population of over seven and a half billion was now closer to five.

Europe had had a casualty rate higher than North America since the main passage to the Realm of Celestial Light was in Rome—the focus of all those centuries of worship from a religion that gave angels a prominent role thinning the veil between the human realm and the light realm. But countries with the densest populations and the densest cities took the worst of it. Easier to exterminate the humans if they were all bunched together. Thankfully Gabriel had stepped up after the first few brutal assaults, making it harder for Michael to target large cities and forcing him to be more strategic in his attacks.

There'd already been a weapons manufacturer on this side of town, and the federal government had confiscated most of the factories and warehouses in the area to increase production. But that had made the area a target and during the height of the war, the nephilim had attacked, destroying or damaging beyond reasonable repair most of the buildings in the area.

As a result, when humanity and supers turned to rebuilding, they focused on city cores, creating areas for supers, hospitals, and schools. Buildings not in use, whether they could be useful in the future or not, weren't a priority. And in reality, the war had only been twenty-three years ago and the rebuild effort had barely begun.

The archnephilim's warehouse stood at the end of the road, which stopped with a metal barrier and a forest growing in and around the stumps and fallen trunks of the original forest, destroyed by powerful magic during the war. The small parking lot looked uneven, riddled with cracks and weeds, and had a massive wave of asphalt cutting through the middle of it, the top curled as if it had actually been liquid at some point. It hid the front half of the building from the road, and I had to pull into the lot and drive around it to get a full look at the structure.

The warehouse was a tall single-story building, with windows up high near the roof, backlit by a blazing red sunset that turned the clouds above ominous. The back half of the structure had collapsed, and parts of the roof had been ripped away. At the end closest to me, one of two wide bay doors hung precariously from broken hinges and creaked in the breeze, while the other one stood about ten feet away, partially embedded in the ground, and twisted into what people were now calling post-war urban art—anything damaged by the nephilim's magic that had yet to be cleared away.

I could sense both the archnephilim and Gideon inside. Their essences burned and vibrated through me. Gideon's jagged electricity was now stronger and made my buzz claw under my skin, while the flares in the arch-nephilim's came farther and farther apart because his overall fire had grown in strength.

This was the worst idea ever.

I shut off the car and got out.

But there wasn't a better plan. While there might be a way to capture the archnephilim, no one would find it before Gideon's hour was up. And even if I wanted to, I couldn't resist the need to go to Gideon and do whatever it took to save him.

I pulled the ring from my pocket and slid it onto my thumb. It was a tight fit, but better that than too loose on my finger and falling off. It would be awkward if I was going to shoot a blast at the archnephilim, but not a problem for pressing it against the brand burned into my biceps. Light flickered from it and power swelled around my hand for a moment then dimmed, ready, waiting. All I had to do was cast the spell summoning divine light to release the power from the ring.

I squared my shoulders and strode toward the creaking bay door, feeling naked without my department-issued sidearm. Funny how I'd gone two days now, talked down a robber and faced the archnephilim three times, without my Glock, and now I wanted the weapon when I knew it wouldn't do any good.

But the sense of self preservation that Marcus claimed I didn't have was screaming at me, proving that it wasn't that I didn't have it, it was that I was practical enough to ignore it to do what needed to be done. I'd grown up understanding that sometimes hard choices had to be made, and this was one hell of a hard choice.

Except it hadn't been my choice at all. I hadn't asked the archnephilim to brand me, or Gideon. The only choice I had left was how many people were going to die before I ended this.

"I knew you wouldn't be able to stay away," the archnephilim said in my head as I reached the bay door.

I hadn't expected the element of surprise since the archnephilim could probably sense me better than I could sense him, but his voice, suddenly within me, still made me jump.

"Myself for Gideon." I entered the gloomy darkness of the warehouse, the air cold and musty. "That was the deal."

Weak light shone through the holes in the roof, while the last of the sunset streaked through the cracks in the wall. Gideon hung from a metal rafter thirty feet from the floor, hands tied behind his back, noose tight around his neck, and hooks—the only thing actually holding him up —sliced into his wings, spreading them taut. Blood caked his wings, the side of his face, and his shirt. Light glimmered on his pants, tracing a thick trail of still-wet blood down his legs to a blood pool beneath him. His head lolled forward as if he were unconscious, and maybe he was, but his eyes were partially open, light radiating across a face swollen and bruised. His electricity was still jagged inside me, almost as painful as the buzz now, and the pull on my strength was now an urgent tug.

The archnephilim stood on the floor near him. He was mostly angel with onyx wings, hair, and even clothes. Hints of smoke curled around him, softening his edges, and half a dozen tentacles writhed around his torso.

The heat from his brand flared in my arm, and I stopped in the doorway, hoping it was far enough away that the archnephilim would have to come closer if he wanted to grab me—as well as to prove to myself that I actually could stop. "Release him and I'm all yours."

"*Release him yourself,*" the archnephilim chuckled in my head.

Yeah, not going to happen. Getting closer was the last possible option. If the archnephilim grabbed me before I could activate the ring, all was lost. But if I couldn't get

Gideon free, or at least the archnephilim away from Gideon, then he was dead, and the connection between us wasn't willing to accept that. "I don't see a ladder."

"Free your wings, little nephilim," he hissed, sending panic racing through me even though he was still in my head and Gideon hadn't heard him... I hoped. *"Or do you not want your mate to know what you are?"*

The archnephilim curled a tentacle up Gideon's leg, around his ankle, knee, and thigh, then yanked down. Gideon's wings bowed, and his head jerked up with a strangled cry of pain. Light blazed from his eyes then sputtered out, leaving him shuddering and gasping for breath.

"Wakey, wakey. Your mate has arrived," the archnephilim said aloud, his voice no longer in my head.

Gideon's unfocused gaze lifted slowly, dragging across the warehouse floor until he found me. For a second his eyes were filled with hope, then realization swept across his expression and his grief rushed around me in a thick mist. He'd thought Zella had come, and just my presence reminded him that she hadn't been his mate and was now dead. His disappointment tightened my throat with emotions I shouldn't have for a stranger and certainly not for an angel. But I couldn't resist the connection, and right now I had other things more important to resist, like the archnephilim's control over me.

The archnephilim chuckled. "Doesn't look like he's happy to see you."

I pushed back my hurt at Gideon's disappointment. "Doesn't matter if he is or not. The deal was him for me. I'm here. Let him go."

"And I said, get him yourself." The archnephilim burst into his wraith form, growing in size, massive tentacles writhing from his smoke, crushing around Gideon's chest.

Gideon cried out, his agony cutting through the mist and stealing my breath.

"Go on. Get him."

"I can't."

"Then let me help you." The archnephilim's power exploded from his brand and fire seared my back with such force I screamed and my knees gave out.

CHAPTER 21

My pulse roared and panic swept through me. I tried to stand, but the archnephilim's power heaved me forward. I caught myself, my palms scraping against the debris littering the concrete floor, but my muscles contracted, freezing me on my hands and knees.

No, please. The power tore through my back, slicing between my shoulder blades. I gasped, fighting to breathe past the pain. I didn't have wings. He couldn't just make them appear. But I convulsed and a new power, something different, not fire or electricity, something else and without a doubt mine, curled tight in my back.

Oh, God. Do I actually have wings?

The archnephilim howled with laugher, his inky darkness sliding from his brand around my heart, while his power ripped at my skin.

Gideon wrenched against the hooks, light blazing from his eyes. Whatever disappointment he'd had that I wasn't Zella was gone and now his electric hum crackled through my buzz with ferocious determination. It set my nerves on edge, my muscles contracting as if the low voltage electric fence of my buzz had been turned up to medium, zapping it through the fire.

The archnephilim's heat in my back shuddered, dimming for just a second, and I jerked myself up, sitting on my heels. The fire flared back with a vengeance, screaming not just through my back but every inch of my body.

I clenched every muscle I had and fought to stay upright. I couldn't let him win. And there wasn't any chance now to ensure Gideon's safety. I had to go ahead and burn the brand.

Except I couldn't move. It took everything I had just to stay up and not collapse on the floor, writhing in agony.

Come on. Just move your hand. That was all I needed to do. But another surge of the archnephilim's power screamed through me, stealing my breath.

Just move.

Come on. Move.

The muscles in my arm twitched, but not enough to raise it.

Come on. Come on.

But the archnephilim was too strong and all his power was focused on me.

He rushed toward me and whipped a tentacle around my neck. "Stop fighting. Become what you're supposed to be."

"No."

The tentacle tightened, choking me, and wrenched me up until my toes skimmed the floor. The fire in my back burned hotter, and I strained to breathe, my muscles still frozen, unable to raise my hands and grasp at the tentacle.

"We could rule this world. All would bow before us and our power."

"You honestly think you can do what Michael couldn't?"

"I control both light and dark power, and with my brand on you, I'm as powerful as Michael." Another tentacle caressed my cheek, and his tone turned low and dark. "And when you accept what you are, I'll be more powerful than him."

"But you'd give that up and still kill me just to kill Gideon?"

"Release your wings and you'll be more powerful than him." The archnephilim's face solidified in his smoke and he sneered at me. "I don't need you sane to reap the benefits of your essence."

The tentacle around my neck squeezed tighter, making me gasp, and the tentacle caressing my cheek plunged into my mouth.

"You might be strong enough to fight me through the brand, but you can't fight me inside you." His smoke poured down my throat, surging around my heart and up into my head.

Gideon yelled and wrenched one wing free, tearing feathers, the bits falling like oversized snowflakes and sticking in the blood pool beneath him. His weight yanked him down on his other wing and the noose jerked tight against his neck, making him gasp.

A red haze swept over my vision and all thought vanished, papers in a fire, leaving only searing heat, consuming power, and fear. Heart-stopping, utter terror as I helplessly felt myself burning away.

Gideon's electricity went first. Then the buzz.

Something flickered inside me. A hint of light? Electricity? My soul? The archnephilim's power devoured that as well. All that was left was a tiny, barely audible voice screaming in fear and agony and desperation.

Then a gunshot roared nearby and the archnephilim's power shuddered.

Another gunshot and the smoke pouring into me vanished.

Strong hands grabbed me as I collapsed. My mind and soul jerked back into my body as those hands yanked me away from the archnephilim.

A barrage of semi-automatic gunfire thundered through the empty warehouse. The archnephilim howled, his form shuddering, and Kol leaped past me. His face was still disfigured and his hands covered in angry red scars from my divine light, but he held both of his daggers as if that didn't affect him and slashed at the archnephilim, as fast and as powerful as I'd seen before.

"You're a God damned fool," Marcus growled, his voice close to my ear.

I glanced back at him and his hands on my shoulders tightened. His piercing green gaze was filled with fear and if my body wasn't still on fire, I was sure the temperature in the warehouse would have plummeted.

"You're not supposed to be here." I tried to pull out of his grip but he held tight. "How are you here?"

"I know you, Essie. I knew you'd do something stupid. So I planted a tracker on you."

"When did—? In the elevator, when we—?" That was the only time he could have done it. Had our moment in the elevator just been a ploy so I wouldn't notice? As much as I craved Marcus, I didn't really know him. Except that didn't make sense. Everything he'd done had been to protect me.

"You made it too easy," he said, and bolted toward the archnephilim. His body turned to liquid flesh, compacting, expanding, twisting, and within three quick steps, never missing a beat, he'd transformed into a massive black wolf, the magic of his lycanthropy permanently consuming his clothing. I'd only seen a shifter transform once before, and it was beautiful and horrific all at the same time. Marcus leaped at the archnephilim, snapping through tentacles, and Kol dove past to a concrete pillar supporting the roof and began to climb.

Behind me, Jacob, holding the HK416 assault rifle from the armory in Operations, fired another barrage of bullets. They sliced through the middle of the archnephilim, drawing a howl. Guess bullets enchanted to take down a greater demon did affect an archnephilim, but one shot, let alone four, still hadn't been enough to bring him down.

The only sure way to do it was my original plan.

I tried to raise my hand, but couldn't.

God damn it.

I gritted my teeth. The archnephilim's smoke wasn't in me any more, but the power from his brand was still strong, still threatening to rip me in half.

Kol reached the rafters and ran to Gideon, who flapped his free wing, trying to raise himself enough to unhook his other wing or, in the very least, not choke on the noose, but his flaps were uneven and yanked him against the hook and noose.

The archnephilim swept out a tentacle to hit Kol, but Jacob fired another short barrage, slicing through the smoke, making it vanish before it struck.

Kol cut the rope securing the noose to the rafters, and Gideon jerked up, above the rafter, and yanked his wing from the hook. He hit the ceiling with a boom and crashed, stomach first, onto the girder. My pulse stuttered with a fear for him that I shouldn't have. Kol grabbed him and steadied him then cut the rope binding his arms.

The archnephilim howled with a rage that made his fire within me burn brighter. He shot two more tentacles at them. Jacob hit one of the two tentacles but didn't completely sever the second one. It bashed Kol off the rafter. Gideon threw himself after Kol and grabbed his arm, but Gideon's wings couldn't get enough air or were too damaged and they crashed to the floor.

The electricity within me flared and yanked on my essence, pouring it into Gideon. I shuddered, my muscles weakening, and fought to maintain what little control I had on my body.

Jacob fired again into the center of the archnephilim's writhing form. The smoke whirled, caught up in a wild wind I couldn't feel, and his fire within me stuttered. Marcus tore into him, and Kol scrambled to his feet his daggers ready, while Gideon groaned and pulled his wings into his body. The electricity from his brand flared again, jagged spikes under my skin, weakening me even more as he stood, swaying.

"Get Gideon out of here," I yelled. I didn't care who did it, just that it was done.

"You can't protect him," the archnephilim said, and a massive tentacle slammed Kol across the warehouse, sending him crashing through the debris littering the floor. "You can't protect any of them."

Dozens of tentacles shot at Marcus, who twisted and snapped at them, but two sliced deep into his side, making him howl. Gideon half lunged, half staggered toward the archnephilim, his sword of light forming in his hand. He slashed at the archnephilim, but a flurry of tentacles batted the blade aside.

Another barrage of bullets cut through where the archnephilim's head would have been, and Kol barreled toward him, daggers raised.

The guys slashed and tore and shot the archnephilim, but it was like the fight in the cafeteria, and for every hit they made on him, the archnephilim gave them two.

I mentally heaved against the archnephilim's control.

Marcus was speared again with another tentacle and his blood splattered on the floor. The archnephilim heaved him up and Gideon took that moment of distraction and rammed his blade into the archnephilim's side. The archnephilim slammed Marcus against the warehouse wall, and Gideon twisted and wrenched the blade through the archnephilim's smoke, drawing a howl of pain.

The fire within me weakened again and I jerked my hand up. My thumb with the divine light ring swept through a stream of weak sunset light and flashed brighter than it should have.

The archnephilim burst out laughing as he sent a tentacle through Kol's chest and tossed him at Marcus.

"You brought a toy," the archnephilim said. "How cute." He whipped a tentacle around Gideon's chest and squeezed what had to be already broken ribs. Gideon screamed and his electricity sliced through his brand. More power rushed out of me into him.

I staggered, trembling, my head whirling. I fought to keep standing, then realized there was no point. I could end this on my knees.

I sagged to the floor. My hand shook. I still had control, but barely. The words of the light strike raced through my head, over and over again, and the new power, the one I recognized as mine, built within me. I squared my shoulders and embraced that power.

"You're not powerful enough," the archnephilim sneered. "That won't kill me."

"Not directly." I rammed the ring against the arch-nephilim's brand and released my power. It poured into the ring, turned to divine light, and exploded into my arm with searing white agony.

Gideon jerked toward me. Marcus yelled my name.

The archnephilim howled. His smoke burst apart, revealing his angel form, and white light blazed out of his eyes.

His fire in my body surged, fighting the divine light, and my hand with the ring trembled. I gritted my teeth, keeping it in place while my body was trapped in the center of a sun, burning up from the inside out.

Tears filled my eyes, and the divine light overwhelmed the archnephilim's fire, consuming it and everything it touched.

"He'll betray you," the archnephilim hissed in my head, dropping to his knees. I could feel him fighting to control me with our mental connection, using his words to dig himself deeper into me.

The agony in my arm was all-consuming. It was too much. I had to stop. Except I couldn't. If I survived, then the archnephilim did. The choice had been made for me the moment the archnephilim had branded me. I was already dead. And I hated that. I hated that I'd spent my childhood scared and hiding. I hated that my mother had given up the semblance of a normal life because of me. And I hated that the one thing I wanted, a normal life, would never be possible.

Even if I survived this, even if I wasn't Gideon's mate, I'd never have a normal life. I wasn't even sure if I could get close to having one. If I got too close to a friend, even a human one, they could become suspicious. Eventually someone would notice and question my temperature issues. And there wasn't any way I could have a romantic relationship. How could I let myself get close to someone when I had to lie to them about who I really was?

"He'll kill you," the archnephilim said. *"That's what angels do to our kind."*

"You'd kill me, too, and then you'd kill others, innocents." At least if I couldn't have the life I yearned for, my death could mean something.

"I'm not killing the innocent. They slaughtered babies."

And that was the true horror of what Michael had done with his war. Forced good people to make the choice between themselves and unnaturally created babies that would, in a matter of months, be mindless, monstrous soldiers. *"So vengeance is the answer? Killing in kind without mercy?"*

"It's the only answer."

"No. It isn't." A seizure jerked me. The ring jumped away from my arm. The divine light dimmed and I yelled the light strike spell again and rammed it back in place.

The light in the nephilim's eyes burned brighter. He screamed and divine light poured out of his mouth and nose. I could feel his pain. It was my pain, consuming both of us down to our very essence. It would be over soon. *Please let it be over soon.* I needed to last just a little longer. *Please.*

But I was weakening and so was the light pouring from the ring. I wasn't going to hold out long enough. I was going to fail and then Marcus and Gideon and the others would be in danger. The archnephilim would torture and slaughter them. I could feel his rage through our connection. He despised Gideon, and all those who'd fought in the war, and he hated me with a consuming fury for turning my back on my own kind.

Except I wasn't anything like the archnephilim, I hadn't been made in a laboratory, and I didn't have his blood lust.

I threw what was left of my essence, the strange power within me, the gnawing buzz grating in my mind, always present, even what little of Gideon's electricity I could feel, into the ring. All of it. All of me. Every bit, every miniscule flicker of magic, every hope and fear and heartache. Everything I had. It went into the ring, and poured through me into the archnephilim in a ferocious inferno a thousand times stronger than the archnephilim's fire.

Cracks snapped through his body, blinding white light slicing out, slicing through me. I fought to see past the blaze, to hold on, and see it through to the end. One of the cracks erupted and the light roared out of him.

He howled and writhed as it consumed him, and collapsed in a smoldering black heap.

The weight of his brand, a weight I hadn't realized had been there before, shattered, and the divine light, with no place left to go, surged back into me.

I screamed as it devoured me, unable to move or stop the power flowing from me and the ring into my body, knowing I'd end up a smoldering black heap like the archnephilim.

But that had been the plan. To save the guys, to save everyone, and sacrifice myself.

CHAPTER 22

THE BUZZ RETURNED TO MY SENSES FIRST, SNAPPING UNDER my skin at pre-nicotine levels and grating against nerves that had been burned raw with the archnephilim's power and divine light. The damp musty smell that had filled the warehouse was gone. So too was the chilly evening air.

I couldn't hear the guys and panic seized me. I must have failed, passed out before killing the archnephilim. Surely if they'd survived, they'd be talking, regrouping, trying to figure out what to do next. But I couldn't hear anything—

No, that wasn't true. I could hear the gentle whoosh of air, the kind of steady, low hum that came from the heating-cooling system of a big building. And the temperature was consistent with being indoors.

Recognizing those two details tripped a switch in my brain, and I realized I lay on my back on something soft, instead of being crumpled on a wet concrete floor, and was covered with a blanket.

I cracked my eyes open and stared up at a white ceiling cast in partial shadow. The fluorescent light above me was off, but, given the way the illumination and shadow painted the ceiling, a light to my left had to be on.

I let my head slowly fall to the side, afraid to discover just how injured I was underneath the biting buzz, not yet ready to take stock of the damage I'd taken from the archnephilim or the divine light ring, but nothing screamed in pain.

My gaze followed the light, stalling on an IV bag with a line trailing toward me. I didn't look to see if it was hooked up to my hand. If I was alive and in a hospital, I was hooked up to the IV. Beyond the bag was a small reading lamp turned away from me, shining on Kol.

He slouched in a chair, one leg up—ankle on thigh—his head bowed, reading whatever was in the folder in his lap. My pulse stalled, but I didn't know if it was desire because he exuded sexual grace—and a hint of danger—or fear for what I'd done to him.

His black hair had fallen forward, veiling most of his face, and I couldn't tell if he was still horribly scarred or not. His body language was loose, not tight with pain, suggesting that whatever had happened with the archnephilim, he'd managed to recover from his injuries. Had Marcus?

My pulse stuttered again and my right forearm ached, but not enough for me to know what that meant. Had Gideon survived?

Gideon didn't have the same kind of self-healing that Kol did, and I couldn't sense his electric power within his brand or the pull of strength from him to me. Of course that might have something to do with the strength of my personal, torturous buzz and that I was too weak to offer him any strength.

No, if I was in the Joined Parliament Operations Building, then I had no doubt Amiah would have taken care of Gideon and Marcus before she'd taken care of me... if they'd lived.

My throat tightened. They had to have lived. All of them. That had been the whole point.

I must have made a sound because Kol's head rose, his warm brown eyes capturing my soul, making my thoughts flicker—and not fully stutter like they had the last time. I wasn't sure what that meant, either.

He was still breathtakingly beautiful. His face was perfect, as if I hadn't badly burned him with divine light, but there was a tightness in his eyes as if he were worried, or holding back, or something.

God, it's bad news. It has to be bad news.

"Is he alive?" I asked, my voice rough, barely a whisper.

"The archnephilim, your mate, or your wolf?" he asked, the tightness melting into relief edged with a hint of wicked sensuality.

"All of them. And Jacob, too." *Please tell me everyone made it and it's over.* I didn't know if I could burn the archnephilim's brand again, especially if I needed to hold out longer to make it work.

"The archnephilim turned to ash when you passed out. He's well and truly dead. Everyone else is alive." The sensuality vanished, his relief the stronger emotion, but his eyes turned glassy.

"Thank God." *Thank God, thank God, thank God.*

"Tell me you're okay. Tell me Gideon's brand protected you and you're all right," he said. "We all hoped it would, but Amiah said we wouldn't know until you woke up. And you've been unconscious for days," he said.

"Days? How many?"

"Five."

"Five days?" No wonder the buzz was going insane. I'd been without nicotine for five days.

Kol grabbed my hand with both of his, holding it tentatively between his palms, careful not to touch the IV needle.

"Tell me you're okay." His gaze flickered to my left biceps and realization flashed through me.

The archnephilim was dead. I wasn't. That meant the outcome for me was insanity. Except I felt fine, or as fine as I could be with the God damned buzz in my body.

"I—" Would I even know if I was insane? Except I didn't feel as if my life had been shattered... I mean, I did and it had been. I had feelings I couldn't ignore for Marcus and wore Gideon's mating brand, both situations risked revealing my secret and endangering my life, but I wasn't heartbroken to hear about the archnephilim's death. I didn't *feel* any of the things the textbooks said I'd feel when someone I was bonded to died.

"I think I'm good. I still feel like I was lit on fire, though."

Kol winced and I regretted using that comparison.

"And probably torn apart from the inside out, too" he said. "That's what Amiah said it looked like the arch-nephilim tried to do to you. Burn you up and rip you apart."

I shuddered at the memory, making the buzz snap within me. "So Amiah healed me?"

"The physical damage, yes. But Amiah can't do anything for the mental. So—"

"So you're sitting at my bedside waiting to see if I'll wake up insane."

"Pretty much." He flashed a full-watt smile with hell-fire flickering in his eyes that made my insides heat with desire. Then his eyes widened, as if he'd realized what he'd just done, and he jerked away, releasing my hand and leaning as far back into the chair as he could get. "That's me. On damsel duty again."

"Tell me you haven't been sitting here for five days."

"It hasn't been a problem. I've gotten caught up on a ton of paperwork."

"So just you." Perhaps that was a good thing. I had no idea what I'd say if I'd woken with Gideon or Marcus at my bedside. But it still stung that they were clearly avoiding me. Jacob, too.

"Jacob is staying away because of the power of his claim on you. He didn't want you to wake and be caught up in his compulsion, not if your mental state was frag-ile." Kol's expression turned somber. "The moment Amiah said you'd live, Marcus made Gideon promise you'd get your life back, no supers, nothing, then left."

Of course he did. I shouldn't have been surprised or disappointed. He'd promised he'd do everything to get me away from the supernatural world, and that meant getting away from him. He hadn't said goodbye the last time. Why would I think this time was different?

Except this time had been different. We'd given in to our desires, at least in part. I ached to kiss him again, even if he'd used my desire against me to put a tracker on me.

But what hadn't changed were my reasons for not being able to stay in the supernatural world.

"And Gideon?" I couldn't believe he'd agree to Marcus's demand to leave me alone, not with how much he'd said the mating brand was a beautiful fated thing.

Of course that was before he'd learned he was stuck with a human.

"He took Zella's body back to the Realm of Celestial Light."

And before he'd lost the woman he'd really loved.

Which left me where?

A part of me wanted to get out of Operations, grab my go bag, and get out of town. If I'd been a cat, I was sure I'd used up at least six, probably seven, of my nine lives just by being caught in this mess. Hell, I had to be down to one life left because somehow Gideon hadn't heard enough of my conversation with the archnephilim to figure out the truth. If he had, I was sure I would have woken up handcuffed to the hospital bed. The longer I stuck around, the greater the chance someone would discover my supernatural nature.

Except if I ran, Gideon would know. And really, there wasn't anywhere in the world I could go where Gideon wouldn't be able to find me.

My best bet was to carry on, life as usual, and hope I,

as well as Gideon, could ignore the compulsion from the mating brand to be with each other. The bond between us made that thought sting, but the rest of me knew it was the right call. Maybe if we cut ties now, before we really had any kind of a relationship and while he was still in love with Zella, our connection wouldn't grow stronger.

Maybe I'd be able to find a magical solution that, while it might not be able to break the bond between us, could mute its affects. I doubted angels with mating brands went to see witches or demons to diminish the strength of their bond.

It was a slim chance, but my best option. Besides, if I was going to risk everything for a relationship with a super, it was going to be with Marcus. Which I wasn't. So I needed to go back to flying under the radar.

Someone walked past the large glass window behind Kol, drawing my gaze up to the dimly lit hall, and I gasped at my reflection. My eyes were glowing. Why hadn't Kol questioned my glowing eyes?

Perhaps I wasn't really seeing the glow, or I was and no one else could, like how no one else could feel the temperature change when someone had strong emotions.

I squeezed my eyes shut, then opened them again.

Still glowing.

"Ah..." I didn't want to ask, but I had to know. If my eyes were glowing, I needed to figure out how to deal with that. "Are my eyes—?"

"Glowing?" Kol asked. "They have been since you passed out in the warehouse. Even with your eyes closed, it bleeds out under your lashes."

"And you're not worried about that?" He was acting the same as always, not like he knew I was a monstrous nephilim.

"You just blasted yourself with who knows how much divine light and you didn't die. I'm surprised your whole body isn't lit up like a Christmas tree."

"Well, thanks for small miracles." That no one knew, and that I wasn't fully lit up.

"Although it would make it easy to always find you," he said with a soft laugh that caressed my senses.

"But impossible to do my job."

"I don't know." He offered a sensual shrug, his mirth making his eyes shine. "You could be the new poster girl for the Union City PD, what with your new *glowing* personality."

I rolled my eyes at him. "Yeah, and I'll never be put on a boring stakeout again. Can you imagine? Me, at night, sitting in a car, trying to look inconspicuous while brilliant white light blazes around me?" I burst out laughing.

It was so utterly ridiculous and amazing and... hell, I was still alive. I'd faced an archnephilim, saved who-knew-how-many lives, and Kol didn't seem at all bothered that my eyes were glowing.

Kol snorted, his laughter growing. "What about trying to sneak up on a perp in the dark?"

"Would it mean I'd never get stuck on the graveyard shift?"

"Or would you always? I mean, you'd never need a flashlight."

I laughed so hard tears streamed down my cheeks. Really, it wasn't that funny, but I couldn't stop. All the worry and stress and fear and heartache that had built up over the last few days needed a release and this was how it was coming out. Which was fine with me.

Kol grinned at me, his smile slightly lopsided and boyish. There was a hint of sensuality to it—I didn't think he'd ever be able to dampen all of it—but it was warm, friendly, and genuine. "I'm so glad you're not crazy."

"Me, too."

I was going to be okay.

"And Amiah did say the glow in your eyes would go away, once all that divine light leaves your system."

Everything was going to be okay.

Marcus had said he'd get me my life back and for the most part, all things considered, he had.

Except did I really want to go back to that life?

It was the safest option for me, but it was also the loneliest. I'd had a taste of what it felt like to be part of a team, and an ache for the kind of physical contact I'd always been afraid to commit to.

I wasn't sure I could go back to the life I'd had before.

DESTINED BLOOD
Nephilim's Destiny: Book Two

Like it or not, she's part of the team... come hell or fiery demon.

Barely a week after a searing wraith battle left me with amped-up supernatural abilities, I'm back to my cover as Essie Shaw, "normal" beat cop. My frostbite-inducing empathic gift and enhanced hearing, I can work with. My combat spell —weak at best—still comes in handy. But it's the 24/7 glowy eye thing that's toughest to hide.

When an encounter with a feral vampire nearly kills my partner (déjà vu, anyone?), the chief of police gives me a make-or-break assignment—join the JP team. Yeah, good luck bridging the aching gulf that's divided us since that near-fatal fight with the wraith. There's Gideon, who electrifies my soul; Jacob, who commands it; and Kol, who tempts it. Then there's Marcus with his ferocious, pulse-pounding energy, who left without even a goodbye.

Amid lingering tensions, we investigate who's creating an army of twisted, insatiable feral vampires. The truth will extract a terrible price from us all—body, magic, and soul.

OTHER BOOKS BY TESSA COLE

THE NEPHILIM'S DESTINY SERIES